. . . Al

"You robbing me.

"Turn out yore pockets an' be damn quick 'bout it. I ain't gonna miss at this range."

Longarm said calmly, "You better pick an easier target, mister."

"You just never mind tellin' me my bid'ness. You just turn and face me so's I can see whatever is in yore mind and put a stop to it before you git up to mischief."

Slowly, Longarm turned. As he came fully around to face the man, he suddenly let his left leg collapse, falling full length to the boardwalk on his side. As he fell, he heard the sharp explosion of the robber's pistol, saw the orange-red flame of the shot erupt in the night, and heard the *whiz* of the bullet through the space where he had been standing.

But he was drawing as he fell. Before his left shoulder hit the boardwalk, his revolver was in hand, the hammer back, the barrel aimed at the spot he'd seen the muzzle-flash. He fired, the hammer of the gun slamming back in his palm. Over the echo of his own shot he heard a muffled "Hummmph!" From the sound, Longarm knew that his bullet had found solid flesh and, more than likely, bone.

TABOR EVANS

LONGARM

AND THE LUSTY LADY

JOVE BOOKS, NEW YORK

LONGARM AND THE LUSTY LADY

A Jove Book / published by arrangement with
the author

PRINTING HISTORY
Jove edition / August 1996

The Putnam Berkley World Wide Web site address is
http://www.berkley.com

ISBN: 0-515-11923-7

A JOVE BOOK®
Jove Books are published by The Berkley Publishing Group,
200 Madison Avenue, New York, New York 10016.
JOVE and the "J" design are trademarks
belonging to Jove Publications, Inc.

PRINTED IN THE UNITED STATES OF AMERICA

10 9 8 7 6 5 4 3 2 1

Chapter 1

"Like hell I will!" Longarm said with feeling.

His boss, Billy Vail, Chief Marshal of the Southwestern District, stared out washed-out blue eyes for a second as if he were trying to see through a foggy window. Then he put his hand up and smoothed down his sparse gray hair, put the hand behind his ear and leaned forward across his desk. "Say what? Guess I'm gettin' hard of hearing. I thought you said something that sounded like you wasn't going to do what I told you."

U.S. Deputy Marshal Custis Long looked back at his boss in disgust. "Now don't start playing that silly old game again, Billy," he said. "You're about as hard of hearing as a she-wolf with cubs and got about the same disposition. But no, I ain't got the slightest intention of having anything to do with any such plan. And you knew that before you brought it up."

"Let me see something here," Billy said, getting out of his swivel chair and coming around the desk to stand behind Longarm. Billy Vail was deceptively small and innocent-looking. Time spent living and behind a desk had finally sanded away at the rough, weathered face and left him looking a little sleek and a little soft. But even though he now gave orders to other men to carry out jobs he'd have liked to handle himself, he was still the Billy Vail of whom an outlaw had once said, "Shoot, I ain't scairt of Billy Vail. I very nearly come close to makin' him tell me *twice* to drop my gun."

And Longarm knew it. He also knew what Billy was up to as he stood behind his deputy and put his head down on Longarm's left shoulder. "Just want to get round here" he said, "and get your perspective on the matter."

Longarm gave him a disgusted look even if he couldn't see it. "Damnit, Billy, this ain't necessary."

"Aw, yeah it is," the chief marshal insisted. "I figured, judging by what you said, that we had different views on the matter. So I come around here to see what you see. Wait!" Billy pointed to something with his finger. "What is that on that desk? That little boardlike thing. See it there?"

Longarm grimaced. "I see it, Billy. Will you just go to hell once and for all?"

"Look what that sign says. What does it say?"

"You know damn good and well what it says. Damnit, Billy, you may be the orneriest old sonofabitch ever walked the face of the earth, and I think you're getting worse."

"Wait!" Billy Vail said again. He squinted. "These old eyes of mine ain't so good no more, but it appears I can make out what that little piece of wood says. Says 'Chief Marshal' on it. What do you think about that? *Chief* Marshal! That's the boss, ain't it?"

Longarm said tiredly, "You will do this, won't you,

2

Billy? Ain't no way you're going to stop, is there?''

Billy Vail straightened up. "There's just the one more thing," he said. "As I recollect, you are a *deputy* U.S. marshal. That's not as high up as a *chief* marshal, is it?''

Longarm set his mouth, folded his arms, and stared straight ahead. Billy Vail went back behind his desk and sat in his wooden swivel chair with the big leather pad on the seat. "Now," he said, "as near as I can figure from all this, I am the one who gives the orders and you are the one who takes them. Is that about the way it falls out?''

"Go to hell, Billy," Longarm replied. "I ain't working with him and that is my last word.''

Billy Vail's pale blue eyes suddenly sharpened. "Oh? You handing in your resignation, are you?''

Longarm raised both arms over his head in frustration. "Damnit," he said, "you don't know Austin Davis. He's a damn smart aleck is what he is and he irritates the hell out of me. He's got such an opinion of himself I'd like to buy him for what he's worth and sell him for what he thinks he's worth. I'd get rich. Billy, just let me go down to Texas and handle that job by myself. I don't want to work with Austin Davis! Hell, he ain't been a deputy marshal much over six months.''

Billy Vail sat and studied his deputy. Where Billy was small and rounded, Longarm was tall and heavy in the shoulders and arms and hands. His face said he could have been pushing past 40, but the easy, powerful grace of his body suggested a younger age. All of him said hard and determined and resourceful. He had gotten the nickname Longarm some years past, partly because his last name was Long, but mainly because it was known among those on the other side of the law that you couldn't run far enough to escape Custis Long. An outlaw once said, "I was buried so deep in the badlands of New Mexico that I swear my Maker couldn't have found me and, first thing I knowed, here come Custis Long sticking that long arm of the law of his in there and plucking me out of the back of a cave."

Longarm worked with other men, sometimes willingly, but more often with no enthusiasm. He was a loner who did not like to consult with others about his plans and his decisions. But now, worse than just working with *anybody*, Billy Vail wanted him to work with that tall talker from Texas, Austin Davis. He said again, "Let me do the job on my own, Billy. Or give me somebody else."

Billy Vail turned and looked out the window of his office in downtown Denver. "Hell, Custis," he said, "you worked with the man before. You deputized him your ownself. And it was you recommended he apply to the U.S. Marshal Service." He wheeled back around in his chair. "Ain't that a fact?"

Longarm looked away. "Yes, but—"

"Ain't no buts about it. In the first place, it's Davis who brought this matter to my attention. He's done some good work getting depositions from Texas cattlemen who have been affected by them Mexican herds. He's done most of the spadework already. And, besides, he knows the Tex-Mex border better than anybody else I got."

Longarm said very softly, "So he claims."

"What?"

"Nothing. Listen, Billy, why don't you send somebody else? Hell, I got a few days off coming and I wouldn't mind cooling my heels a bit."

"All you been doing is cooling your heels here lately. You've got more time in town than I have. You surely have had time to make it through your list of lady friends more than once. Now, are you telling me that this Austin Davis ain't a dependable man in a tight place?"

Longarm grimaced. "No, I ain't saying any such thing," he said grudgingly.

"You telling me he can't handle himself?"

"No."

"You remarking on his character?"

Longarm looked unhappy. "No, I ain't bad-mouthing his character. Damnit, Billy he is such an arrogant son-ofabitch. He irritates the hell out of me. Why that bastard thinks he could walk into a Mexican whorehouse without a penny in his pocket and come out with a satisfied look on his face."

Billy Vail cocked his head. "Now there's a curious thing. Davis said you told him he couldn't get laid in a two-bit cathouse with a thousand dollars in his pocket."

Longarm looked off toward the corner, a disappointed expression on his face. Shaking his head, he said, "Now that's it right there. Just the kind of remark he would pass."

"You didn't tell him that?"

Longarm looked uneasy. "Well, yeah," he admitted reluctantly, "but only because of remarks he passed about my poker playing. He said the only way I'd make a small fortune playing poker was to start with a big one."

Billy Vail smiled and looked away, then remarked, trying to sound serious, "He said you told him the only chance he had of breaking even in a poker game was not to play. Any truth to that?"

Longarm was squirming. "See?" he said. "See? See why I don't want to work with that lying, miserable sonofabitch! Telling tales behind my back. And not only that, but the sonofabitch drank the last of my good Maryland whiskey when he don't know the difference and there was enough of the rotgut variety around to swim in."

"Marshal Davis said he done it for your own good," Billy Vail replied. "Said he didn't think a man of your age ought to be putting so much of that juice away. Said it made you creaky in the mornings."

"Well, that does it!" Longarm exclaimed. He got up, picked up his hat, and put it on his head. He gave Billy Vail a grim look. "Give me the particulars. I can guarantee that *Marshal* Davis will be damn sorry to see me come and damn glad to see me go. I reckon he won't ask for me on a job again. All right, I'll go wet-nurse the smart-aleck little bastard. Where and when?"

"Oh, he didn't ask for you," Billy Vail said. "In fact, he put up a bigger squawk than you about working with you. Damn near said the same things you did." The chief marshall let a small smile work on his face. "Seeing as how the regard is mutual on both sides, y'all ought to get along just fine."

Longarm felt the heat rising. "That sonofabitch," he said. "He come at you in exactly that way to trap me. All right. So be it. He's a sneaky sonofabitch, but I reckon I can put up with him for the good of the service. I just hope the little bastard don't forget who the senior deputy is. I hope you made it clear to him."

Billy Vail leaned back in his chair and twined his fingers across his ample little belly. "No," he said, "I figured you'd get him straightened out on that. Now, sit

6

down and let me lay the matter before you." He smiled a little. "You wouldn't want to go down there and have Davis know it all and you be in the dark."

Longarm sat down and said, "I just hope the sonofabitch has got a wad of money in his pocket and feels fearless enough to play me a little head-up poker. If that happens, then this damn trip will have been worth it."

"Funny thing, but Austin Davis said—"

Longarm waved his hand. "No, no. Don't tell me he said the same thing, because I ain't going to believe you."

The chief marshal looked at his deputy intently. "Custis, do you really not want to work with the man? Is he that bad?"

Longarm worked his head around on his shoulders for a few seconds and picked a piece of lint off his pressed, starched jeans. Then, looking away, he acknowledged grudgingly, "Aw, he ain't that bad. Fact is, he's all right. I wouldn't be one to go around damaging a fellow marshal's reputation. But he's got his ways, I'll tell you that. Just so long as he don't come on with he's the expert down along the border. I ain't going to abide that. Last time I looked, there was seven or eight agents working out of this place could draw assignments on the border, but I always seem to get that card. So I want the smart aleck to understand this ain't my first stampede when it comes to matters down along the Rio Grande."

Billy Vail was fighting to supress a smile. Putting concern in his voice, he said, "Well, Custis, I hate like hell to send you off unhappy. Like you said, there are other deputies I could send."

Longarm sighed. "No, no. Ain't no point in that. I'd never ask another man to do work I wouldn't do myself." He looked off across the room again. "I swore an oath to do my best at whatever duties come my way and I ain't backing down on that. No, I'll go. I'll make the best of it. Maybe *Marshal* Davis might learn a thing or two. Though you'll never get him to admit it."

"Is he really a better poker player than you, Custis?"

Longarm's eyes flared as he replied, a little louder than necessary, "Hell no! Double hell no!"

"Then how come he claims to have taken your money? Is he lying? I need to know if I got an agent here who lies."

Longarm still looked outraged. "He might have got away with a little of mine, but he is the most uncommon lucky man you ever saw in your life. But, like I told him, he sits in that chair long enough, that luck will even out and then it will come to skill. Then we'll see who takes the money home."

The chief marshal was still fighting a smile. "And is he better with the ladies than you, Custis?"

For a second, Longarm straightened as if he was going to come out of his chair. Finally he subsided and studied the same corner of the room he'd looked at before. He flicked at his trousers. "I ain't even gonna answer that."

"I asked," Billy Vail said, "because, if he is, you better get your ashes hauled tonight. You've got to be on a train tomorrow, and I wouldn't want to see you down there doing without for a long haul."

Longarm slowly swung his eyes around to his boss. He studied him for a second, realization slowly dawning. "Billy Vail," he said, "you are a mean old man. You've been sitting there, spurring the hell out of me and having yourself a quiet laugh. Well, I reckon you got some chickens going to come home to roost one of these days.

I'll just file this little incident away for future reference.''

Billy Vail smiled big. "Either way, you still got to be on a southbound train in the morning," he said.

Mrs. Spinner, Longarm thought, was about the most aptly named woman he'd ever met, even if she was still carrying the name of a former husband. She could set your mind spinning, your body spinning, your senses spinning, and even cause the hands of a clock to spin slower or faster depending on her whim. When she put her mind to it, she could get the both of them spinning and that included the bed and the walls and ceiling of the room. She was a lady of short acquaintance, relatively speaking, but one he intended to maintain good relations with as long as she was willing. She had moved into his boarding house a month previous and Longarm had immediately set out on a deliberate plan of seduction. Which was when he discovered that Mrs. Spinner—Lila was her given name—was also one of the most forthright people he'd ever encountered. As he'd begun his early, foundation work she'd suddenly rounded on him and said, "Marshal, are you trying to get me in bed? If that be the case, then let us dispense with these walks in the moonlight and talks in the porch swing and meals in expensive restaurants and get right to the business at hand."

The "business at hand" had left him breathless and drained, and longing for more strength and stamina, anything to keep up with Lila. She was a woman of thirty but she had the body of a girl. In her tight-fitting bodice and corsets she looked slim, almost boyish. But when she took off the restraints, her hips bloomed and her

9

breasts blossomed in a way that left Longarm short of breath before the actual "business at hand" ever got started. But even with her ample breasts and the wonderful flare and curve of her buttocks and hips, she was still as smooth and firm as a satin doll. She worked as a chorus dancer at one of the theaters in Denver that furnished popular entertainment, but, before that, she had been an acrobat in a flying trapeze act in the circus. The main performer in that act, the "catcher," had been her husband. She had left both him and the act when the drink he'd taken to had taken him over. She'd said to Longarm, "Marshal, I can tell you that a drunken acrobat is not a laughing matter. No, sir. Not fifty feet in the air. I never cared for the stuff myself and I can see where it might not cause much harm to, say, a banker or a cowboy or a storekeeper, but I do not believe it has any place in a trapeze act and I told my ex-husband that very thing. It was a wonder that none of us were killed."

Part of Longarm's irritation at being sent off on assignment, with or without Austin Davis, was that his affair with Mrs. Spinner had only been in progress for about a week and he was far from satisfied. To suddenly be told that he had to leave at once had left him with an almost physical ache. He reckoned that Austin Davis was going to feel a little of that dissatisfaction.

But Mrs. Spinner had given him a very memorable sendoff the night before. He had never, he was sure, been involved with a woman who was more inventive, or willing to be inventive and certainly none more supple. They had begun last night by facing each other, both naked. He had taken her around the waist, lifted her straight up, and then lowered her on his erect member. She had wrapped her arms around his neck and her legs

10

around his waist and they had walked all over his room at the boarding house while she writhed and gyrated and pumped against him. Because she knew how to distribute her weight, she had felt light as a feather and he'd had no trouble carrying her even with her wild movements. She had climaxed very quickly, as she often did, clawing his neck and kissing him with deep, sucking kisses. He had held off until he'd felt her rising again, and then they both went off almost simultaneously. He had been near the bed and he fell on it with her as his own explosion began. It had given him the strange sensation of floating for a long time in midair while thunder and lightning and fireworks exploded all around him. He had not been aware of hitting the bed until some moments later when she moved in his arms, freeing herself so she could move down his body and bring him back to arousal.

The amazing thing about Lila Spinner, he thought, was how she could look so hard and smooth and then, when he took her in his arms, she just seemed to melt into him and around him. She could go from a marble statue with beautifully formed breasts with upturned tips, flat belly above a wheat-colored thatch of hair that protected the warm, pink, soft flesh within, softly rounded hips, straight legs, and small feet, into a flashing, body of flesh, which was like warm dough in the way it could envelop him and suck him into her.

He sat on the train seat in the back of the car, thinking about last night and about Lila Spinner. She was so formal, so serious out of bed. So dignified. But once the shades were drawn there were no holds barred. The memory made him shake his head. He did not believe he had ever been in more intimate positions, not just

11

with any other woman, but maybe with the sum of half of the women he had been with. And all that in just a week.

And she was insatiable. She could reach climax in a a matter of a very few moments and then continue to reach the top of the mountain for as long as he could last. It shamed Longarm how early he often had to quit. He resolved that he was going to cut back on his drinking and smoking and get in better shape so as to be more worthy of a woman like Lila Spinner. He also resolved that this border matter was going to get settled a hell of a lot quicker than anyone reckoned, and that included Austin Davis. He was not going to be separated from this incredible woman any longer than need be. He knew she loved and missed the circus and the job of being an acrobat. His greatest fear was that a circus might come through Denver and she'd join up with a troupe before he could talk her out of it.

As the train rumbled down the grade from Colorado and crossed into Oklahoma, Longarm let his mind wander over the infinite variety of Mrs. Spinner's pleasures. On their third or fourth assignation she had invited him to come up to her room after dinner to take "tea." He had been quite surprised, since he'd expected something else, to discover her fully dressed in a severe frock that buttoned to the neck, and an actual tea service laid out on a small table. For the first fifteen minutes he'd been off balance and not quite certain what to do. Finally he had moved his chair around next to her and made a small advance. It had been immediately repulsed. She had even said, "Why, Marshal, what kind of girl do you think I am?"

Since he'd had ample proof on their previous engage-

ments of just what sort of girl she was, he'd been confused and unsure what to do. But she had turned coy
and flirty and, encouraged, he made another sally in the
direction of her breasts. Once again he was rebuffed,
only this time with much batting of her eyelashes and
coy looks and little slaps on the back of his hand. It had
finally dawned on him what the game was. He assaulted
her then with vigor and determination. She'd resisted
sometimes to the point where he thought he might be
following the wrong trail, but he had kept on. The frock,
though intended to cover all, buttoned all the way down
from neck to hem. Button by button he had slowly won
his ground, fighting for every inch of it over her breathless protests and feeble cries and faint attempts to push
his hands away. After the dress it had been a succession
of petticoats and then a chemise and finally an under-
bodice and bloomers. When he finally got her stripped
down naked and felt and tasted her, he knew she was as
ready as any woman he'd ever had. She'd lolled back
in her chair, arms outflung, and said, "Then take me if
you must, you cad."

He had picked her up, carried her to the bed, and laid
her down gently. She lay on her back, legs spread wide,
gently massaging herself through the silken wheat-color
hair with one long, slender finger. She was making soft
little outcries as he frantically tried to tear off his clothes
so he could join her before it was too late. She was
starting to heave her hips up when he finally covered
her and entered the soft, warm vagina. She had climaxed
the instant he'd taken himself fully into her, and his
excitement had been such that he had followed only a
few seconds later.

Longarm suddenly became aware of a fine sheen of

sweat on his forehead. It was June, and warm in the passenger car, but not warm enough to sweat. The heat was being generated from within and he reckoned it would be a good thing for his health, as well as his general appearance, if he put Lila Spinner's infinite variety of pleasures out of his mind for the time being. His assignment could last a week; it could last a month. He certainly didn't want to be tormenting himself with a slice of pie he couldn't have because it was out of reach. Better to think of the job ahead and think of Mrs. Spinner at such time as he might be able to take her in hand.

It was early afternoon. On the floor next to Longarm's feet was a sack of biscuits stuffed with ham that his landlady had made up for him. There was also a bottle of his good Maryland whiskey sitting in the seat between him and the side of the coach. Having had nothing to eat since breakfast, and that had come at six A.M., he dug into the sack of biscuits and began to eat the ham sandwiches one after another as he stared out the window at the countryside rolling by at forty miles an hour. They had slipped only briefly though a corner section of Oklahoma and were now running due south through the northern part of Texas. The train had just stopped at Lubbock to drop off some passengers and take on some new ones. Still, the car wasn't very crowded and Longarm had had a seat to himself all the way. Usually it was his luck, if he rode the passenger coaches rather than accompanying his mount in the stock cars, to draw some stout old lady who crowded him and objected to his cigar smoke. He knew that lady was waiting at some station between here and San Antonio, but, so far, his luck had held.

Outside, the landscape was bleak and arid-looking.

Longarm didn't reckon a man could raise ten cows to a thousand acres. Now and again they passed the cabin of a sodbuster. Usually the wife and children would be standing out in front of the weatherbeaten cabin staring at the train with big eyes while the farmer was out behind a plow hoping like hell to make a crop of wheat or corn or cotton before weevils or wind and rain or hail, or just plain bad luck, took it. Longarm always thought the women, especially, had such a hopeless look about them. He wondered how they felt, alone on a great prairie, no neighbors, no pretty things, nothing but hard work and bearing children and waiting for the next crop to fail so they could load the wagon and move on to another piece of soil in an equally unwelcoming place so another crop could go down and then wither under the killing sun and lack of rain. He guessed that was why they had so many kids. There wasn't much else to do. And, as the train passed, he could pretty well figure how long a couple had been married by the number of kids they had. The children always stood in a rank, the youngest next to the mother, who generally had a baby in her arms, and then they stair-stepped upwards to the oldest. You could tell that there was usually just about a year between them.

He yawned and took a moment to unplug his bottle of whiskey and take a short drink. He still had a long way to go. Even though they were well inside Texas, it would be about eight hours more before they reached San Antonio. Texas, Longarm reflected, was just too damn big. You could travel and travel and still be in the same damn state. A man liked a little variety. Texas was like making love to a fat woman. More was not necessarily better.

Austin Davis was supposed to meet him when the train got in, but Longarm had his doubts on that score. Most likely, Davis would get captured by a bottle or a poker game or a woman or all three and completely forget about meeting the senior deputy marshal. It made him mad just to think about it.

He had met Austin Davis some fourteen or fifteen months back, in Mason County, Texas. Longarm had been called in to run down a gang that the local authorities couldn't seem to handle. Davis had shown up with some wanted paper on several of the supposed bandits and claimed he was there doing a little bounty hunting. Given the quality of the local law, Longarm had sworn him in as a provisional deputy. No one had been more surprised than Longarm himself when Davis had panned out pretty well. In a rash moment Longarm had recommended him for the Marshal Service, and then damned if he hadn't been accepted.

Longarm calculated Austin Davis to be in his mid- to late-thirties. He was as tall as Longarm—a little over six feet—but wasn't built quite as heavy in the shoulders and arms. He figured Davis was probably a pretty good man in a hand-to-hand fight. He knew he was good in a gun fight, but he reckoned he could also use his fists. The man was deceptively strong. When they were setting up an ambush in front of the mercantile in Mason, Longarm had seen him lift an eighty-pound bag of feed like it didn't weigh anything. Besides, Davis' face was virtually unmarked, and for a man with his turn of tongue that was a sure sign he could handle himself. Austin Davis was a smart aleck. No, Longarm thought, reluctantly trying to be fair, that wasn't quite true. Davis was smart. Plain and simple smart. But he knew it, and he didn't mind letting folks around him know it. That was where the "aleck" part came in, and that was what irritated the hell out of Longarm. He didn't mind Davis being right once in a while, but he hated to hear him announce it.

And, on top of everything else, Davis was just close enough to being handsome to be certain that all the ladies were standing in line waiting to get a piece of him. Longarm looked out the train window, brooding on his new partner's defects. Some things were going to have to change and he, Longarm, was just the man to adjust matters. For a moment Longarm let himself speculate on what Mrs. Spinner would think of Austin Davis, but he quickly banished that line of thinking. Mrs. Spinner, he firmly decided, was well above the station of some ride-and-shoot *pistolero* like Austin Davis, and he would never allow a lady of her accomplishments to come anywhere near a rounder like the junior deputy marshal. He was confidant, though, that if she did happen to meet the man, *she* wouldn't be fooled by his flash-in-the-pan looks or his sassy mouth.

He stretched in the seat, sticking out his long legs and extending his arms over his head. It was a most uncommon long ride. And then, once in San Antonio, there was still the business of getting down to Laredo, which was another two hundred miles. Longarm had not brought a horse with him, but there was a military installation at San Antonio, several in fact, and he could requisition whatever mounts he needed from the cavalry.

The train kept rumbling along. The afternoon had worn down and dusk wasn't far off. Longarm got out one of his two-for-a-nickle cigars, bit the end off, and lit it up with a big kitchen match that he struck with his thick thumbnail. When it was drawing good, he took a swig of whiskey to sweeten his mouth and then leaned back and blew out clouds of smoke, most of it whipping out the open window by his side. He'd be glad to get off the train and he didn't care who knew it. He wanted a steak and a bath and a good bed. People said he was crazy, but he would rather sit a horse for twelve hours than ride a train for the same amount. Riding a horse was a whole hell of a lot less tiring as far as Longarm was concerned, but he couldn't get anybody to agree with him. Some folks claimed they *liked* to ride on trains. He considered that just plain silly.

It got dark and he ate a few more of the biscuit sandwiches and had another drink or two of whiskey. A candy butcher came through the coaches selling various things to eat and smokes and soda pop. Longarm bought a bottle of strawberry fizz and found it went very well with his corn whiskey, though not at the same time.

He didn't know a great deal about the job that lay ahead, but that was all right. It seemed there was a customs inspector in Laredo, an official with the United States Customs Service, who had been allowing cattle from Mexico to cross the border without staying in quarantine for the prescribed number of days. The result had been considerable trouble for the South Texas ranchers through whose ranges these herds of illegal Mexican cattle passed. The problem was that Mexican cattlemen did not dip their stock to rid them of the ticks and fleas and lice that could cause half a dozen plagues in clean, American stock. For that reason they were supposed to be held on the border for ninety days to make sure they weren't suffering from some disease, primarily Mexican tick fever, before they were allowed to cross onto United

States soil. But holding cattle in corrals, large herds of cattle, was an expensive business. There was no grass for them to graze off, so they had to be fed hay and grain and feed, and for a herd of any size that could run into a considerable amount of money. Also, standing around like that, the cattle tended to become sore-footed and get on the prod with each other, which meant fights, which meant dead cattle. But the worst thing about the quarantine, for the man who was buying cheap Mexican steers with an eye toward bringing it into the U.S. and turning a profit, was that, just as the quarantine was intended to discover, the cattle might get sick and all of them up and die. When that happened, the U.S. speculator lost all the money he'd spent on the cattle, all he'd spent gathering them and driving them to the border, and all the money he'd spent feeding them before they got sick. The best way around all that trouble was to bribe a customs official to fake your quarantine and give you papers that would let you through in a hurry and legally. The problem was that most inspectors wouldn't take a bribe because it was too easy to get caught. Smuggling a thousand head of steers across the border was a lot harder than dealing in any other kind of contraband, like gold or weapons.

Of course many herds were taken across "wet," meaning they were driven across the Rio Grande at a secluded spot along the border. The problem here was that the owner had no papers to prove he'd crossed the cattle legally through quarantine, and he was subject to being stopped by any range inspector and having his herd taken away from him. Also, it was very difficult to sell "wet" cattle, since the buyer knew he was not only buying cattle but trouble.

But according to Billy Vail, Austin Davis had gotten the goods on an official at the customs station in Laredo who had apparently found a way to take bribes without getting caught. The cattlemen who had been having their herds infected had appealed to the Customs Service first and hadn't gotten any satisfaction. Customs had claimed that their investigations showed all their people to be in the clear. After that, the ranchers had turned to the Marshal Service, and Austin Davis was sent to look into the matter. He'd apparently found enough going on to warrant a full scale investigation. And that, as Billy Vail had said to Longarm, "is what is going to put you in Laredo."

Billy had been about to give his deputy some of the details, but Longarm had waved him away, saying, "Naw. Save that for Davis. Them few little facts is about all he's going to get to tell me, and I'd hate to deprive him of the chance of swelling around and feeling important."

Billy Vail had looked a little worried. "Now, Longarm," he'd said, "we ain't ever had no killing between our marshals. You ain't fixing to break that string, are you?"

Longarm leaned back fretfully in the coach seat and yawned. He stared at the blackness out the window, relieved only here and there by a pinpoint of light. Would the damn train, he wondered, ever get to San Antonio? Hell, as bored as he was, he was even beginning to look forward to seeing Austin Davis.

Chapter 2

To Longarm's great surprise Austin Davis was there to meet him when the train finally pulled in to San Antonio a little before eleven at night. He was waiting on the passenger platform and he came forward as soon as he spied Longarm He said, putting out his hand, "Hell, Grammaw was slow but she was old. Where the hell you been, Marshal."

Longarm had to put his saddle down to shake Davis' hand. He had his saddlebags in the other hand with a small valise hung off his thumb. It was awkward, but if Davis wanted to shake hands instead of getting part of the load, Longarm wasn't going to complain. He hadn't made the trip expecting any fun. "How are you, Austin," he said, "Still wearing that border hat, I see."

Davis was wearing a black, flat-crowned, stiff-brimmed hat favored by the kind of men who hung around the border for their health. He was also wearing a soft black leather vest with silver conchos for buttons. Davis shook hands and then touched the brim of his hat. "Hell," he explained, "I got to stay in the role. I'm

21

supposed to be a border desperado dealing in illegal cattle. Supposed to be a bad man.''

Longarm picked up his saddle and slung it over his shoulder. His thumb was about to break off holding the small valise the way he had it. ''It suits you,'' he told the junior deputy.

''What, the hat?''

''Naw, acting like a desperado. I ain't so sure but what you ain't. But if you don't get this valise off my thumb, you're going to be a bad man in pain.''

Austin Davis jumped around and took the valise, relieving the pressure on Longarm's thumb. ''Well, hell, why didn't you say you needed some help? Last time I helped you without you asking, you like to have taken my head off.''

Longarm just gave him a glance. ''I want a steak and a bath and a bed,'' he said.

Davis chuckled softly. He had a pleasant voice when he chose to use it. ''I got you all set. I know you're a man who likes his comfort. We got rooms over at the Gunther Hotel. Ain't two blocks from here. And the cook will still be there. I warned him there was a bad ol' bear coming to town and if he didn't get a steak or two, he might eat the hotel and everybody in it.''

''Well, that's a fair start, Davis,'' Longarm said. ''Could be we'll get out of this with you still alive. That is if somebody else don't kill you.''

Davis laughed. ''Yeah, and I'm glad to see you, too. Hell, I was scairt you might have changed and turned human. I bet ol' Billy Vail had to twist your arm plumb off to get you to come down here.''

Longarm looked at him. ''Hell, I heard it the other way around. The way Billy told it, you wanted anybody but me. Somebody, I reckon, who didn't know all your sly ways.''

''Billy's sly ways,'' Davis corrected. ''This is kind of a tricky setup we're going into and I told him I didn't reckon was anybody else but you could pull it off.''

They had left the train depot and were walking down the street toward the hotel. Longarm stopped dead. ''Now listen, smooth-mouth,'' he said, ''that kind of silver tongue bullshit might sell in some markets, but it won't fit me. I ain't rising to that kind of bait.''

Davis shrugged. ''You can believe me or not. Don't make a damn bit of difference to me. Things have changed since you swore me in in Mason County. Now I wear the same badge as you do and they ain't no place on the back of it where they stamp in the years you got in the saddle. Me and you is equal, partner, and you can like that or lump it. I ain't smooth-mouthing you about nothing. I don't have to. I asked for you and that is a fact. And by the time we are halfway through this little deal I expect, unless you get taken by a serious case of the dumbs, that you will see why. But, like I say, it's all the same to me. We ain't got to be friendly.'' With that, he turned and continued walking toward the hotel, his back very straight and rigid.

Longarm, startled, stared after him for a moment. Finally, when he could find his voice, he yelled, ''Hey, wait a damn minute! Davis! Hold up there, you sonofabitch!''

Austin Davis slowed and stopped some ten yards down the street. He turned halfway around. He was still holding Longarm's valise in his hand. ''What?'' he said.

Longarm walked toward him. When he'd arrived so that they were facing each other he unslung the saddle from his shoulder and dropped it at Davis' feet. Staring the other man flat in the face, he said, "I have carried that saddle better than halfway from the station. If we're going to be partners, it seems only right that you carry it the rest of the way."

Austin Davis stared back for a half a moment. Finally he shrugged and said, "All right. That sounds square." But before he bent to pick up the saddle, he held out the valise. "But then you ought to take this."

"Fine," Longarm said stiffly.

Austin Davis picked up the saddle and slung it over his shoulder. "The hotel is just another block yonder," he said.

"I know where the damn Gunther Hotel is as well as you do."

"You still ain't shucks as a poker player."

"Listen," Longarm said with some heat, "before this job is over I am going to have every cent you got and a lien on your next year's salary."

Davis replied amiably, "You just keep on dreaming, partner. And I wouldn't count on no comfort from the ladies, not while I'm around."

As they resumed walking toward the hotel, Longarm said, "If you're a real good boy I might let you have some of my leavings so far as the females are concerned. But I can guarantee you they will be gnawed down to the bone by the time I'm through with them."

"My, my. That is brave talk for a man of your years. You sure you got the strength for it?"

"If we don't get to that hotel and get me a steak, you will shortly find out about my strength. And I just hope you haven't already got the situation screwed up where I can't save it. I'm down here to do a job and I can only hope you don't get in the way with your big feet.''

The Gunther was an old institution in San Antonio, known for miles around as the best cattleman's hotel in the West. It had a big, spacious lobby with a first-class bar that served liquors and whiskeys not found in the ordinary saloon. Their rooms were of good size and their resturant was famous for the quality of its menu. A man could walk across the Gunther's marble floor, go up to the desk, drop his saddle, and say what he wanted and expect to have it happen faster than he could put his name in the hotel registry. When Longarm told the clerk what he wanted, the man just nodded and snapped his fingers. In an instant porters were there to relieve him of his gear and luggage and the clerk recommenderd they have his supper, following which, Longarm's bath would be waiting for him in his room. And if he didn't feel like shaving himself or wanted his hair cut, the clerk would have a barber sent up.

And that at eleven o'clock at night.

As they went into the dining room Longarm said, ''These folks know how to run a hotel. I come in here one morning at about three A.M. with a bullet in my side and a terrible thirst for some goat's milk. I guess I was half out of my head with the wound, but it seemed like somebody had told me goat's milk would keep your strength up. Well I don't know how they did it, but they had a glass of goat's milk in my hand before the doctor arrived to take the slug out of me.'' He made a face. ''My word, I can still taste that damn goat's milk. But I drank it. Man gets an idea in his head, he can't shake it. I asked the doctor about it later and he said he'd thought it was a little strange to find a gunshot victim drinking goat's milk, but he figured it was probably some kind of superstition. Said it wouldn't hurt me, but he doubted it would have done me as much good as getting the bullet out."

Austin Davis gave him a glance. "Is they a point to that story?"

Longarm shrugged. They had come to the big double doors of the dining room. A uniformed waiter was hurrying toward them. "Naw, not really," Longarm said. "Just makes me wonder how many other hotels there are around could come up with a doctor and a glass of goat's milk at three in the morning."

"Not many, I'd guess." Davis remarked dryly.

The waiter came up and said, "Mister Davis, I seen y'all when you come in the lobby. I done told the cook and he's already got y'all's steaks on. Big T-bones. Got some potatoes and some corn, and some apple dumpling for desert with sweet cream. Let me get y'all set down an' I'll bring you what you need from the bar."

As they followed the waiter, Longarm said to Austin Davis, "See what I mean? They not only can produce a glass of goat's milk, they can remember you."

Austin Davis looked amused. "Wasn't my face that they remembered. Was that of Abraham Lincoln."

"What are you talking about?"

Davis sat down in the chair the waiter had pulled out for him. "That's the face on the five-dollar bill I gave him to remember."

"Don't be so careless with my money," Longarm said. "I got plans for it."

"Your money? How you figure that?"

Longarm smiled thinly. "When this job is over, sonny boy, I'm going to send you home with nothing but lint in your pockets and a vow in your heart to never play

26

poker with the big boys again.''

Austin Davis yawned. "In your dreams, Marshal."

"So how does it fall out?" Longarm asked.

He was in a galvanized tub, soaking the train tiredness out of his bones in the hot water. Austin Davis was sitting on the bed, drinking whiskey out of a glass and smoking a cigarillo.

"Well, Jay Caster is the man we want. He's the chief customs inspector for all the cattle that cross the border at Laredo. There are other custom folks there dealing in other matters, but he is the honcho on the cattle and the horses and any other kind of livestock that has to be quarantined. He's got about four other men working for him, but only one of them is a customs officer. The rest are just Mexican hired hands that work the livestock."

Longarm reached an arm outside the tub, and found the bottle of whiskey sitting there. He poured a measure in his glass, took a sip, and worked it around in his mouth. A tooth had been bothering him lately and he hoped to hell it wasn't going to get serious. There were damn few things he was out-and-out scared of, but a dentist was one of them. "You reckon the rest of them are in it with him?" he asked Davis.

Davis took a puff on his cigarillo. "They'd have to be." He blew a smoke ring. "Hell, moving a herd of cattle around ain't like palming the ace of spades."

"Well, how does he do it? I mean, does he just get paid off and then clear the cattle right on through without even the show of a quarantine?"

"Naw. Nothing so raw as that. He puts up a front. It ain't a good one, but it seems to satisfy his superiors. That, by the way, is the crux of the matter. How far

27

uphill does the water run? Caster is crooked. We ain't going to have no trouble proving that. But he's got a boss. In Brownsville. And that boss has got a boss. In Galveston. So just how high up the tree are the branches rotten? Boss on top of a boss, right on up to Washington, D.C., I reckon."

Longarm took another mouthful of whiskey and soaked his tooth in it. After a moment he swallowed and said, "Why don't we just catch one crook at a time? The whole thing kind of irritates me, anyway. Why doesn't the damn Customs Service clean up their own messes? Hell, we got other hooligans to gather up."

"The way I get it," Davis said, "the cattlemen complained about them diseased herds coming through and infecting their cattle and the customs folks never gave them no relief. Claimed the herds must have been wet, illegal, though any damn fool knows you can't get twenty miles in this country driving a herd up from the south without proper papers. But the more they complained, the more the customs folks said it couldn't be none of their bunch doing anything wrong since they was all good boys and put a dime in the collection plate every Sunday."

Longarm glanced over at Davis. "Reckon they've been laying behind the log?"

Davis nodded. "I would reckon. I would reckon they've been looking out for each other. Been a little back-scratching going on to my way of thinking."

"And we got called in how?"

"Cattlemen went to their legislators and asked did they want to keep their soft jobs or get voted out next election. The senators and congressmen got right on to our outfit and that's how come you're taking a bath in

San Antonio and I'm sitting on this here bed.''

Longarm gave a little bark of laughter. "You do have a way of cutting right to the nub of the situation, Austin. But you ain't told me yet how this Caster fellow passes the illegal herds through without being so damn obvious about it. Does he just hand out paper giving them a clean bill of health and let them wade on across?''

Davis shook his head. "Even he couldn't get away with that. The herds have got to come through the port of entry, as they call it, at Laredo. They got to actually cross the International Bridge there. They get a trail brand, or mark, to see them through the border country and on up toward the north where most of them are bound. To the railheads, to Oklahoma, Kansas, wherever.''

"So how does it work? I've seen the big corrals around the bridge. Here and down at Brownsville. I guess there's one up at Eagle Pass also.''

Davis took another drink of whiskey. "Yeah, they get put in the holding corrals. They got a system the way they handle the situation. As you can well imagine they is one hell of a lot of cattle comes in to the quarantine stations. I mean in the thousands. What they do, when a fresh herd comes in, is slap a daub of paint on the side of each head of beef. It's red paint for them coming in new and getting ready to be penned up for ninety days. After that, they stage the herds. The ones moving up, getting ready to go out in another thirty days, gets a daub of white paint. Then, when those cattle are free and done their time, they get slapped with a swipe of green paint. Maybe you've seen that on herds down here in South Texas. It wears off pretty quick, but some of it can still be seen after a time.''

29

Longarm scratched his chin. He'd shaved while in the bath and the razor had nicked the point of his jaw. "Yeah, I've seen that," he said. "What's that got to do with us? Looks like a good way of keeping up with the inventory."

Davis shrugged. "There's a lot of folks around, watching those herds. Caster can't just run a herd in, slap it with green paint, and then run it across the bridge. Too many interested parties."

Longarm stepped out of the bath, picked up a towel, and began drying himself. "So he's got some sly way of going about it, is that what you're saying?"

Davis nodded and exhaled a cloud of blue smoke. "Oh, yes. And he does it right under folks' noses, too. You're getting the floor wet."

Longarm gave him a look. "How the hell am I supposed to get out of a bathtub without dripping on the floor? Hell, they expect such things. What is this cute way Caster's got?"

Davis pondered for a moment, studying the tip of his cigarillo. "I don't know," he admitted.

Longarm threw his towel down, took a clean pair of jeans off a chair, sat down, and began pulling them on. "You what?"

"I said I don't know." Davis gestured with the glass in his hand. "Don't you wear no underclothes?"

"Naw."

"How come?"

Longarm glared at him. "How come? What the hell business is that of yours? I never wore underwear because I never seen the need. Besides, it gets crosswise and rides up on you. But what the hell has that got to do with a bribe-taking custom inspector? I thought you had this play all figured out. How come you don't know how he does it?''

Davis stood up and walked to the bedside table where there was another bottle of whiskey. He poured a little more liquor in his glass, then said, ''Because I just don't. He's slick, damn slick. And there are an awful lot of cattle in an awful lot of pens and they get moved around. One day a bunch is in one pen with white paint on 'em, and the next day they've moved clear on around to a pen at the bridge and are wearing green paint and getting their papers. I've watched for two weeks, and I still can't see how he's been doing it.''

''You sure somebody hasn't made you for the law?''

Davis shook his head. ''No. I ain't showed a badge around here in two months. Anybody I've run into that knowed me before don't know I'm a federal officer. Caster puts this show on for everybody. I think he naturally expects the law to be watching him and he goes along under that assumption. I know he's moving cattle out of here illegally, because I've seen it done. I've picked me out a few steers from a fresh herd that I was pretty sure would be bribed through. Knew it from what I'd heard. And I've watched those steers as close as I could, allowing for a few hours of sleep and eating, you understand. Somehow they got from the red paint to the green in a week and were on their way. But I still don't know how it happened. Thousand head.'' He put his head back and took a long drink.

''Huh!'' Longarm said. ''This is sounding more like it. But you said there wouldn't be no problem proving this Caster is crooked. You said your big worry was how far up the tree we could reach. Now it sounds like you ain't even got anything on Caster.''

Austin Davis laughed. "Oh, hell, he'll be easy. I got a herd being put together about fifty miles south of Laredo. When I bring them up I'll simply bribe the sonofabitch and arrest him at the same time. But that's just Caster. I'd like to get his boss in Brownsville."

Longarm was pulling on his boots. "I can't believe that man can get a thousand head of cattle past me without me seeing how he's doing it. Like you said, it ain't like palming an ace."

Davis said patiently, "We don't have to know how he's doing it. All I got to do is catch him in an illegal act, like taking a bribe. Or we could follow one steer and see how he manages to move up to the green corral so quick. I'll tell you one thing it ain't hard to tell the cattle that ain't being bribed through. They stand around and stand around and stand around. Get damn little feed and less water. You can watch them losing flesh in the course of one afternoon. I think Caster does it to drum up business. It's the same as saying, Hand over the cash or sit and watch your cattle wilt away."

Longarm stood up and stomped his boots on the floor, settling them to his feet. "This still an all night town?" he asked.

"Oh, yes." Davis replied. "You can get anything at midnight that you can get at noon. Why?"

Longarm picked up a clean shirt and started putting it on. "I reckoned we'd go out and play a few hands of poker. Kind of put our ear to the ground. I don't know about you, Austin, but damned if I'm content to just arrest that man. If he's stacking the deck, I want to find out how. And I intend to do so before we put his ass in jail. Ain't a sonofabitch alive can slip a herd by me."

"You do know it's after midnight?" Austin Davis

yawned. "A good bit past midnight."

"You ain't got to go. Where you bunking?"

Austin jerked his thumb. "Next room. How we going to play this? Do we know each other?"

Longarm thought a moment. "Hell yes, I don't see why not. You're the man bringing in the herd. I'm the fellow what is buying them. Gives me a reason to be in on all the transactions. You coming?"

"Not without it's an order. I been up since four this morning. I don't hanker for no night life right now."

"Then I reckon I'll see you for breakfast. We can talk it over a bit more then. What time?"

Davis shrugged. "You're going to be out late. Say eight o'clock?"

"I'll be too hungry by then. Say seven."

Davis yawned again and stood up. "Well," he said, "you try not to get into no trouble before I'm up good and had my coffee. We still got a few things to talk about."

"Seems to me the main thing is how we're going to reach up the tree and get one more branch."

"That would be it." Davis stretched his hands over his head. "Hell, I'm plumb give out. I'd of thought you'd be the same."

"I been cooped up on a damn train all day. I got to get out and see a little of the world up close before I can unwind. Besides, I ain't been in South Texas in a time. I need to get used to the place again, even if this is just San Antonio."

Austin Davis was at the door. He turned the knob and shook his head. "That," he said, "ain't going to happen. I been in this country on and off for twenty-five years and I ain't got used to it yet. You don't understand this

33

place, you just try and survive it. Wear your eyes and ears out there. They is folks walking around will kill you for the boots on your feet, let alone your revolver and what change they think might be in your pockets. And we're still a hundred and eighty miles from the bad part."

Longarm said dryly, "I'll be real careful, Marshal Davis. Wouldn't want to bring no discredit on you. You lose a senior deputy the first day on the job, wouldn't look good on your record. What time is our train for Laredo tomorrow?"

"Supposed to leave at eleven. Most times it does. I ain't kidding about this town. San Antonio ain't the border, but it's still Mexico on both sides."

"What about horses? I could requisition some mounts at one of these calvary stations right here. We could hire a stock car."

"I got the horse situation all tended to," Davis said. He pulled the door open. "See you at breakfast."

"I hope you understand I am mighty particular about my riding stock," Longarm said.

Austin Davis gave him a slow smile. "Tell me, Marshal, just what ain't you mighty particular about?"

When Davis was gone, Longarm buckled on his gun belt. He carried a Colt .44 caliber with a six-inch barrel. He had another of the same model in his saddlebags, only with a nine-inch barrel. He seldom had use for it, but when he did, it was a mighty handy instrument for a distance that was a little too long for regular pistol work but too close for a rifle. His gun belt featured a big, concave silver buckle. From the outside it appeared to be an ordinary if somewhat outsized buckle. But inside the curve of the buckle there was just enough room to conceal a .38 caliber derringer, kept in place by a strong steel spring. It had saved his life more than once. His lever-action carbine was the same caliber as his Colt revolver, which eliminated the necessity by buying different ammunition.

Lastly he put on his hat, a high-crowned pearl-gray beauty with a four-and-a-half-inch brim that curved up gracefully. It was a new hat and had cost him $45. Billy Vail had predicted it would be a wreck before he got back to town, but Longarm had vowed that this was one hat that was not going to see hard usage as most of his hats did. Billy Vail had just laughed.

He left his room and walked through the lobby, his boot heels echoing loudly in the deserted expanse. All around were big, overstuffed chairs and divans. In the morning they would be occupied by cattlemen talking business, but now those buyers and sellers were in bed, sleeping the sleep of men who knew they could trade cattle or horses with the best of them.

Longarm stepped out into the cool night. He stood a moment orienting himself. Some three blocks away was the big Military Plaza. When Texas had been a province of Mexico, the plaza had been a parade ground where the Mexican calvary had wheeled and manuevered. Now it was a bricked-over park with trees and fountains and benches. But it was still bordered by the governor's mansion and other government buildings that had been taken over by the Republic of Texas and later by the state when Texas entered the Union.

Longarm turned left out of the hotel and began walking in the general direction of the center of town. Even though it was late, he could see several saloons going full blast. There were not many people on the streets, but now and again he met a man walking or a woman sidling along, practicing her profession. Occasionally a horseman went by.

Peering in the window of the first saloon he passed, Longarm decided it looked like poor pickings and continued up the street. He really didn't intend to stay out late. He'd simply been cooped up too long on the train and felt the urgent need to get out and stretch his legs. As he walked along, he mulled over the problem of the cattle inspector in Laredo. On the surface it seemed pretty easy, but Longarm was damned if he could figure how Jay Caster moved whole herds around without being obvious about it. As much as Longarm hated to admit it, Austin Davis was no slouch and if he hadn't caught on to how it was done, it was a gut cinch that they had a job of work cut out for them.

He stepped into the second saloon he came to and stood at the bar for a drink of inferior whiskey while he looked over a couple of tables where poker was being played. After a few hands had been dealt, he could tell both were limit games and not worth his trouble. He preferred a dollar ante, pot limit game. It was the only way a man could use his money as a weapon. If you couldn't bet enough to make a man check his character, you might as well turn all the cards face up and just play to see who had the best luck. Luck wasn't something a real poker player counted on. Poker was a game of skill and science, requiring a thorough knowledge of human nature. Longarm had had some of his biggest nights when he never made a hand better than two pair.

He paid for his whiskey, leaving it half undrunk and then stepped out of the saloon and started for the next block. It was a dark area and, just as he was passing an alley, he heard a voice, close by, say, "Psst! Hey! You there!"

Longarm stopped. The mouth of the alley was dark to almost black, but he was able to make out a form there, for the man who'd hailed him was standing no more than ten feet away. Longarm also caught the glint of something in the man's hand. "You talking to me?" he asked.

"See anybody else?"

"What do you want?"

The man chuckled hoarsely. "Now what you reckon I want? I want what's in yore pockets. And I reckon I wouldn't move was I you. I'm holding steady on yore middle, an' I'll blow a hole through you a horse could climb through if you so much as bat an eye."

"You robbing me? Is that it?"

"Enough of this palaver. Turn out yore pockets an' be damn quick 'bout it. And while you be at it, move over this way a mite. An' I wouldn't let my hand git near my iron was I you. I ain't gonna miss at this range."

Longarm said calmly, trying to see the robber more clearly, "You better pick an easier target, mister."

"You just never mind tellin' me my bid'ness. You just turn and face me so's I can see whatever is in yore mind and put a stop to it before you git up to mischief."

Slowly, Longarm turned to his left. He knew that the man was going to order him to drop his gun, and he knew that once you let a situation start getting bad it never got better by itself. As he came fully around to face the man, he suddenly let his left leg collapse, falling full length toward the boardwalk on his side. As he fell, he heard the sharp explosion of the robber's pistol, saw the orange-red flame of the shot erupt in the night, and heard the *whiz* of the bullet through the space where he had been standing.

But he was drawing as he fell. Before his left shoulder hit the boardwalk, his revolver was in his hand, the hammer back, the barrel aimed at the spot he'd seen the muzzle-flash. He fired, the hammer of the gun slamming back in his palm. Over the echo of his own shot he heard a muffled "Hmmmmph!" as the man grunted. From the sound, Longarm knew that his bullet had found solid flesh and, more than likely, bone.

He lay a second, letting his eyes come back into focus from the blinding flash of his shot. As he stared into the alley his eyes gradually adjusted to the dark. At first he couldn't see anything. But then, looking closer, he saw what appeared to be a heap of old clothes lying on the ground in the mouth of the alley. For half a moment Longarm lay still, his revolver covering the heap, watching for any sign of movement. None came and he slowly got to his feet and advanced on the fallen man. He lay on his side, his revolver nearby in the dust. With his boot toe Longarm turned him over. He could see, from the dark stain on the fellow's shirt, where his bullet had struck home, midway up the chest and just to the left of the breastbone. The impact would have knocked the man down and probably killed him before he could hit the ground.

Longarm reached down, picked up the man's pistol, and stuck it in his belt. He looked at the man's face. It wasn't anyone he'd ever seen before; just one more robber in a town full of robbers.

He sighed and said softly, "Damn, damn, damn!" For a moment he was tempted to just walk away and leave the body. But he couldn't do that. Someone else, some innocent party, might be charged in the shooting. No, as much as he hated it, there wasn't but one course of action open to him. He'd have to go to the local law. The least of that was that it would take time and put him to bed later. The worst was that it would call attention to himself and his presence in South Texas. But there was no help for it; it had to be done. He sighed again and started toward the downtown section, where he reckoned the sheriff or police office would be. So much for a relaxing walk and a quiet drink and a few hands of poker. Why hadn't the stupid sonofabitch waited for an easier mark? Why did he have to pick on a U.S. deputy marshal? Well, Longarm decided, it was just bad luck for both of them.

Chapter 3

Longarm waited until they'd finished breakfast and were on their first smoke and second cup of coffee before he related what had happened the night before. When he was through, Austin Davis raised his eyebrows slightly and whistled. "Well, I'd have to say you done the town up a little better than what I was expecting."

"Hold the comments to yourself," Longarm said. "What do you reckon? Am I exposed? I know how tight this country is around here. What do you think? You figure we can proceed as planned?"

Davis thought a moment, then said, "Hell, Longarm, I don't rightly know. I got to say there is a well-worn path between San Antonio and Laredo. They might be a hundred and eighty miles apart, but I swear you can see a man in Laredo one day and then run into him the next right here in San Antonio. They've been hooked together for two hundred years, back when this was part of Mexico. But I hate to abandon the plan we got, because I don't know of another one. How many you reckon saw you or heard about you?"

Longarm shook his head, remembering. "Like I told you, I went over to the jailhouse. Sheriff wasn't there, but a couple of deputies were on duty. I told them what had happened, hoping I could get out of the business without declaring myself. But I was a stranger to them and they weren't about to take me at my word. They insisted on sending for the sheriff, and away we went with all boilers blasting. Sheriff come down, and then me and about half a dozen deputies went around to look at the body. Collected quite a little crowd."

"But they still didn't know at that point who you were?"

"Naw," Longarm said. "I just give my name as Long and hadn't said anything else. The feller I killed was known to them as a small-time crook around town. But what caused the trouble was they insisted he'd never tried armed robbery before, and kind of took the attitude I might have just shot him for the hell of it. Wasn't nothing but my word that he'd been holding a gun on me. Naturally I'd turned it in when I got to the jailhouse, but they took the position that that didn't mean he'd ever been holding the gun and threatening me with it. In fact, they come about as close to calling me a liar as you can get."

Davis smiled slightly. "I reckon they couldn't understand how you could kill a man who already has the drop on you and your weapon is in your holster. I can see how they'd wonder about that."

"Naturally that point got made. The way they were going on I could see it wouldn't be long before they decided I'd been robbing the dead man and had killed him to keep matters clean." Longarm shook his head. "Just was bad luck."

Davis blew a smoke ring into the air. "I reckon the dead man might have been thinking along the same lines if he could have been thinking."

"Well, I finally had to own up." Longarm said. "I got the sheriff aside, hoping to limit the publicity, and kind of told him on the quiet and showed him my badge." He made a disgusted sound. "For all the good that done. We was back in the office by then and it didn't take ten seconds for word to get around that I was a federal marshal."

"Did they know you? Recognize the name?"

Longarm looked up at the ceiling and sighed. "Sometimes I don't think matters shake out fairly. I been a good marshal. That ought to have been enough."

"I take it they knew you."

"It's that damn nickname of mine. I wish I'd never heard the word Longarm. I'd like to find the man that first pinned that on me and do him a great harm."

"How many you reckon heard about you?"

Longarm grimaced. "No telling," he said. "I reckon they was a dozen collected together there in the sheriff's office."

"All law?"

"Oh, hell no! Bunch of them wasn't nothing but loungers and busybodies and I don't know what all. So if a dozen heard it, how many you reckon knows this morning that a U.S. deputy marshal is in this part of the country?"

Davis laughed ruefully. "Enough so if they was voters you could get elected mayor. This is a talking town. This whole part of the country is talking towns." He shook his head and put his cigarillo out in his saucer.

Longarm looked across the crowded hotel dining room. "Damn!" he swore.

"The famous Marshal Longarm," Davis said waggishly. "I reckon I'd heard about you for ten years before I finally clapped eyes on you in Mason. I figured you to be nine feet tall."

"Cut it out," Longarm said.

"Hell, some of them stories I heard about you would have stretched the mind of the world's biggest sucker. But they was told for the truth."

Longarm gave him a cool look. "I didn't make the stories up, sonny boy."

"I'd hope not. Hell, if you'd run down and caught every crook I heard about, there wouldn't be a horse left alive in the Southwest. You'd have ridden them all to death."

Longarm smiled slightly. "All right, all right. Let's get off that. You're the man on the scene. What do you think this does to our plan?"

Davis leaned back in his chair and took the time to light another cigarillo. After a moment he said, "Well, they know there's a federal marshal in San Antonio, and folks in Laredo will hear about it and they'll figure that the marshal will naturally come on down to see them. But there ain't no reason for anybody in Laredo to suspect that the marshal is you. Not unless you kill another alley robber. I mean, your name is a hell of a lot better known than your face. I can't see any reason anyone would recognize you. You say there was a dozen men at the jail last night? What's the odds on them, anyone of them, showing up in Laredo and being there at exactly the wrong time? Pretty slim, I'd say. Naw, I don't see no reason to alter our plans."

44

Longarm said, with feeling, "If there's a chance it could cause matters to go wrong, I won't take it amiss if we bring in another man. We can wire Billy Vail and have somebody else on the next train."

Austin Davis glanced across the table at Longarm, then said evenly, "You really don't want to work with me, do you?"

Longarm pulled his head back to look at Davis from a greater distance. "I didn't say that. Where'd you get that idea? You reckon I went out and got in that shooting scrape to get out of working with you?"

"You been passing remarks ever since I picked you up at the train. Ain't no skin off my nose either way."

Longarm looked at Davis coolly. Speaking of skin," he said, "thin skin don't go with this job. It don't turn no bullets. You understand me?"

"I understand you appeared to be looking for a way out of the job. You was quick enough to talk about wiring Billy Vail."

Longarm sat still for a moment, not speaking, not doing anything. Finally he said, "Davis, I'm the one wrote the recommendation that got you into the U.S. Marshal Service. I don't do that for men I don't trust with my life and who I don't want to work with. Now, you either get this idea out of your mind about me or we will have to figure out something else right here and now."

The junior deputy stayed his hand as he was about to take a puff on his cigarillo. He was sitting slightly sideways to Longarm. Glancing at him, he said, "You actually wrote me a letter of recommendation?"

"You just heard me say it, didn't you?"

"Hmmmm . . ." Davis said. "That kind of puts a whole new light on the matter. Maybe you ain't all that

45

bad of a feller after all. I reckon I'll have to take back some of them things I been spreading around about you."

Longarm cocked his head. "Do you ever plan to get serious? We got us a job to do."

Davis blew out a cloud of blue smoke. "I'm trying to say I'm sorry and to thank you, you dumb sonofabitch. Yes, I can get serious. Now, if you ain't going to run out on me and head back to Denver, where you ain't got no competition for the poontang, I reckon we better settle our bill here, get packed and get out of this hotel and catch a train. You do realize we're going to Laredo, don't you?"

Longarm got up. The hot coffee had started his tooth to acting up again and he wanted to get to his room and give it a dose of whiskey. "If I've got to go anywhere with you," he said, "I reckon I'd just as soon it be Laredo. Even you can't make a trip to that hellhole any worse."

"Listen," Davis replied, "don't put the knock on Laredo. I've been hanging around there for two months. With a little help I might be able to make myself go back."

As they stepped into the lobby, Longarm said, "I'll meet you back here in half an hour."

Davis was starting toward the desk. "It's still two hours till train time," he said. "You reckon you can go that long without killing anybody?"

Longarm didn't pause. "So long as you stay out of my sight I can." But he couldn't enjoy the banter for the pain in his tooth. It was getting worse and he cursed his luck as he strode down the hall toward his room. The only thing he could think of that was worse than being in Laredo was being in Laredo with a toothache. For a moment he wondered if he had time to go to a dentist while they were still in San Antonio, but he immediately put the thought aside. Better to suffer a little longer than go straight to the sure hell of a dentist's chair.

As he gathered up his few belongings, Longarm couldn't stop worrying about the previous night's experience. He knew it was just an unlucky break but he couldn't shake the feeling that it was some kind of bad omen. He wasn't, by nature, a superstitious man, but he wished feverently that the incident had happened some other time. He and Austin Davis were going into a delicate and potentially explosive situation. Anytime you tried to catch officials in a fellow service and not only shut them down but put them in jail, you were taking on an extra load of law work that usually didn't go with the job. If you made one misstep or didn't play it exactly by the book, making damn certain you had your evidence cold and in black and white, you could come up against a storm. The Marshal Service was part of government, as was the Customs Service, and anytime you got to messing around with government that meant politics and politicians and beauracracy and all the back room dealing you could imagine in your worst nightmare. If they didn't catch Caster and his henchmen clean and sure and square, Longarm hated to think of the trouble they'd be in. It would make being in the middle of a tornado seem like a ride in a front porch swing. So the last thing he wanted was to have inadvertently called attention to himself beforehand. But maybe it was nothing, he told himself. Maybe he was just being over anxious. By the time he'd soaked his tooth in several mouthfuls of whiskey and then swallowed the whiskey, the situation no longer seemed so worrisome. Whiskey, he noted, had a way of giving you that feeling. He also had serious doubts that young Mister Austin Davis really knew what kind of bad country they were heading into. Davis hadn't been a marshal long enough to have had the pleasure of arresting a well-placed government officer. He probably thought a crook was a crook and handcuffs fitted a circuit court judge just as easily as they did a horse thief. Mister Davis had an education coming.

The train pulled out of the station no more than fifteen minutes late. They had a five-hour ride ahead of them. The coach had not been crowded and they'd managed to get one of the double sets of chairs that faced each other. Longarm took the side facing the engine because he didn't like to ride backwards. Austin Davis sat down across from him and piled his duffle and some paper parcels in the empty seat at his side. Longarm nodded at the parcels. "What's all that?" he asked.

Davis yawned. "Oh, I took the opportunity to buy a few clothes. You can't get nothing in Laredo."

Longarm's eyebrows went up. "More clothes? Lord, as near as I can tell you already got more clothes than any four men I know." Davis was wearing his soft black leather vest with the silver conchos down the front. Longarm nodded at it. "What'd you pay for that vest? I bet a family of four could live six months off the price of it."

"Was a gift," Davis said. He smiled. "Lady give it to me. Sort of a thank you present."

"What for? Getting out of town?"

The train rolled along. For the first fifty miles, running

due south, the country was hilly and rolling and covered with oak and sycamore and elm. It was more brushy than pastoral, but now and again a green valley could be seen, decorated with cattle and horses. Then, abruptly, they came out of the hill country and entered the southern plains. The land turned increasingly arid with every passing mile. The oak and elm disappeared to be replaced with mesquite groves and greasewood thickets. Longarm had the window up and it seemed to him that the temperature had risen ten degrees as soon as they'd plunged into the rough rangeland.

"Pretty, ain't it?" Davis said.

Longarm looked out at the drab scene. "How the hell does anyone raise cattle in this scrub?"

Davis said, "They don't. Not in this part anyway. This is called the big *brassada*, the big brush country. There's old mossy-horned longhorns back in them thickets might have got off the ark with Noah. They can make a living here, but ain't no other cow or critter can seem to. No, but you go fifty miles east and you're in the coastal plains and that is rich country. *Muy rico.* That's where the big cattle ranches are in this part of the country, and that's where the hombres live who are kicking up a storm about those diseased Mexican cattle that are being driven through their range."

Longarm glanced out the window again. "Why don't them as is driving illegal cattle take them through here?"

"No water. No grass. You ever tried to drive a thousand cattle a hundred miles without water or grass? It's a little better to the west, and sometimes somebody will try and sneak a wet herd through there, heading for the railhead or maybe trying to get them to Fort Worth or someplace they can sell them without being pressed too close about the origin of the cattle or what paper the sellers got.''

Longarm reached beside him in the seat and uncorked the bottle of whiskey he had handy. He took a mouthful and let it deaden his tooth for a moment. Then he swallowed and said, ''What makes it worthwhile for a man to go to all this much trouble? The prices that different?''

Austin Davis nodded. ''I would reckon. You can buy steers in Mexico for between six and seven dollars. They'll bring twenty dollars in Fort Worth and thirty if you can get them to Abilene, Kansas. Most settle for railhead delivery at the first point they can make north of San Antonio—Waco, or Austin or some such. Ain't no use trying to sell cattle in San Antonio. That place is already full to overflowing with wet beef.''

Longarm took another swig of whiskey, held it in his mouth for a moment or two, and swallowed it. ''Well, now I can see where it's worth the while of cattle crooks to bribe the customs folks. You got any idea what they're getting? What the going rate is for not quarantining cattle?''

Austin Davis was studying Longarm intently. ''You got a toothache?''

Longarm said quickly, ''You just never mind about my teeth. I asked you about the customs people. What do they get for their work?''

Ignoring the question, Davis said, ''Ain't nothing more bothersome than a toothache. Man can't concentrate on his work. We gonna have to get you to a dentist first thing we get to Laredo. That whiskey trick won't work long enough for the water to get hot. I know, I've tried it.''

50

"Listen," Longarm said with heat, "I ain't going to say this but once more. You forget all about my teeth. And I ain't going to no dentist! Now, tell me about the customs inspector."

"Just trying to help," Davis said, looking put off. He thought a moment. "Caster ain't really got a set price. It depends on how many cattle you got and how fast you want them through. I've heard if you've got a thousand head and you want them straight on through—that takes about a week—the going price is about three dollars a head. If you can afford to feed them for a couple or three weeks, he'll come down to two dollars. Less chance of him getting caught that way. If you only want to halve the ninety days, he'll accommodate you for as little as a dollar and a half a head. That is if you got enough cattle."

Longarm cocked his head and whistled. "That ain't bad pickings."

"Especially if you reckon on how many cattle pass through there a month. Caster ain't getting it all, but I roughed it out at about a minimum of five thousand dollars a month. That kind of money would make a judge turn crooked."

Longarm looked out the window. "I arrested a judge once," he said.

"Yeah?"

"But he was just a county judge, so that didn't amount to anything." He paused and then shook his head slowly. "But once I arrested a federal bank examiner." He let out a sigh and shook his head again.

Austin Davis waited a moment, and when Longarm didn't go on, he said impatiently, "Yeah, so you arrested a federal bank examiner. What about it?"

Longarm lounged back in his seat. "I'd rather have gone up against a barrel of wildcats wearing barbed-wire britches than got involved in that mess." I let out a breath. "Hell, before it was over I wasn't sure who was going to jail, me or him."

Davis wrinkled his brow. "Didn't you catch him clean? Wasn't he guilty?"

"Hell yes, he was guilty, guilty as sin. The man had left a trail of thievery a mile long by the time I put the cuffs on him. Every time he went into a bank to examine it there was always less money in the vault than when he came. After a while that kind of thing starts to get noticed. Of course you couldn't tell it from the books— he had them well doctored. I followed him around for two months after we got called into the matter, and couldn't get within a day's ride of him. Finally I just arrested him as he was departing a bank one day and confiscated his little leather satchel where he kept all his papers and whatnot. Found five thousand dollars all done up neat in the bank's wrappers. Them little bands that banks mark packets of money with. As it turned out, after the bank counted up that was exactly the amount they were short."

"Well, hell," Davis said, "you had him dead to rights."

Longarm nodded. "Yeah," he said with a trace of bitterness. "You'd think so, wouldn't you? But I got some news for you, young Mister Davis, dealing with folks like that ain't like catching bank robbers or road agents."

"How so?"

Longarm looked weary, thinking back over the incident. "First of all, they got their ways that we don't know nothing about. He was a bank examiner. What the hell do I know about that? Maybe he was taking that money out of the bank just to test their safeguards. That's what he claimed. Second, they work for a bureau of the government, and if there's anything that protects their own it's bureaucracy. They pack up worse than wolves. I think they operate on the theory that if one gets caught they might all get caught.''

''But you caught him with the damn money!''

Longarm shook his head. ''Don't mean a damn thing. I had to be able to get at least two more federal bank examiners to swear that what the crook done wasn't proper and part of procedure, and that took some little doing. Billy Vail said that at best I could be out of a job and at worst might go to prison for drawing a gun on a high government official. I tell you, it was nip and tuck there for a while.''

''How'd you finally get him?'' Austin Davis was looking puzzled and worried.

Longarm shrugged. ''Well, it took a little bit of luck. A bunch of bankers who'd lost money every time the examiner paid them a visit come forward and helped out. But the biggest help was the man's wife. She got spiteful because she was pretty sure he was running around on her, and she come forward and told us where we could find an account he had hidden that had better than a hundred thousand dollars in it.'' Longarm gave Davis a look. ''Bank examiners don't make that kind of money.''

Davis said, ''Yeah, but wait a minute. Hell, we are a branch of the government. Why the hell should a bank examiner carry more clout than a deputy marshal?''

Longarm explained. ''Because we're on the rough

side of the bench. We carry guns. Some folks ain't sure we're the law or outlaws. We are supposed to be willing to risk our lives for poor pay and no credit and be damn grateful and damn quiet about it.''

Davis was riled. "Why, that is a hell of a note."

"Ain't it? Listen, to have any whack in the government you need a desk and a couple of clerks to write outraged letters for you. I tell you, before that deal was over with the bank examiner we had the Federal Reserve system down on us and the Treasury department and I don't know who all. All Billy Vail done for about a month was answer letters and telegrams that would burn your hand you picked one up. Didn't make me any too popular with him.''

"But he knowed you done right, didn't he?"

Longarm sighed and shook his head. "Austin, that part don't make a damn. I put my boss to considerable trouble. Right or wrong, he didn't care for it. He told me—and I ain't too sure he was kidding—that next time he'd appreciate it if I'd just shoot the sonofabitch and not bring him in.''

Davis suddenly cocked his head and stared at Longarm. "Would you be telling me this story for a reason?" he asked.

"I might."

"Would this have anything to do with the customs people?''

Longarm shrugged. "I don't know. I would reckon, at a guess, that they are a close-knit bunch. I reckon they wouldn't want it getting around that any of them are crooked, if you take my meaning.''

Davis looked angry. "Are you telling me that if we catch that sonofabitch Caster, and any other fish we can get in the net, we are going to have political pressure put on us? Are you telling me that because they belong to a big outfit like Customs, we are going to get some grief?''

Longarm held his hands out, palm upwards. ''They is a bunch of them. They got a strong union. They collect a lot of tariffs. Bring in a lot of money. What do you want me to say?''

Davis was outraged. ''I think it's a damn sin, is what I think!'' He leaned forward, jabbing his forefinger. ''Listen, Longarm, I got two months in, working on this job. I put in some piss-poor days scouting the back country of Mexico and, believe me, that ain't no church social. I put in enough time hanging around cattlemen's saloons to be a drunk. I've took more than my fair share of chances. *That* sonofabitch is guilty. And so is his boss in Brownsville! And I can prove it. And now you come along and tell me we might not can make it stick? Hell!''

Longarm lifted his hands. ''Wasn't it you that said we jerk on the rope down here when we arrest Caster, they'll feel the tug in Washington? I ain't got no friends in Washington, D.C. Do you?''

''Hell!'' Davis said again. He sat back in his seat and folded his arms. ''This makes me mad as hell.'' Then he glanced at Longarm, a glint of suspicion in his eye. ''You ain't playing me for the greenhorn, are you? This ain't another one of your tall tales just to tie a can to my tail?''

Longarm, looking at Davis out of hooded eyes, said evenly, ''Some things I don't joke about, sonny boy. Before this is over, you may wish you'd shot Mister Customs Inspector Caster and told Billy Vail he died of a bad cold.''

Davis stared back. "You ain't kidding," he said slowly. "I got Jay Caster dead to rights and I mean to have him. I got his boss in damn near as tight a bag on information I've picked up about his doings in Brownsville. I intend to have him also."

"What's his name?"

"James Mull. He's the head honcho for the whole southwest border district in Texas. Jay Caster couldn't move one illegal cow without his say-so."

Longarm stretched out his legs and looked out at the unchanging landscape. "The further up the tree you reach, the further you got to fall. All I'm telling you is what might happen."

"You're not saying we should back off, are you?"

Longarm swung his eyes to Davis' face. "Now who's doing the kidding? I just wanted you to know the situation might be a little stickier than you'd figured."

Davis tipped his hat forward so the brim hid his eyes, then said, in a disgusted voice, "Well, if this wouldn't kill knee-high cotton. Damn! I thought I had me a bird's nest on the ground and then you come along and tell me the damn game is rigged. What the hell we going to do?" He pushed his hat brim back up and gazed at Longarm.

"I reckon we are going to do what we come to do, arrest as many crooked customs officials as we can. And hope they get sent to prison."

Davis slumped back in his chair, got a cigarillo out of his pocket, and lit it. With the first mouthful of smoke, he blew a smoke ring that came out small and then grew and grew until it finally came apart. "So," he said, "you're saying all this politics don't mean nothing."

Longarm nodded. "That's right."

"Well, what in hell did you tell me for? Hell, I was much happier when I was ignorant."

Longarm gave a short bark of laughter. "Oh, that ain't changed. You're still about as smart as a sack of sand."

"You know what I mean, you bastard."

Longarm shrugged. "I wanted you to be prepared, wanted you to know we had to mind our *P*'s and *Q*'s on this one. Do it up special with no mistakes. Wanted you to understand it was going to be somewhat different."

"So do we change the plan?"

Longarm laughed. "Well, if you recollect, I don't know what the damn plan is. It's your plan. You ain't told me about it yet. I ain't worked a cattle case in a long time and I don't reckon I ever worked one involving the customs folks. How you got it laid out, other than you don't know how Caster moves the cattle?"

"Well," Davis said, "I'm gathering up a herd of about one thousand a little ways into the interior. Bought with money supplied by the Ranchers Association of South Texas. I'm gonna bring them up to the outskirts of Nuevo Laredo on the Mexican side and then either me or you are supposed to approach Caster about letting us cut down on the quarantine time. Get him to take a bribe. I was hoping we could get his boss, Mull, down for the doings, but I haven't figured out how to do that yet." Davis bent forward and flicked ashes on the floor. "I ain't got much more than that worked out." He smiled. "I was kind of hoping for some help from the senior member of the company as to how we should proceed on the finer points."

Longarm thought for a moment. "You're going to

leave me in Laredo while you go into back country in Mexico?''

Davis nodded.

"How long?"

Davis shrugged. "I don't know. Long as it takes to drive them cattle the short distance to the border. Three days. Maybe four."

"Listen, one thing I ain't never understood. Where the hell are the cattle kept in quarantine? On the Mexico side or the Texas side? You said something before about the cattle going over the International Bridge. I ain't up on all these matters you understand."

Davis said, "The pens are on the Texas side, Longarm. I reckon they'd have to be unless we had some sort of arrangement with the Mexican government to lease ground on their side of the river. But Customs takes charge of the cattle the minute they leave Mexican soil and hit that bridge. From there they go straight to the pens and get the paint smeared on them. I didn't figure all that had anything to do with it. I had it figured that I'd just show up with this herd I'd put together and offer to grease my way through and he'd take the money and it would be wham, bam, thank you ma'am."

Longarm shook his head. "Naw, it ain't going to work quite that simple."

"Then what do you reckon? You ain't actually talking about holding these cattle for any time, are you? Hell, they didn't give me that much money. You got any idea what it costs to feed one thousand steers a day? Plus hay and water? Listen, the second he takes the money, ain't he guilty right then? Ain't he caught?"

Longarm held up his hand. "Don't rush me, boy. I need to get on the ground and kind of nose around. This is a little bigger operation than I'd thought at first.''

Davis gave him a flickering smile. ''You mean there's a chance I ain't got the great man out on some penny-in-the-posy kind of business?''

''Will you put that smart mouth of yours away for a while? Give me a rest.''

''Sorry,'' Davis said. ''I can't help it. But you reckon it's all right for us to be seen together in Laredo, even on the Mexican side?''

''I don't see why not. After all, I'm the big money who is buying the cattle. I reckon I'll need to hire some drovers to take them up the trail once we get them clear of Customs.''

''Wait a minute. Like I said, they didn't give me all that much money.''

Longarm gave him a sour look. ''I ain't gonna actually hire any drovers, just kind of act like I'm seeing what's available. I mean, you don't actually reckon to drive your herd to Texas, do you?''

Austin Davis laughed. ''I can see I'm gonna have trouble keeping you up with when I'm playacting and when I ain't. I got to remember we are not actually smuggling cattle, but arresting customs inspectors.''

''What are you supposed to do with that herd once its served its purpose?''

''Beats the hell out of me. I reckon that cattleman's organization will take over from there. It's their money, their cattle, their problem.''

Longarm was silent for a moment, thinking. Then he took out his watch and checked the time. ''I reckon we're about an hour out of Laredo. Where you got the horses?''

"At the livery of the Hamilton Hotel. Do you know it?"

"Oh, yeah. Best in town." The Hamilton, like the Gunther in San Antonio, was an old, solid, traditional hotel that catered to the traveler with both the means and appreciation for comfort and quality. It was a big, square brick building that sat on one side of the big plaza very near the end of the International Bridge.

Davis said, "I got us rooms there."

Longarm thought for a moment. Something was starting to kindle in his mind but it wasn't ready to be spoken about yet. "No," he said, "*I* got a room there. You're going to be leaving in the morning to see about your herd anyway, ain't you?"

"Well, yeah. Why? What are you thinking?"

"I'm thinking maybe it would be a good idea if we wasn't seen together right off. You'll be out of Laredo for three or four days and that will give me some time to scout around and get the lay of the land. I'm still thinking on how we can pull Caster's boss, Mull, into this thing."

"Where the hell am I supposed to stay?" Davis asked.

Longarm looked at him. "Hell, Austin, I don't give a damn where you stay. Right now I just come to the conclusion that it might be helpful for me to move around on my own for a time. So I don't want us to be seen together at the Hamilton. In fact I don't even want us to get off the train together."

"But you still ain't give me no good reason."

Longarm uncorked the whiskey bottle. "I ain't got to give you no good reason. You go along like you were really planning to bring a herd up to sell me. I ain't seen you before and you ain't seen me. When you get off the train you go over and get your horse or horses out of the livery stable and tell the stable keeper that you've left one for a cattle buyer. That would be me. That's all you got to do. Just go ahead and get your herd together and then meet me back in Laredo in three or four days. We'll act like we're strangers to each other. Fact of the business, I'll lallygag and you go by the Hamilton and leave a message for me, Mister Long, that you've been called out of town suddenly but you'll be back and I'm to wait."

Austin Davis shrugged. "I hope to hell you know what you're doing."

Longarm smiled slightly. "If I did, it would be the first time."

Chapter 4

Once off the train, Longarm killed some time in a nearby saloon and then, when he was sure that Austin Davis was cleared out of town, he took himself to the Hamilton Hotel. The bogus message from Davis was waiting for him, and he got a room and settled himself in with a long drink of whiskey and a slow cigar. By then it was going on for four in the afternoon, the town just waking up from the siesta hours, and he took himself on a tour of the place, between the river and the central part of the town which was mostly built around the big square. Walking toward the river, he was able to see the holding pens for the quarantined cattle and he was a little surprised at their size. He'd expected a big operation, but it was nearly twice what he'd imagined. His view, however, was not the best since he'd held himself back about a quarter of a mile, not being ready as yet to be seen taking an interest in cattle.

He walked around the town with no particular route in mind, but he did have an objective. He was looking for a man. He didn't know the man's name or what he looked like or what line of work he was in, but he knew he'd find him. It had been Longarm's observation that in every Western town he'd ever been in there was always one fellow who was in the know on nearly all matters. He might not necessarily be an important man or hold an important job, but he always seemed to hear the latest, see the newest and be able to tell you where to go if you wanted to find something or somebody.

The hard part was finding that fellow and getting a fix on him bypassing imitators or replicas who claimed to be the real article. Longarm had found that bartenders were the best guide to what he thought of as "telegraph operators." He'd go from saloon to saloon and, as casually as he could, ask after different matters around town, none of them necessarily having anything to do with the information he was seeking. But that part didn't matter. The "telegrapher" usually knew a little or a lot about everything, and if one name kept coming up from several sources it was a good bet that Longarm would find his man. It had always amused him that the "telegraph operators" were a mixed lot, seldom having any one common trait from town to town. In one place the "telegrapher" might manage the hotel or run a saloon or even a livery stable. In another town he might be some old man who spent his time in front of the general store whittling and spitting tobacco juice. Of course they were never officials such as judges or mayors or sheriffs. "Telegraphers" couldn't be in a business where their gathering of information might be viewed as self-serving or done for gain. No, as a general rule they were just townspeople who had big ears and good memories and liked to stay current on events. They weren't gossips in the sense that they went around telling everything they knew and passing on information just so they could appear important. In fact, the opposite was true. The better the source was at getting the lowdown, the harder it was to pry any of it out of him. Sometimes they would sell what they knew if they figured nobody was going to get hurt, but they were not busybodies or malicious or men who collected information for any other purpose than to simply possess it and watch to see how it all, in the end, came together.

So, for that reason, Longarm spent the last hours of daylight going from saloon to saloon, hunching up to the bar for a beer and striking up a conversation with the barkeep or some of the hangers-on who happened to be there. He started off by wondering aloud who would be a good man to talk to about hiring a half-a-dozen drovers, and worked his way from there to what old head had been around when they first started bringing cattle across the bridge. In a few places he asked for the name of the leading authority on gathering a herd in Mexico, and in others he came closer to the point by wondering if anybody knew any citizen who was in tight with the customs officials.

One name finally began to surface enough that Longarm felt fairly certain he was on to his man. The last bartender had shrugged and said, "If anybody knows about switching sides of the border it would be Jasper White. Don't know if he'll have much to say to you, though. You being a stranger and whatnot."

It was a warning Longarm had heard more than once about other "telegraph operators." But he had found that cash money would loosen the rustiest tongue. From all accounts the Tejano Cafe and Saloon was Jasper White's main hangout. It was a small place on the south side of town, near the International Bridge and almost in the center of the border traffic. The bartender said Jasper sometimes sat out front on a bench and sometimes could be found inside drinking coffee. "But that be during the day. Nighttimes he roams around most of the saloons. Don't drink much and don't talk much. Listens mostly."

It was going on for half past six and twilight was fast approaching. In an hour it would be dark. If he was to get to the cafe and have a look at White before the man started his nightly rounds, Longarm would have to move quickly. Since, by now, he'd managed to amble at least half a mile into the town from the river, he had a good walk ahead of him in his high-heeled boots. He wished mightily that he'd taken time to get the horse Austin Davis had arranged for at the stable. Now there was no other way to get down to the bridge except by shank's mare. Once, Longarm had been caught in a desperate situation and was forced to walk ten miles across the New Mexico desert. He'd promised himself then that he would never, under any circumstances, walk farther than he could shout back to have someone bring him a horse.

Then, in spite of breaking that promise, he still arrived at the Tejano too late to meet up with Jasper White. The proprietor, a light-skinned Mexican with a scar on his upper lip, said that White had left not more than ten minutes past. "He go a leetle early today. But maybe I can help you with your business. What do you require?"

Though the cafe and saloon was small, Longarm could see that it was clean and well run. He hadn't had his supper and this looked like as good a place as any. He sat down at a table. "Well, right now I'd like a steak and some eggs and some potatoes and whatever kind of vegetable you might have.''

The proprietor was dressed in a suit, obviously to indicate that he wasn't a waiter. ''I meant your business with Señor White,'' he said stiffly. ''I will send a girl over to bring you food. But you should know that Mister White keeps close counsel with me.''

Longarm gave the slightly built man a look. ''Do I look that green?'' he asked. ''Hell, I ain't going to put my business around just anywhere. Now, how about that chow?''

The owner went off without expression and, after a wait, a pretty Mexican girl came over to take Longarm's order. The food did not disappoint his expectations, though he was still slightly mystified at the owner inquiring into his business. That sort of inquisitiveness was not the usual practice along the border. But then maybe Jasper White was more than just a mountain of information; maybe he was in some sort of smuggling racket and the little Mexican was in it with him.

But it didn't matter to Longarm, since it had nothing to do with his job. He finished his meal and then went sauntering back toward the Hamilton Hotel and its bar. He had heard there was a fairly decent poker game there most every night. And, if his luck was bad, it wouldn't be far to bed.

On his way to the hotel he wondered how Austin Davis was doing. He expected that the younger deputy had reached the herd by now and, if he'd gathered enough cattle, would be starting for the border in the morning.

He played until midnight on average luck and with only part of his mind on the game. He quit forty dollars ahead and didn't receive so much as a nod or a look when he left the game. Longarm had played poker in many a border town and it had always amazed him how quiet the games were. Over the years he'd given some thought to the condition, and had come to the conclusion that border-town poker players weren't more serious than their counterparts inland. They didn't talk any more than was necessary because of the dangerous climate of the border and the greater chance of giving offense by some offhand remark. Most men who played poker along the border were hard cases, and it didn't take much to get a fight started. As a consequence it was just safer, all around, to keep your mouth shut and your eyes open. But it did make for a fairly dull game, especially if your luck was only lukewarm.

He went to bed that night thinking about Mrs. Spinner and her amazing ability to get into such a variety of positions. She was truly a woman born to please a man. He could only hope that no circuses came to town while he was gone and that she would be there, waiting for him, when he got back to Denver.

He woke up the next morning with his tooth aching even worse, and sat on the side of the bed, soaking it in whiskey while he sourly contemplated the idea of going to a dentist in Laredo. It would probably be less painful to get it knocked out in a bar fight. Of course there was always laudanum. You could buy laudanum at the apothecary and it was guaranteed to stop pain for a while even if it did make you slightly lightheaded.

Finally his tooth let up and he was able to get up and shave and put on clean clothes. He took breakfast in the hotel dining room, doing well on the ham and eggs, but passing, reluctantly, on the hot coffee. Instead he had a lukewarm mixture of half coffee and half milk, which was almost no coffee at all but at least didn't set his tooth to singing.

After breakfast he killed time until ten o'clock by sitting outside on the porch with the rest of the railbirds, watching the traffic heading to and from the bridge. When he figured that Jasper White would just about be in place, he went around to the hotel livery and collected the horse Austin Davis had left for him. Longarm hated to admit it, but his fellow marshal appeared to have a pretty good eye for horseflesh. The animal, a big roan gelding that was mostly quarterhorse, had a nice way about him and looked, judging by his deep chest and long legs, to have some staying power. The horse was frisky from standing in the stable for a few days, so Longarm mounted him outside and let him jump around and kick up his heels a little until he'd got the shivers out of his spine. After that he settled down and acted as if he'd been raised right with a good set of manners. Nevertheless, Longarm rode him out to the edge of town and fired off his revolver several times just to see how the horse would react. He tensed up some, but the sound of the gunshots didn't seem to scare him over much. The gun test had been an institution with Longarm since a dozen years past, when he'd fired a rifle off the back of an animal who tried to turn himself inside out at the explosive sound. Longarm had been in the midst of a running gun battle with some cattle thieves, and the horse's actions had come at a very bad time. It had cost him the thieves, the horse, and a broken finger when he'd bucked off into a pile of rocks. There were still a few men around who would have liked to make reference to the incident, but didn't out of respect for the look that came into Longarm's eyes when the conversation wandered anywhere near the subject.

Finally satisfied with the horse, Longarm rode directly over to the Tejano Cafe, dismounted, and looked around for Jasper White. The bench out front was unoccupied, and Longarm went on into the cafe. It had a small bar and he slouched up against it while he looked the place over. It contained no more than ten tables and only a few of them were occupied. The pretty Mexican girl who'd served him the night before brought him the beer he asked for. As he looked back at the tables, he asked the girl which of the men would be Jasper White. She nodded at a man seated at a small table by the window. He was drinking coffee and smoking a cherroot, and looking out the window toward the bridge. "That is the Señor White," she said. "But he ees not welcoming to the stranger who just come up. You unnerstan'?"

Longarm reached in his pocket, took out a silver dollar, and spun it on the bar in front of her. "Why don't you take that and put it in your pocket and go over and ask Mister White if he's got time to talk to a cattleman from out of state. Tell him I'm buying the coffee or whatever he'd care to have."

The girl shrugged and went around the bar. Longarm slouched against the counter while he watched her approach the table. White was younger than Longarm had expected. Usually, town "telegraphers" were older men, but Jasper White looked to be somewhere in his mid-thirties. A tall man who could have used a little filling out, there was nothing unusual about him except for a high, balding forehead. Longarm watched while the girl bent over to speak with him. After a few seconds White glanced around, his gaze directed at the bar. Longarm looked away. He wondered what White had to be so careful about. You'd of thought he was sitting on a key to Fort Knox, the way he protected himself from strangers.

Finally the girl came back and said that Señor White would spare him a few moments of his time. Longarm spun another silver dollar on the bar for the girl, took his beer, and sauntered over to the small table where White was sitting. There was an extra chair, but White did not invite Longarm to take it. "Mister White," the deputy marshal began, "my name is Long. I'm a cattleman from Oklahoma. From what I hear around town you're the man to talk to about getting articles from one side of the border to the other. Being a stranger and not knowing the ways of the country, I thought I'd come to you for advice." Longarm stood there waiting, his mug of beer in his hand. White didn't pay him the slightest bit of attention.

At last the man loooked up. Longarm noticed how pale his eyes were. "So you be a stranger to these parts," White said. "Don't know yore way about."

"That's right," Longarm said.

"You be from Oklahoma."

"Yep."

"You be in the cattle business."

"Yes," Longarm said with a little irritation. He'd said all this before.

"And you want to know how to get some cattle across the border. Do that be it? But you don't know how to go about it."

"That's about the size of it."

Jasper White nodded slowly, then played his eyes

over Longarm. "Say you are new to these parts? Say yore name is Long?"

"Yes," Longarm said, wondering if he'd come to the right man.

White was drinking black coffee. He nodded at Longarm's beer. "I don't hold with strong drink."

Longarm, now more than a little irritated, said, "I don't hold it any longer than I have to myself. Quicker I can drink it down, the more good it does." To illustrate, he turned his beer mug up, drained it, and then signaled for the girl to bring him another.

White ignored the gesture. "I take it you want to get these cattle across the border without gettin' 'em wet."

"That would be the general idea. But I want to do it as legal as I can."

"You mean you want papers to say you done it legal. You don't actually want to do it legal, else you wouldn't be huntin' me up."

Longarm just looked at him silently. The girl brought his beer and he took a sip, waiting for the man to go on.

White said, "Tell me, Mister Long, you are in the business of selling cattle for a profit. That about the size of it? I mean, cattle is yore stock in trade."

"That would be about right."

"So you don't give cattle away. That right?"

Longarm, seeing where the man was headed, said, "Mister White, I had intended to pay you for any information you might supply me. I ain't here looking for a handout, just the name of the right man to go to."

"And you figger to pay a fair price fer that?"

"I do."

White nodded toward the extra chair. "Sit yoreself

72

down and let's see what we can work out.''

Longarm took the back of the light wooden chair, spun it, and sat down astraddle. He said, "I take it you would know."

White nodded again. "I reckon we better understand one another, Mister Long. You do be talking about keepin' them cattle dry and moving them right along without no bothersome delays here at the border. That be right?"

"It would."

White seemed to think a moment. Finally he heaved a sigh and said, sounding almost sorrowful, "Well, that information is worth exactly forty dollars. You got forty dollars, Mister Long?"

Longarm reached into the pocket of his jeans and pulled out his roll, flashing enough of it to inform White that he was pretty well heeled, but not enough to seem extravagant. He peeled off two twenty-dollar bills and laid them on the table between himself and White. "You said that would get me a name." He stuck the roll back in his jeans.

White looked at the money and then looked up at Longarm. He said, chuckling a little, "Well, Mister Long, you seem like such a nice feller, I'm gonna go you one better. For the price of one I'm going to give you two names. One man is Jay Caster. Works for the customs people. The other is Rudy Thomas. He does the same." As he reached for the money, White started to giggle.

His fingers never quite picked up the bills. With a swift motion Longarm whipped his revolver out of its holster and brought the barrel down forcibly onto the back of White's hands. The blow wasn't hard enough to break the skin, but hard enough that the man jumped and cried out. Longarm kept White's hands pressed to the tabletop with the barrel of the revolver. White looked at him, his eyes wide and suddenly scared. Stuttering a little, he said, "Da-Da-Damn, mister! That hurts. Cain't you take a little joke?"

Longarm kept the pressure on the man's hands. "Yeah, if it was a joke. I got an idea one of them names is the right man. The other would be the wrong man. I don't like paying forty dollars for the chance to guess right. But I suppose you were just teaching the greenhorn stranger a little lesson in border odds. That right?"

White suddenly jerked his hands out from under the barrel of Longarm's gun. It scraped off a little skin, and a thin line of blood formed on the back of his hand. He looked at it sullenly. "Something like that," he said. "Damn, you done gone and cut me."

"You cut yourself. Now, you just figure I taught you a little lesson in how to make a stranger feel welcome. I'm still willing to do business with you, but we're going to go outside, where I can be seen talking to you. Anything happens to me, folks are going to notice that me and you had a conversation. You *savvy*? In fact, me and you are going to walk down to the bridge and take a look at where they hold the cattle in quarantine. Maybe you can point out Mister Jay Caster and Mister Rudy Thomas to me and tell me if there is any difference to the pair."

White was still looking belligerent. "You ain't got no call for that kind of acting up. You're on the border. I was givin' you a little lesson about who you could trust down here." As he said it, he cut his eyes over Longarm's shoulder.

Longarm smiled. "And I was just giving you a little lesson in who to try and steal from. What you looking at so hard there? That little Mexican runs this place coming up behind me? He better not be. This here revolver is pointing right at your belly. You better go to nodding and smiling and quit worrying about your damn hand or I'm going to ease the hammer back on this big *pistole* of mine. You *savvy*?"

White looked at Longarm and then at the muzzle of the revolver that had crept up to aim at his midsection. He said, calling toward the bar, "It's all right, Raymond. Everything is fine."

"That was sensible. Now pick that forty dollars up and put it in your pocket. You are going to earn it before we get done talking."

White swallowed, his Adam's apple jerking up and down. His eyes were all for the gun in Longarm's big hand. "I—I don't want it."

"Put it in your pocket." Longarm said the words quietly, but there was menace in his tone. "And then get up and start for the front door. I'll be right behind you."

"I ain't going nowhere with you."

Longarm started the hammer back with his thumb. It made the first *clitch* sound, and White was instantly on his feet, exclaiming, "I'm going!"

He came around the table as Longarm rose. When he was on his feet Longarm turned toward the bar, the revolver still in his hand. He half expected to find the little Mexican standing there with a shotgun leveled at him. The owner was behind the bar, but he was simply standing next to the girl, staring at Longarm through narrowed eyes. Longarm took two steps in his direction, holstering his pistol at the same time. "What would your name be, señor? You seem to take a big interest in my affairs.''

The man's eyes got even narrower. "This is my place of business, señor. I take an interest in all that happens here." He spoke excellent English with only a trace of Spanish accent.

Longarm said, "You still didn't tell me your name. You ashamed of it?"

There was a hard expression on the owner's face. "My name is San Diego," he said, "Raymond San Diego. Be careful how you use it should you have occasion to speak it."

Longarm smiled and nodded. "My name is Long. You can use it any way you want to. I ain't all that proud. Just stay out of my business. I may not be proud, but I'm touchy about money. You *savvy*?"

"I think we meet again."

"Don't see why not. You serve good grub at good prices. I reckon I'll make this my eating headquarters while I'm in town."

Longarm could feel the man's eyes on his back as he followed Jasper White through the door and down the steps of the cafe. The proprietor wasn't very big, but then you didn't have to be very big to handle a big revolver. Longarm was confused as to what the connection between his "telegrapher" and the owner of the cafe was, but he had no doubt that Raymond San Diego would make a dangerous enemy.

Once outside, Jasper White stopped and turned around. He was holding the two twenty-dollar bills in his hand. On his feet he was an even less impressive physical specimen than he was sitting down. Holding the money out toward Longarm, he said, "Look here, mister, I don't want yore money. I played a little joke and it blew up in my damn face. Now I'd jest like to forget the whole matter.''

Longarm was slightly confused. His original intention in seeking out Jasper White had been to establish a contact with Jay Caster independent of Austin Davis. He'd thought that it would make any connection between himself and Davis even more remote, nothing more than a buyer and seller of cattle. Rather than having Davis introduce him to Caster, he'd hoped to be able to go to the customs man and say he'd been recommended to him by another party, Jasper White. But now he was running into this strange alliance of a Mexican cafe owner and the town information bank. It was an unlikely combination.

He pushed the money back to Jasper White. ''Put it in your pocket, I said. I'm nearly sorry I pulled a gun on you. And I'm nearly sorry you caused me to do it. But that's all over and done with. I still got business with you, and that is what we are doing standing out here on the street.''

Pushing the money forward again, White said doggedly, ''I don't want no part of you, mister. You look like trouble to me.''

Longarm looked at him intently. ''Did that Mex tip you a wink on the way out? He give you some kind of sign not to fool with me or not to do no business with me?'' He paused, waiting for some reply, but Jasper White just looked steadily away, staring out toward the river. Longarm tried again. ''There's something between you and that Mex. You two are in cahoots about something. Yesterday I was in the cafe and asked after you and he the same as said your business was his. What are y'all up to—a little smuggling? Or are you part of passing cattle over the river?''

White swiveled his eyes around to Longarm. "Mister," he said, "you better get on back to Oklahoma. You ain't going to last long on this border.''

"What's that fancy gent's name? San Diego? Raymond San Diego? That's a hell of a lot of name for a man runs a Mexican greasy spoon. And dresses like he owns the county. Where does a man like that get money for them kind of clothes?''

Jasper White made an attempt at a fierce look. It did not come off as much more than a sneer. "I'll tell you this much, an' I'll tell it to you for nuthin'. Was I you, I'd leave Raymond San Diego the hell alone. He ain't a man to be foxed around with. And he's got a brother that is triple trouble. You do any business with Jay Caster and you'll have his brother looking over your shoulder. His name is Raoul San Diego, and the last thing in this world you want is trouble with him!''

Longarm smiled slowly. "So the customs man I want is Jay Caster.'' He gave a little laugh. "You earned your money after all, Mister White.''

Jasper White looked sullen. "Don't think you be so smart. You could have gone in any saloon and found that out in five minutes. He don't make no secret out of it.''

"Pushing cattle through quarantine? He better start making a secret out of it. The way I understand the matter, it's against the law.''

White shrugged. "Is it? You'll have to find out how he does it before the law can step in.''

Longarm said, "I ain't interested in the law stepping in. I'm just interested in getting some cattle across the border fast.''

"Well, now you know, don't you?"

"Yes, and I'm much obliged. Mind telling me how I go about it?"

"You be so damn smart, you figure it out."

"How about you approaching him for me? I got a feeling you already know how."

White glared at Longarm with his close-set eyes. "Mister," he said, "I ain't sayin' nothin' except I don't want to do no bid'ness with you. Not no more, not the way you do bid'ness." He lifted his injured hand and looked at it as if in silent accusation.

"Now, c'mon," Longarm said. "You brought that on yourself, and if you're fair about it, you'll admit as much."

But Jasper White shook his head. "I don't know nothin' about you, feller. You could be the law for all I know."

Longarm gave a short laugh. "That's a hot one. I'm standing here talking to you about rushing some cattle, and you think I might be the law. Look, there's nothing to know about me. I got a herd due up from the interior of Mexico in the next couple of days. I want to get them on the road to market as quick as I can. I ain't going to make any money with them standing around in cattle pens waiting to see if they got tick fever."

White pursed his mouth and seemed to be contemplating. "I don't know," he finally said.

Longarm gestured at the forty dollars he was holding. "I got the balance of that would make a hundred-dollar bill in your pocket was you to introduce me to Jay Caster."

White looked interested. "Sixty dollars more?"

Longarm put his hand in his pocket. "Cash money.

On the spot. All you got to do is walk up with me to the man and give him my name. Give me a howdy and a handshake to him. Nothing more.''

"You don't want me to tell him what you be looking for?''

Longarm shook his head. "Nosir. Not at all. Wouldn't ask you to do a thing that might seem like trouble. Ain't no law against introducing one man to another, now, is there?''

White glanced toward the cafe, looking thoughtful for a moment. "I reckon not.'' he said at last. "But I want the money in advance.''

"When you want to do it?''

White spit on the ground and scratched his head. "Well, I don't exactly know. I don't know if Mister Caster is in his office right now or not.''

Longarm pulled a look. "You mean you don't know if you ought to go in the cafe and check with your partner first. Ain't that about it?''

White raised his head. "I don't got to ask Raymond nothing about this kind of bid'ness. He ain't my boss.''

"No, but you two are in some kind of business together, ain't you.''

"That wouldn't be none of yore affair.''

"Well, while we're at it, seeing as you're a man knows his way around the town, can you tell me where I can scare up some drovers? I'd be willing to pay you for your help on that score.''

Longarm could see the greed starting to build in White's eyes. He had counted it. "How many men you looking for?'' White asked.

"Enough to handle a thousand steers. Say eight drovers and a cook. You find me good men and I'll pay you ten dollars a head.''

White hesitated only a beat. He said, "I reckon I could handle that. Let's see, that would bring it up to a hunnert and fifty dollars what you'd owe me. That right?''

Longarm said, "Only if I can make a deal with Caster. I'll pay you the sixty for that as soon as you can get me met up with him. But I can't pay for no drovers until I get a herd through. Now, what about it? Reckon you can make time to get me within handshaking distance of the customs man?''

The lure of money was proving irresistible to Jasper White. He glanced at the cafe and then over his shoulder toward the river. "Well," he said, "I don't see nothing wrong with us walking down to the pens and seeing if Mister Caster ain't handy.''

"Let's go," Longarm said. "Ain't me holding us up.''

Still Jasper hesitated. He looked down at the money in his hand, slowly folded it, and slipped it into his pocket. "When was you thinkin' 'bout payin' me that other sixty?''

Longarm gave him an impatient look and jerked out his roll. He peeled off four tens and a twenty. "Hell," he said. "How about right now? One of us has got to start trusting the other. I guess it might as well be me.''

"What if Mister Caster ain't there?''

Longarm took White by the shoulder and turned him toward the river and the holding pens. "Then you'll make me acquainted with the gent at some other time. Hell, Jasper, quit acting like you ain't already done this a hundred times before.''

Jasper White looked at him. "You been talkin' to folks about me."

Longarm shook his head. "No, I've been talking to you about you. That's been enough."

Chapter 5

They stood in front of the whitewashed lumber-and-adobe building. A sign hung from the porch announcing the place as the offices of the United States Customs and Tariff Service. The building, about the size of a small house, wasn't near as grand as its title. Off to their left stretched the holding pens, crowded with cattle. Longarm could see half a dozen hired hands working in among the steers, feeding, watering, haying, moving the steers, slapping paint on some. Not too far from where he and White stood was a slim man in a brown uniform. "Which one is that?" Longarm asked.

"That be Rudy Thomas."

"He not in on it?"

Jasper shook his head. "I couldn't say about that. But if he is, I ain't heard."

"How the hell does Caster operate without him catching on?"

Jasper gave Longarm a worried look. "You shore ask a lot of questions, mister. Was I you, I'd worry about my cattle getting across and not how Mister Caster runs his business.''

Longarm shrugged. "You got a good point. Where you reckon Caster is?''

Jasper bent over and peered through one of the big windows that was covered by a screen. "He be in there. I can see him sitting at his desk. C'mon and I'll take you in."

Longarm put out a hand and stayed him for a moment. "Now, you're going to tell him I'm an all right fellow, ain't you?''

Jasper gave him a long look. "I never heard that was part of the bargain.''

Longarm looked disgusted. "Well, hell, I'll just be another yahoo if you just walk me in there and say my name. I need the man to have some trust in me so we can do business. Them cattle I've bought are due in here any day.''

Jasper blinked and frowned. "Well I don't *know* that you're all right. Hell, I don't want to get crosswise with Mister Caster. What if you don't pay him?''

"Thought you said he had this mean Mexican worked for him. Thought he was supposed to keep the business straightened out.''

"Raoul?" Jasper's face brightened. "Yeah. I forgot about Raoul. Don't nobody cheat Mister Caster. Not as walks away.''

"Hell, I'll pay the man in advance. C'mon, Jasper, you got to fix me up with this hombre. I already figured you get a cut."

Jasper glared at Longarm. "You better not believe everything you hear," he said.

Longarm slapped him on the back. "You're already

a hundred up on the day. Now usher me in there and set me up with Jay Caster and I'll take it from there. You can't lose.''

Jasper looked doubtful, but he stepped up on the porch and pulled back the screen door. Longarm followed right behind him. Inside he saw a thickset man in a brown khaki suit sitting at a back desk. The fellow glanced up as they entered. ''Jasper,'' he said, ''what the hell you doing up and around this early? You liable to get heatstroke, boy.''

''Howdy, Mister Caster. How you be?''

''Pretty good,'' Caster said, but he had switched his attention to Longarm. ''Who you got with you, Jasper?''

''Cattleman, Mister Caster. Feller name of Long. From Oklahoma. Looking to have a little visit with you.''

Caster frowned. He had a heavy mustache that covered his top lip. ''I'm pretty busy right now, Jasper. Another time might be better.''

''Well,'' Jasper said, ''he's an obliging feller, Mister Caster. I wouldn't reckon he'd take up much of your time.''

Listening, Longarm felt sure that Caster was doing more than saying he was busy. He was asking Jasper if he, Longarm, was worth the trouble.

Jay Caster leaned back in his swivel chair. ''So, you be saying he wouldn't be wasting my time.''

Now Longarm was sure they were talking in a kind of code.

''Pretty shore, Mister Caster. He done right by me.''

Jay Caster looked back at Longarm, giving him a slow going over. Finally he nodded and said, ''You run along, Jasper, and I'll spare the man what time I can.''

''Yessir,'' White said, and was out the door in three

strides. Longarm turned to watch him go. When he turned back around, Jay Caster was staring at him.

"What'd you say your name was?"

"Long. Out of Broken Bow, Oklahoma. Oklahoma Territory."

Jay Caster hooked his fingers behind his head. "Pretty wild country, that, ain't it?"

"Oh, it's calmed down a little." Longarm was still five or six feet from Caster's desk and wondering if he was going to be invited to sit down.

"What can I be doing for you today, Mister Long?"

Unbidden, Longarm took two steps forward and said, "I'm in the cattle business, Mister Caster. I'm expecting a herd of about a thousand cattle in here in the next day or two."

"Mexican cattle, I assume."

"Yessir, from the interior. The deep interior." He added delicately, "Where they ain't got no tick fever. Cattle are clean as a whistle."

Caster smiled as if he'd heard that story one more time than he cared to. "Yeah," he said, "but they got to pass through tick country to get here to the border. We don't think of them as clean cattle, Mister Long. That's why we got all them pens out there. Now, if you could get them cattle to fly up here to the border, might be a different story."

Still unbidden, Longarm sat down in a straight-backed wooden chair directly across from Caster. He took his hat off, crossed his legs, and put his hat on his knee. "Uh, they say money can do a powerful lot of things, Mister Caster. Maybe it can make them cattle fly up here so they can get rushed right through and be on their way to Oklahoma. I got a government beef contract to feed

86

Indians. Ain't the most generous contract you ever saw. I shore know it ain't going to stretch far enough to feed them cattle for ninety days while they stay in quarantine.''

Mister Caster was chewing tobacco. He leaned sideways and spit in a bucket, wiped his mouth with the back of his hand, and then said mildly, ''I've heard of drovers who went clean on around this little customs station of mine here and swum their cattle across.''

Longarm laughed without humor. ''Yeah, I tried that one time. Luckily it was a fairly small herd, so I didn't lose everything. Four hundred head. I reckon I fed cavalry soldiers with that one instead of Indians. Let's see, I reckon I wasn't no more than fifty miles inland when a range inspector come up and wanted to see my papers. Naturally I didn't have none, so he said he reckoned they weren't my cattle, and damned if he didn't fetch them off with him.''

Caster nodded and spit again. ''Yeah, I hear that will happen. Man needs papers on cattle he imports into the United States of America from Mexico. I understand that is the law.''

Longarm scratched his head. ''I wasn't planning on driving through any settled country on the southeast side of the range,'' he said. ''Not through any ranches where I might cause trouble. Naw, I was going head northwest out of here. Wouldn't cause nobody no trouble. And I shore wouldn't be passing on no tick fever.''

Caster shook his head sympathetically. ''Law don't make no allowance for that, Mister Long. Law don't care which direction you're headed. Law says you got to keep your cattle penned under government supervision—that would be me—for ninety days. If they don't show no signs of fever, why, you're free to go on your way. Of course if they come down sick, we got to turn you back. But, then, I reckon this ain't no news to you."

Longarm fiddled with the crown of his hat. It was important to not be too bold with Caster. A sure enough smuggler wouldn't be. "Yeah, I know all that part," he said casually. "I just keep thinking about how nice it would be if them cattle could just fly right on over the border and be on their way to Indian territory. Looks like the right amount of money could make that happen. What do you think, Mister Caster? What do you reckon it would take to get them cattle rushed on through the rigamarole and on their way to feed some hungry Indians?"

Caster leaned over slowly to spit again, and then, even more slowly, straightened back up. "Now, Mister Long," he said, "you wouldn't be talking to me about bribe money, would you? That's illegal. Maybe you didn't know it, but a customs official has got police powers. That means I could arrest you right here on the spot. What do you think of that?"

Longarm cocked his head. "Well," he replied, "I don't know what you'd be arresting me for. All I asked was your opinion on how much money you reckoned it would take to make cows fly. Ain't no law against that, is there? I didn't hear anybody in this room offer nobody a bribe. Did you?"

Caster grinned, showing his tobacco-stained teeth. "You kind of got a cute little way about you, Mister Long. Tell me," he said, "did you hear around town that I might be the man to see if you wanted to get some cattle sailed on through in a hurry?"

Longarm shook his head slowly. "No, can't say I did,

Officer Caster. Is that what you call a customs official—
officer?''

"Not generally.''

"Well, you was talking about police powers. I didn't
want to be taking too big a chance. No, I just got in
town late yesterday evening. Ain't really had time to talk
all that much to anyone except bartenders.''

"You seem to have found Jasper White quick
enough.''

"Oh, that.'' Longarm pulled a face and brushed at the
brim of his hat. "There's a Jasper White in every town.
They ain't hard to find.''

"So you and him ain't old buddies?''

Longarm looked up and locked eyes with Caster.
"Met the man this morning. Over at a little cafe.''

"The Tejano.''

Longarm nodded. "That's the one. I was having
breakfast. Being so close to the bridge, I figured the
owner might know something about how this place operated. I never brought cattle through here before.''

"So you spoke to Raymond.''

"Yeah. Raymond. Got a long last name.''

"San Diego. His brother works for me.''

"Does he now? He a customs official?''

Caster showed his brown teeth again. "Not exactly.
He kind of works for me privately. Sort of makes sure
things run smooth, if you take my meaning.''

"How would that be?''

"Oh, he just does.'' Caster hunched forward and
leaned his elbows on the desk. "You said you never
brought cattle through here before. Of course I know
that—I'd have remembered you otherwise. But this is
kind of far to the southeast for a man driving cattle to

Oklahoma. What caused you to pick Laredo?''

Longarm gave a whisper of a smile. "Oh, just seemed like a good place," he said easily. "Get to see a different part of the country."

"Have a little trouble up north of here, did you? At Del Rio and Eagle Pass?"

Longarm let himself look the slightest bit uncomfortable. "Oh, they could have made matters easier," he said. "Anyway, this was where the man I'm buying the cattle from wanted to deliver them."

"Jasper didn't tell you I could make cows fly, did he?"

"Now, why would he do a thing like that? I told you, Mister Caster, I just met the man this morning. We talked a bit about my business and I wondered if he knew the chief customs inspector. He said he did." Longarm spread his hands. "That's the sum of the matter."

Caster drew his head back a little. "Well, I reckon you can appreciate my position, Mister Long. I'm a government official. Got my duties and my reputation to think of. Wouldn't want talk getting around town that I can make cows fly." Caster gave a little imitation of a laugh. "But you say Jasper was the only one you had a talk with?"

"Well, the only one where the talking come to anything. Like him bringing me up here and giving me a howdy-do to you."

Caster tried for another smile, but his stained teeth wouldn't allow it. He leaned further forward. "How much money you give him?"

"What makes you think I give him any money?"

"Because," Caster said dryly, "I know Jasper White. He wouldn't help an old woman up from a mud puddle 'less there was something in it for him. How much?''

Longarm frowned slightly. "That kind of sounds like we are talking about my business here. What's it got to do with you?"

Caster leaned back in his chair, rocking it back and forth slightly. "Oh, I was just curious as to what Jasper's going rate was these days. I'm gonna guess fifty dollars. Would that be about right."

Longarm shrugged. "If it suits you to believe that."

"Did you tell him how many cattle you had? Did you let on or look the least bit desperate? Did you tell him your cattle was due here in a couple of days?"

Longarm shrugged again. "I might have. Though I don't see what that's got to do with our business."

Caster swiveled his chair around so that he was presenting his side to Longarm. "It's got a lot to do with our bid'ness," he said. "I don't know you, Mister Long. Don't know a damn thing about you. And here you come to the chief customs inspector and the same as ask me to make it easier on your cattle then them as belongs to other folks." He waved his arm toward the pens outside. "Hell, I bet I'm holding near five thousand head right now. Why should you get any different treatment? How the hell do I know you are who you say you are. And just who *are* you? Tell me about yourself."

"Ain't much to tell, Mister Caster. I been in the cattle business man and boy for thirty years, ever since I could get up on a stump and get a foot in the stirrup. Always operated in Oklahoma. I don't owe nobody and I never went back on a deal. But don't take my word for it. You can wire the bank in Broken Bow and ask after me." Longarm said the last with a careless bravado. But he wasn't too worried. He didn't think Caster would check

91

up on him, and anyway, he planned to wire Billy Vail as soon as he could and have him inform the bank in Broken Bow that if any questions were asked about Custis Long they were to say that he was a good and valued customer and a cattleman of the first water.

Caster looked around at him. "I might just do that, Mister Long. I just might. But tell me something else. You got a contract to provide reservation beef. What the hell you doin' coming all the way down here? Hell, ain't they no cattle up where you ranch?"

Longarm stared at him for a long moment before he replied. "Mister Caster, you got any idea what the Bureau of Indian Affairs pays for a beef? If you knew, you wouldn't have to ask why I was buying Mexican cattle."

Caster chuckled softly. "What are you paying for those cattle you're having brought up?"

"Well now, there we go again, straying over into my business. Why would that be of any concern to you?"

"Weeelll . . ." Caster said slowly, "I was just trying to figure out if you had the price to get them cattle to fly over the border. You're telling me the Indian Bureau ain't leaving you much leeway. That means you better be buying the cattle on the cheap side. I know what range cattle are selling for in South Texas. It's clear you can't afford that price. I'm just wondering if you know what a set of cow wings costs."

Longarm kept silent for a moment. To cover the lapse he fumbled in his pocket, got out a cigarillo, and lit it. This was the first indication Caster had given him that he'd do business. When he had the little cigar drawing good, he leaned back in his chair and looked up at the ceiling. "All right," he said. "What does cow wings go for these days?"

Caster swiveled back around so that he was facing Longarm. "One thing you better understand is that there ain't no such thing as flying cows." He gave a little chuckle. "Them cattle are going to have to stop off with me for at least a week. You can't take them straight through. I ain't writing no papers on wet cattle. So they at least got to stop off here for a week."

Longarm blew out smoke. "Yeah, so I heard. That part don't come as no surprise."

Caster straightened up. "I thought you said you hadn't been talking to nobody."

Longarm quit looking at the ceiling and lowered his gaze. "I told you I hadn't been talking around town. That's a fact. But I know an awful lot of other men in the cattle business. Men who have bought Mexican cattle. After I lost that herd of four hundred I went to asking around." He looked at Caster. "Know what I mean?"

Caster grinned. "And they told you I was the man to see."

Longarm studied his cigarillo. "I'll talk about my business, Mister Caster, but I won't talk about other folks'. If you take my meaning. Whether they said anything about you or anybody else just plumb escapes me."

"But they told you that a week is the shortest time?"

"That's right."

"You understand that's the express service. Damn near the price of a set of wings. Price goes down the longer I hold them."

"Yeah, but the feed bill goes up."

Caster leaned back again. "What's it worth to you to get a thousand head through in a week?"

Longarm looked over toward a corner. "Oh," he said,

"I figure two dollars a head would be a fair price. Taken all around."

Caster laughed without humor. "You can double that for starters."

Longarm leaned forward and rounded on him. "*Four* dollars a head? Hell, Caster, there is no way I can make any money on this deal at that price."

"Now, that wouldn't be my worry, would it?" Caster said evenly.

Longarm pulled a frown and shook his head. "And I heard you was a man would do business. Hell, four dollars a head I might as well not bother to take delivery of the cattle."

"You seem to have heard a good deal about me. That all you cattlemen got time to do is gossip like a bunch of old maids?"

"Gossiping and talking business ain't the same thing, Mister Caster. You seem considerably touchy about folks talking about you. You doing something you're ashamed of? That damn quarantine law is something to be ashamed of. That's keeping a lot of honest folks from making a living."

Caster leaned over to spit in the bucket, then straightened back up and said, "Long, I don't care what you and yore friends say about me, or what tales you tell. I run this customs station and I'll run it any damn way I please. I ain't a damn bit ashamed of anything I do. But I'd be damn careful, was I you, of making remarks like that. And such remarks ain't going to get you a better price, that is for damn sure."

Longarm got up abruptly and walked over to the window. He could just see one corner of the long row of cattle pens. Without looking around, he said, "Well,

Caster, I'll tell you straight out I can't pay the four dollars. I'm going to get sixteen dollars and six bits a head from the Indian Bureau. I'll be paying between six and seven dollars a head for them Mexican cattle. Say six seventy-five to keep it in round numbers. That leaves ten dollars a head. I give you four and that leaves me with only six dollars a head to work off of. And I got the expense of feeding them here for a week and then the cost of hiring drovers for a month to get them to Oklahoma. Not to mention what I'll have to spend on the road, paying tolls through fenced ranches and farms. Times have changed, and you just can't march cattle in a straight line no more. And then I know at least half of them cattle will be poor and wore out by the time that they get here to Laredo. I stand to lose a good number of them on the trail to Indian country. I get there with eight hundred I'll be damn lucky. And of course I got to pay the contractor that is gathering them for me."

Behind him Caster yawned and he said, "Sounds to me, Long, like you're in the wrong business. You should have knowed what we charge before you got here."

Longarm wheeled around. "I heard two dollars. And from more than one man."

Caster shook his head. "Not for just a week."

Longarm nodded. "Yeah, a week. Two dollars a head." He paused and regarded Caster for a second. "I will say, however, that I might have been mistaken about who they said. It might have been Brownsville, and it might have been your boss—Mull, ain't that his name?"

Caster leaned back slowly in his chair. After a pause he said, "You are uncommonly full of surprises, Mister Long. You are talking about the Regional Director of the Customs Service, James Mull. You telling me you've talked to people who have done business with him?''

Longarm shrugged. ''I done talked too much. What y'all do is your business. I'm just interested in getting some cattle across the border, and I can't pay but two dollars a head.''

Caster's voice rose slightly. ''Well, somebody is lying. Either it's you or whoever told you they got cattle through at Brownsville for two dollars. And I know that for a fact.''

Longarm walked slowly back to his chair. His mind was racing. The man was the same as admitting that both him and his boss in Brownsville were involved in smuggling for a bribe. It was all going much faster and easier than he'd expected. His inclination was to push Caster even harder for more revelations, but a small voice of caution warned him to go slow. He said, sitting down, ''You seem mighty sure of what you're saying Mister Caster. But it's my money we're talking about here.''

Caster shot his arm out. ''Then go somewhere else. Hell, go back up to Del Rio. Go to Eagle Pass. See how yore luck runs. Hell, drive yore damn cattle down to Brownsville if you think you can get a better deal. I'll write a letter you can carry with you to Mister Mull. Take off—See where you can do better.''

Longarm looked thoughtful, as if he were considering what Caster had said. Instead his mind was busy, thinking over how they, he and Austin Davis, might catch two fish on one hook. Finally he gave a little rueful laugh. ''I take it you are a poker player, Mister Caster.''

''I've looked at a few cards. What the hell does that have to do with it?''

Longarm crossed his legs, took his hat back off, and put it on his knee. ''I'm trying to figure out if you're bluffing or trying to buy the pot. Four dollars a head is four thousand dollars. That's a lot of money for doing nothing.''

Caster snorted. ''Doing nothing? That what you reckon? I done plenty to get into this job. Worked my ass off. Say a doctor takes a bullet out of you and it only takes him ten minutes and he charges you twenty dollars. You ain't going to say to him that's two dollars a minute. No, you're going to figure he spent a lot of years learning how to take that bullet out, so you ain't going to say nothing. Well, you can figure the same about me.''

With a little hesitation Longarm agreed, ''Well, yes, there's that. And I reckon there is some risk involved for you.''

Caster stared at him. ''Risk? What risk?''

''Hell, I'm just trying to look at it from your side. I don't reckon the law would look kindly on matters of this kind. But then, the law is always mixing in where they ain't got no call to, and interfering with business.''

Caster laughed out loud. ''Risk?'' he said, ''You think I'm taking some kind of risk letting you get a few cattle through a little early?''

''Well, I wouldn't exactly call a thousand head a few, and I wouldn't call a week against ninety days a little early.''

Caster leaned back and smiled. ''Tell you what, Mister Long, you follow me around the whole week yore cattle is in my pens, and you find me doing one thing even looks illegal, I'll let you take yore cattle through for nothing.''

Longarm frowned. ''Hell, Mister Caster, I ain't interested in your business or how you do it. I done told you

97

my concern is my cattle. But I can't go no four dollars. I got to make some profit or they ain't no reason for me to make the deal. I might could go two and a half, but that is my top.''

Caster shrugged. ''Then you need to be somewhere else, because you're wasting my time.''

''Well, I don't understand that. I know my information is reliable. You've done it for two dollars. I know you have.''

Caster got an impatient look on his face. ''Look, Long, let's get something straight. This is my operation and I'll run it as I please. Maybe I did let a few herds through for two dollars, but them days is over with. That old dog won't hunt no more. If it wasn't you sitting in that chair, it would be somebody else. I got cattlemen lined up from here to the Brazos waiting for what I got to sell. You got some idea in your head that I'm taking a risk with the law, and that gives you some kind of hold over me. Well, you've been invited to watch me all week and see what you can see.''

''I don't see why you're singling me out, Caster, to go high priced. Is it because I mentioned a risk? Well, hell, I'd like to have you explain to me how there wouldn't be no risk when I hand you several thousand dollars. Wonder how that would set with the sheriff.''

Caster waved his hand as if driving off a pesky fly. ''In the first place, Long, you ain't gonna hand me no cash. You heard me speak of that fellow who works for me, Raoul San Diego. That's who you pay. And, believe me, he is the last man in the world you want to short-change. And I ain't singling you out. I raised my prices for the same reason the farmer raises his. He can get it. If corn is in short supply corn costs more. Well, they is a hell of a demand for Mexican beef right now. I don't know the why of it and I don't care. But the price is four dollars a head. Take it or leave it. Like I said, there'll be somebody else sitting in that chair, either later today or tomorrow or the next day, singing the same song. I can only run just so many cattle through a month and I intend on taking advantage of the situation while it exists. You *savvy*?"

Longarm took his hat off his knee and put it on his head. He sat back, rummaged around in his shirt pocket until he found another cigarillo, then stuck it in his mouth and lit it. As he was shaking out the match, he said, "Well, Caster, you've picked a hell of a time to tell me about your new policy. I've hired a man to gather a thousand head of cattle and I'd reckon he's about near finished. What am I supposed to do with the cattle? I can't go back on my word to the contractor. But it will cost me money to give you four thousand dollars right off the top. Hell, I ain't right sure I have got four thousand dollars. Not after I pay the contractor."

"Who'd you hire to gather your cattle? Deep down in the interior, I believe you said."

"What difference does that make?"

Caster pulled at the ends of his ample mustache as if to stretch it out a little further. "I'll tell you why. Was a man come around to me about two weeks ago. Said he was getting up a herd and had a buyer and wanted to know what my rock-bottom price was for slicking a herd through. He was bold as brass. And since you seem to have been talking to every other sonofabitch in Texas about me, I wondered if you wasn't connected to this hombre. Reason I ask is, he is trying to cheat you."

Longarm gave him a look. "I doubt that. I've known

the man a good many years.''

"Man in his mid-thirties? Kind of dandified looking? Wears a soft black leather vest with silver conchos and a black, border hat?''

Longarm looked uncomfortable. "Might be. How was he trying to cheat me?''

"Like I said, he was bold as brass. I'd never seen the feller before but he claimed he'd pushed more than one herd across the border at different spots. Just like you, he was under the impression the price was two dollars a head. He said if I'd give him a half a dollar a head he'd tell you that the price was solid at three and nothing to be done about it. I'd make an extra half a dollar and he'd make the same. Sound like yore man?''

"Well, I'm a sonofabitch," Longarm said softly, "Me and that gent is gonna have a little talk." He looked angry, but secretly he was pleased. To Caster, it made both of them look like crooks, and Caster, being a crook, would feel comfortable with his own kind. "He give you a name?''

"Davis, I think. Yeah. Davis. Don't remember much else, but he said he was gathering a thousand head for some greenhorn from Oklahoma.''

Longarm looked up. "Called me a greenhorn, did he?''

Caster laughed. "Yeah. Beginning to look like you are one, too. He's gathering cattle you can't get to market. But after the way he come at me with his proposition, I wouldn't feel all that bad about just leaving the cattle with him and seeing how he liked it.''

Longarm looked grim. "Well, I ain't been proved a greenhorn just yet. I got an idea or two. Might be I can handle that four dollars a head after all. A thought has come to mind.''

''Yeah?'' Caster raised his eyebrows. ''One minute it will break you and the next you can see yore way clear. Ain't even going to offer me three and see if I'll take that?''

''I would if I thought you was so disposed, but I don't.''

Caster smiled wryly. ''Sounds like you're beginning to catch on.''

Longarm let a pause build up and then he said, ''In fact I'll give five.''

Caster stared at him, unblinking. Finally he said, ''What?''

''I said I'd give five dollars a head. But I got a condition.''

''Well, if that condition is you run them across the bridge and keep on going, you can damn well forget it because that ain't going to be. You and me and your cattle are going to spend a week in my pens.''

''That ain't the condition.''

''Then, pray tell, what is?''

''I want your boss, Mister Mull, to sign my road papers along with you. I want them signed by the both of you.''

Jay Caster stared at Longarm. ''Have you gone loco? My boss is in Brownsville. This is Laredo, or have you lost yore way as well as your head?''

Longarm leaned back in his chair and stuck his boots out. ''So what?'' he said. ''Hell, it ain't but a three-hour train trip. Round trip six hours. You're going to split it with him—hell, I know that. You couldn't be running this business without his okay on the matter. And I can't see anything but a fifty-fifty split. That's twenty-five hundred dollars each. Hell, *I'd* spend six hours on the train for that kind of money.''

Chapter 6

Caster was quiet for a long moment. Finally he shook his head and said, "Well, I'll give you this much, Long. You take the prize for out and out gall. Whatever in the world would make you think I'd try and get Mister Mull down here? What makes you think he'd even consider coming?"

"Same answer to both questions. Money. You and him both know this can't last much longer. One of you will get transferred or something will happen. You both figure you'd better get it while you can. You the same as told me that when you raised your price."

Caster stared at him. "Long, you are starting to give me an itch. Might be I'm going to remember any minute that I got police powers."

"Oh, come on, Mister Caster. We both know you ain't going to do that."

Caster cocked his head. "I'm curious about something. You seem to have in mind what you want to do. Maybe you did when you walked through that door, and me and you have just been waltzing around without any music playing. But how come you need Mull's name on yore quarantine papers, too? How come just mine won't do?"

Longarm smiled just enough so that his lips weren't dead straight. "I done a little looking into this before I come to Laredo, Mister Caster. I talked to a couple of stock contractors who had cleared your quarantine and had their road papers, signed by you. You alone. Theirs was a one week deal also. Only they paid two-fifty a head. Well, they commenced to try and drive those cattle straight southeast across the coastal plains, figuring to take them to Galveston and ship them out to Cuba or New Orleans or some other place. They knew they could get twenty dollars a head. Only problem was them ranchers along the coastal plains. That's mighty rich range land. Them ranchers along in there raise some fine beef and they are mighty protective about it, especially when it comes to Mexican cattle might have tick fever." Longarm paused. "They got turned back, Mister Caster. Turned back by the law and some armed citizens. Ended up driving to the northwest, and didn't make enough to buy lunch." Longarm paused again. "Seems like you got a bigger reputation than you've been letting on, Mister Caster."

Caster studied Longarm for a moment. "Yes," he finally said. "And it appears like you been playing dumb all along."

Longarm gave him an innocent look. "Oh, sometimes I don't have to play. Sometimes it just comes natural. But not this time. This time I have a pretty good idea what I'm going to need to get them cattle to the Galveston port. And it's a little more than your signature on some papers. They know about you along the coast,

Mister Caster. Those rich ranch owners. And they got the law in their pocket. And you and I both know that no cattle slip through quarantine in Brownsville. Mister Mull keeps his reputation slick as a whistle. Here in Laredo is where y'all do your business. We both know that. Don't take a schoolteacher to figure it out. Of course you can tell me to take my cattle to Brownsville and cross them. You can tell me that, knowing I damn well will be obliged to hold them for ninety days.''

Longarm nodded his head. ''It's slick the way y'all run it. I got to give you that. But I want Mull's name on that paper and I want my port of entry to say Brownsville.''

''Long, you are either crazy or you think I am. I got half a mind to have my Mister San Diego pay you a visit.''

''You ain't going to do that.'' Longarm shook his head. ''No, that is not something you would do.''

''Why not?''

''Because it is bad business. You can't do business with a man who is halfway back to Oklahoma Territory.''

''You'd run?''

''I ain't no gunfighter, Caster. I'm a businessman, just like you. And when you give this some thought you'll see it's a good deal. Like I said, this end of your operation is playing out. To drive cattle out of here a man has got to go to the northwest, and that's too far. The ranchers along the coast have cut off any herds coming from here. You'll have to do it my way or get out of the game. I figure you can get herds through with Mister Mull's signature for at least another year. That's a good chunk of money you can make between now and then.''

Jay Caster opened a drawer of his desk and rummaged around until he found a toothpick. He stuck it in his mouth and rolled it around, regarding Longarm all the while. Watching this made Longarm conscious of the dull ache in his own tooth. He needed to get some laudanum. Caster said, "Where you staying?"

Longarm told him. "If I ain't there, I'll be in a poker game at a saloon close by."

Caster nodded. "Well, why don't you get up and get the hell on out of here for the time being. I'll give what you said a good thinking over."

Longarm put on his hat and stood up. "Just remember," he said, "my cattle are due in here any day now. We got to have a deal before I put them in quarantine."

Caster smiled. "You don't trust me, Mister Long?"

"Trust ain't got nothing to do with it, Mister Caster. This is business. Trust is something you have when you loan somebody money. I ain't proposing to loan no money I'm proposing to pay money for a service. You're mighty sure about what you're doing without no risk. I want to have the same feeling."

"I don't know if you'll get to feeling that secure," Caster said, "but we'll see what we will see."

Longarm turned toward the door, but before he'd gone but a few steps, he said, over his shoulder, "I'm obliged to you for telling me about my cattle gatherer trying to cheat me. Obliged, but not surprised."

"Oh? How come?"

Longarm shrugged. "The last two tried the same thing. I done a little lying today but I reckon you can understand about that."

"Oh, yes," Caster said. "I can understand lying."

• • •

Longarm didn't hear from Jay Caster for nearly twenty-four hours. He spent the intervening time moving around the town, acquainting himself with the layout and the country, getting to know the horse Austin Davis had furnished him, playing a little poker, and drinking a little whiskey. He avoided the Tejano Cafe, since he felt that Jasper White would be carrying tales back to Caster, besides which he didn't want to risk a run-in with Raymond San Diego, mainly because he was the brother of Caster's gunman and go-between. Once on the downtown street, he saw a Mexican woman who was nearly as beautiful and voluptuous as any woman he'd ever seen in his life. She was walking near the plaza, wearing a gaily colored gown and carrying a parasol over her shoulder. She had long, shining black hair and very light skin that set off her dark eyes and her full red lips. Longarm's eyes fastened on her square-cut bodice, where he could clearly see how her breasts mounded up and strained against the thin material. Even at a distance the sight of her made his mouth go dry. A man standing nearby had looked around at him and smiled crookedly. "I reckon it's all right to look," he said, "but I wouldn't get too close. That's Dulcima."

"Who the hell is Dulcima?"

"That's Raoul San Diego's woman, and if you don't know who he is, then more the pity you."

"Bad, huh?"

The man had spit on the ground and ground it in the dust with his boot heel. "Bad enough for me to stay clear of him."

Now Longarm was in his room having just finished breakfast in the hotel dining room. He'd been soaking his tooth in whiskey and vowing to go straight to an apothecary and get some laudanum. He'd bit down wrong on a piece of bacon and the pain had nearly killed him. Now however, after five minutes of soaking it was starting to dull down just a little. There was knock at the door. Longarm swallowed the whiskey, then took another quick drink from the bottle. He was sitting on the side of the bed and he swiveled to his left so as to be facing the door and to clear his draw in case he had to go for his weapon. He called, "Come in," hoping it would be Austin Davis, though it was a couple of days early.

The door opened, pushed from the outside, but no one entered. A man stood in the doorway. He was tall and slim and was wearing a flat-crowned border hat just like Austin Davis's. To Longarm's thinking, he was not Mexican, though he looked Mexican. He might, Longarm reflected, be a half-breed. His face had regular features, and was not unpleasant to look at. But his eyes were flat and hard and looked like agatee. He was clearly a man used to settling disputes with the big revolver he wore at his side, and since he was still alive, it appeared he must have won all of them. Longarm had no doubt that this was Raoul San Diego.

The man made no move to come in. "You Long?" he asked. He had very little accent.

Longarm nodded. "That would be me. As a guess I'd say you'd be Señor San Diego. Raoul San Diego."

San Diego ignored the remark. He said, "Señor Caster say you are to come see him this morning. You ready?"

Longarm shook his head. "No, not just at this moment. I got a little business I need to tend to. Tell him I'll be there in an hour."

San Diego stared at him, not blinking for half a moment. He was wearing a white shirt that appeared to be silk. Longarm figured that being the gunman for a crooked customs official must pay pretty good. San Diego shrugged. "Mister Caster send me to bring you. Maybe he don't want to see you in no hour."

Longarm stood up. He often used his size to make a point. "You tell Mister Caster I got a tooth is causing me a lot of pain. I got to go find something for it. Tell him I'll get there quick as I can. Maybe in less than half an hour."

San Diego looked at him for a second or two with his flat eyes, and then he shrugged again. Without a word he turned and disappeared down the hall. But he was wearing big roweled Mexican spurs and Longarm could follow his progress by their *ching chinging*.

He went over and closed the door, thinking the sonofabitch didn't have manners enough to do that. Manners or not, Raoul San Diego was someone he didn't intend to give much of an advantage to. If it came near to shooting time, Longarm determined he would kill the man first and worry about if he'd done right later. Any other course of action might result in a man not having any time to think about anything later.

But there was still the problem of his damn tooth. Laudanum made a man a little slow and groggy, and if he was to be coming up against Caster in serious discussion, Longarm didn't want to be either. Then again, he couldn't be sure what Caster wanted. Maybe he just wanted to say they didn't have a deal and Señor San Diego was going to shoot him for all the trouble he'd caused.

But somehow Longarm doubted that. He spent another ten minutes doctoring his tooth with whiskey until it was down to a bearable ache. After that he put a couple of fresh cigarillos in his pocket along with some matches, checked his revolver, put on his hat, and left the hotel.

It was a pleasant morning. Longarm walked around to the stable got the roan out, mounted him, and set off for Caster's office. It wasn't but half a mile or less, but he had no intention of doing any more walking.

The place looked empty when he rode up and dismounted. The sign that hung from the roof of the porch swung gently in the breeze, creaking a little. There was no sign of any horses or wagons. Off to his left the cattle pens hummed with activity, as before. Longarm climbed up on the porch and let himself in through the front door. Caster was sitting where he had been before, at his desk in the back of the office. Coming in from the sunlight, Longarm paused an instant to let his eyes adjust to the gloom. But Caster waved him forward impatiently. ''Come in, damnit. I ain't got all day.''

Longarm walked forward. Once again Caster did not invite him to take a chair, but Longarm did so anyway. ''Sorry I couldn't come right away,'' he said. ''I expect your Mister San Diego explained.''

''I ain't interested in yore damn teeth, Long. We're doing business here.''

''Are we?''

Caster leaned back in his chair and frowned. There was a letter-sized piece of paper on his desk. He nodded slowly. ''I sent a letter to Mister Mull outlining your proposition. There's his answer.''

Longarm looked surprised. ''You sent a letter? How the hell did you get an answer so fast?''

Caster gave him a look. ''I sent a man down on the

train. How the hell did you think? He brought the answer back last night on the return train. What did you think I was going to do, put that kind of business on the telegraph?"

Longarm shrugged. "I guess I never thought about it."

Caster showed him his tobacco-stained teeth. "That's how come you're settin' where you are and I'm behind this here desk. It's also the reason yore money's going to be in my pocket and you'll be following a bunch of cows for yore share while I'm spending mine."

Longarm kept his face impassive. He knew he had to play the role of a-not-so-bright beef contractor, but he was getting just a little tired of this crooked customs inspector and his lordly ways. But, he reminded himself grimly, it wouldn't be too much longer before their roles were reversed. Contenting himself with the thought of arresting Jay Caster, he said submissively, "Yeah, I reckon you're right. But somebody has got to do the work, such as it is, or you wouldn't be able to sit behind that desk."

Caster laughed. "Never thought about it that way, but, yeah, that's so. I'm just glad it's you and not me."

Longarm spoke with studied innocence. "You said my money was going to be in your pocket. Does that mean we got ourselves a deal? Did Mister Mull go along with it?"

Caster suddenly frowned. For a moment he didn't say anything. Finally he tipped his swivel chair back and said, "Yeah, in a manner of speaking. There will be some conditions, however."

Longarm was instantly alert. "Conditions? I don't see no room for conditions. Can't be a rise in the price, because I'm stretched thin as a guitar string as it is. And I ain't taking the herd to Galveston without his John Henry and stamp on them papers. So what conditions you talking about?''

Caster looked away for a second. When he turned back to Longarm he said, ''Well, one of the conditions is he ain't going to meet with you. You ain't never going to set eyes on him.''

''Well,'' Longarm said slowly, ''I don't see how that's going to work. Ain't no way I'll be able to make shore I got his okay unless he handles the papers himself. Hell, anybody could write his name, sign his name.''

Caster's eyes got hard. ''You accusing me in advance of planning something like that?''

''Well, no. But you got to agree it would occur to a man.''

Caster tipped his chair forward and picked up the piece of paper on his desk. ''If I was to let you read this, you would know that he's going to go along with it. He'll be in Laredo the day you leave with your cattle and he'll endorse your papers and put his seal on them.''

Longarm reached out his hand. ''Can I read it?''

Caster pulled the paper back. ''Hell, no! Who the hell do you think you are? I deal with you cattle bums all the time. You've all breathed so much trail dust it's affected your minds. No, you can't read this letter.''

Longarm shrugged, letting the insult pass but determined to remember it. He wondered what kind of dust Jay Caster had been breathing—the kind you absorb from being crooked? ''Then what's the good of showing it to me if I can't read it?'' he said. ''How come you don't want me to read it?'' He had half an idea, but he

112

wasn't going to voice it. From the sour way Caster was acting, he suspected that Mull hadn't gone for a fifty-fifty split. He'd almost have bet money that somewhere in the letter it said that if Mull was going to have to make the trip to Laredo and back, he'd take three dollars out of the five a head and Caster could have two. Of course Longarm didn't know that for certain, but it seemed likely. He said again, "How come you don't want me to read it?"

"How come? Hell, Long, it's official government business."

That was too much. Longarm had to laugh. "Official government business? That he's coming down here to slick my cattle through quarantine. Hell, Mister Caster, I doubt you want that letter falling into 'official government' hands. You want to borrow a match from me and put a flame to it? What happened he decide to split the money different than the way you had it figured?"

Caster's face went red. He half rose from his chair. "Listen, you sonofabitch, you better watch yore mouth or you'll be swimming those cattle. That, or have them confiscated. Where the hell you get off with that kind of talk? Who the hell you think you're talking to, some saddle tramp drover?"

Longarm wondered why the corrupted hated those who corrupted them. The offer didn't have to be accepted. It could be refused and honor retained. He reckoned that Jay Caster had to despise the "saddle tramp drovers"—the alternative was to despise himself, and Longarm didn't think Caster was man enough to do that. But he had to get him sweetened back up. "Mister Caster," he said earnestly, "I am plumb sorry I said that. It was meant as a joke and I see it didn't come off. It ain't none of my business how you and Mister Mull conduct y'all's affairs, and if I give offense I am mighty sorry for it.''

Caster sank back in his chair, looking somewhat mollified. "Well, just watch it, Long. You cattlemen got a bad habit of coming in here and acting like you own the place just because you pay a little money to get yore cattle to market sooner. What you're buying is time and the cost of not having to feed a herd. Don't worry about me flaring up, but they has been a couple of occasions where I've had to send Mister San Diego to straighten out a few hombres. Trust me, you don't want that to happen.''

"Was it him took the letter to Mister Mull in Brownsville?"

Caster laughed. "Yeah, and he didn't want to.''

"He scared of Mister Mull?"

Caster was in the process of scratching his forearm. He stopped and gave Longarm a look. "Scared of Mister Mull? You talking about Raoul San Diego? Hell, boy, he ain't scairt of nobody and that includes me. I pay him, so he wants me to stay alive. Scared of Mull? Sheeet!''

"Then how come he hated to go so bad.''

Caster laughed. " 'Cause he didn't want to leave that woman of his and be gone all night, that's why.''

"His woman?"

"Dulcima? You ain't heered about her?"

Longarm shook his head. "No, I reckon not. Am I supposed to have?"

"Well, you're staying at the Hamilton and she takes a stroll around the plaza right in front of the Hamilton twice a day. All the men line up on the sidewalk with their tongues hanging out about a foot, panting like hound dogs after a hard run. And don't she know it.''

''Know what?''

Caster frowned. ''Say, are you a little slow? She knows all them ol' boys are standing around watching her, dreaming about what it would be like to get in her britches.'' He looked away thoughtfully. ''I've wondered myself. But I want to stay alive. So I just look, like the rest of them.''

''And she enjoys that, does she?''

''Why, hell yes, she enjoys it. Gets a hell of a kick out of it. I've heard her tell Raoul about it.''

''What does he think?''

Caster shrugged. ''I never asked him. Where that woman is concerned it's best to stay off the subject.''

Longarm got out a cigarillo and lit it. ''Say, is he Mexican? He don't quite look it.''

''Half-breed. His daddy was Mexican. His mother was a schoolteacher from Louisiana or Tennessee or some such place. Fell in love with a Mexican *bandito* if you can figure that.'' He stopped and frowned. ''Long, we ain't getting our business talked about. We still got a couple of conditions to cover. Besides, the less you know about Raoul San Diego the better off you'll be.''

Longarm drew on his cigarillo. ''Now about that first condition. I ain't all that pleased about that. I done told you why, and I ain't gonna run the risk of putting another burr under your saddle blanket, but that condition kind of brings me up short. What else is on the bill of fare?''

''You said you were going to drive for Galveston. Well, you ain't going to make a beeline for there from here. I ain't going to have it looking like you come out

115

of Laredo. You may not want to, but you're going to turn those cattle east for fifty miles and trail in that direction alongside the Rio Grande before you turn them back north toward Galveston or Houston or wherever you plan to take them. I ain't having those coastal ranchers thinking you come from here.''

"Hell, you won't get no argument from me about that. Ain't I already told you I want my papers to say I come out of Brownsville? I don't know that it's necessary to go fifty miles. Hell, that's a three-day drive.''

"Fifty miles. No argument.''

"You going to send Mister San Diego to make sure I do?''

"I will if I have to. But I'll know if you don't go as far as I tell you.''

Longarm stared at Caster for a moment. "All right. What else?''

Caster scratched his forearm and did not look at Longarm. "You're going to pay half the money up front. Soon as we take your cattle into quarantine. Twenty-five hundred. Cash on the barrelhead.''

"The hell!'' Longarm was startled in spite of himself. He'd gotten so into the playacting that he was genuinely outraged. "You want me to give you twenty-five hundred dollars and you got my cattle penned up? Boy, you must think I'm the biggest sucker ever come down the pike. I'll pay the way it's always paid. I'll pay when you give me my cattle and my signed and stamped trail papers.''

Caster shook his head. "No. I want the money as soon as your herd gets here.''

"And what's to keep you from taking my money and just leaving my cattle in quarantine? Listen, Caster, I never heard of such a proposition and nobody I know ever heard of one like it, either. You got something against me personally? You have, why just spit it out. I'd like to know, because you seem to be causing me a world of grief here.''

Caster spit in his bucket. "Long," he said in a bored voice, "you ain't nothing to me but money. I don't know you and don't want to know you, so there ain't nothin' personal. I didn't like you wantin' to drag Mull into this, but maybe it be a good thing. I don't know. And you made a few other remarks weren't none of your business, but let it pass. Now, you want this deal or not? The conditions ain't up for argument.''

Longarm furrowed his brow as if he were making a decision, thinking. Actually, he was thinking. He didn't know how much money the ranchers had given Austin Davis, but he was almost certain it didn't include any five thousand dollars in bribe money, especially twenty-five hundred up front. He sat there for a moment trying to figure out how he was going to lay his hands on that kind of money. He didn't know if Laredo had a federal bank or not, but it didn't make any difference. He wasn't going to tell anyone in Laredo he was a U.S. deputy marshal, even a federal banker. He knew Laredo, he knew the border. You might not be corrupt when you came to Laredo, but if you stayed long enough it would corrupt you sure as hell. The border lived by the *mordida*, the bite, the bribe. That was the way business was done, and it was so natural no one thought anything of it. But that wasn't going to help him get twenty-five hundred dollars. "Look here, Mister Caster," he said at last, "I'll take your deal because I ain't got no choice. I'll just have to take it on trust that Mister Mull is going to sign and put his seal on my road papers. But I got to tell you that I ain't got twenty five hundred dollars I can lay my hands on as quick as you want it. You say you have to have it in hand when my cattle arrive. Hell, that could be tomorrow.''

Caster frowned. "What the hell is all this? You telling me you didn't bring any money with you? Wasn't you prepared to pay at least two dollars a head? You were also going to have to pay the man who gathered the cattle.''

"Of course. But that give me a week. I was going to wire my bank for the money. I figured my cattle would be held a week and I'd have time to get the money down here by wire. But if I got to take and hand over half that five thousand when my cattle come in—well, hell, there ain't going to be enough time.''

Caster's look turned sour. "Hell, you are some hombre to do business with. I reckon you had better get yore cornbread ass over to the bank and get them busy on the transaction. As long as it's in the works I'll go ahead and receive your cattle.''

"Mister Caster, you know what day of the week it is?''

"Of course, it's Saturday. So what? The banks are open till noon. Go find one.''

"They may be open till noon here, but they ain't in Broken Bow. Monday morning is the soonest I can get this wagon rolling.''

Caster slapped his fat hand on the desk. It made a loud thud. "Well, sheet, Long! You are trying my patience. How much money *do* you have with you?''

Longarm tried to look worried. He said, "Not much. Few hundred dollars. Man with any sense don't carry a lot of cash in this country. You ought to know that. I done business this way for years and never had no trouble. Hell, Mister Caster, what is the rush? You'll have my cattle in your pens when they get here, and I won't be able to move them without your say-so. Ain't that security enough?''

Caster leaned forward and rubbed his thumb and forefinger together. ''That's the only kind of security I believe in, Long. Tell you what . . . How long will it take you to get hold of your money?''

''Two days, three at the outside.''

Caster stood up. ''All right,'' he said. ''I'll give you three days starting Monday morning. By Wednesday you better have twenty-five hundred dollars to put in Raoul's hand. You *savvy*?''

Longarm stood up, too, put on his hat, and worked it around to get it set comfortably. ''Put like that, I don't reckon there's much way I can't *savvy*. All I can do is find me a bank Monday morning and get them hopping. You give me to the close of banking hours Wednesday?''

''That's three o'clock. Yeah, you can have until then. But if you're wise, you'll get it to Raoul as quick as you can. You're just about to get where you ain't worth all the trouble.''

Longarm stared at the customs man for a long moment, wondering what all the rush was about. It sounded like Caster was up to something on his own. He was setting up to cheat someone, but Longarm couldn't figure out if it was him or maybe even James Mull. But he let it pass just as he let pass the casual insulting remarks that Caster liked to make. All he said was, ''You drive

119

a hard bargain, Mister Caster. And I don't see no call for it.''

"Don't you? Well then, I reckon you wouldn't. But then you ain't spent ten years dealing with the likes of yourself. Now go on. I've got work to do.''

Longarm walked out of Caster's office very deep in thought. Letting the screen door bang behind him, he stepped off the porch, climbed into the saddle of the roan, and looked around, half expecting to see San Diego watching him, but the gunman was nowhere in sight. He rode slowly back to the hotel, and turned the animal in at the stable, figuring he wouldn't need him for a while. Still deep in thought, Longarm went into the old hotel and walked across the empty lobby. It was almost noon, but he wasn't hungry. He went in the bar, got a large whiskey and a mug of beer, sought out an empty table in a back corner of the almost deserted bar, and sat down to think. The first problem he had to deal with was where in hell he and Austin were going to get the kind of money they needed. He could wire Billy Vail and the money would be sent without any question, but he sure as hell couldn't telegraph from Laredo to the headquarters of the U.S. Marshal Service in Denver, Colorado. And there wasn't another telegraph office within seventy-five miles. And the hell of it was he didn't know where Austin Davis was or when to expect him. Caster seemed determined to have the money and have it within the time specified. Longarm could not figure out why the customs man was being so adamant about it, but the reason didn't really matter. If they were to catch Caster, and Mull, he had to have some cash money in his hand to pass across. That dodge about handing it to San Diego wasn't going to protect Caster, no matter what he might think. He'd already made it clear that San Diego was his employee, and handing the half-breed the money was the same as giving it to Caster.

But there was still the puzzle about Mull. Longarm wasn't sure if Caster was trying to pull a fast one on Mull or not. He was halfway persuaded that Mull had been contacted and was willing to go along with the scheme; he just wasn't willing to be directly linked to it in person.

The money, though—that was a real poser. He guessed, once Austin Davis got in with the cattle, he could take what money the junior deputy had and put it with what they both could scrape up and maybe they'd have the twenty-five hundred that Caster was demanding. Then again, how much money Austin would have depended upon how much the Texas coastal cattlemen had given him and how much he'd had to pay for the Mexican cattle. Longarm pressed his hand against his forehead trying to remember what Davis had said having to do with bribing Caster. Had he been going to actually bribe him, hand over the money? Or was he just planning on making the offer and arresting Caster when he accepted? Longarm could not recall. They'd talked about so much, and he hadn't been on the scene, and he really hadn't paid that much attention. Not that he hadn't been interested—it just hadn't seemed necessary at the time, and he'd figured there'd be plenty of other opportunities to get matters straight. Besides, he hadn't much planned on using anything that Austin had mapped out, anyway.

He sighed and took a drink of whiskey, chasing it with a long swallow of the cool beer. Longarm didn't much care for beer unless he was thirsty, but it went down well enough when a man was doing hot work, like heavy thinking about where to lay his hands on a lot of money.

He was chewing the matter over in his mind when Jasper White suddenly appeared in the door of the saloon and, after pausing to look around, came marching straight over to Longarm's table. Longarm glanced up as the lanky man with the pale eyes came to a stop. "I reckon you owe me money," Jasper White said. "And I reckon you know why you do."

Longarm stared at him for a moment. Finally he said, "Well, Jasper, I think I counted that hundred out right, but if I made a mistake, you set down here and tell me about it. You want a drink?"

"Don't drink," Jasper White said. But he sat down stiffly in a chair across from Longarm. "Never did drink. Don't hold with it."

Longarm half laughed. "Well, all right. That's your business. Just leaves more for the rest of us. Now, what is this about I owe you money."

"You jest paid me fer Mister Jay Caster. Was a hunnert dollars for him. Wasn't nothin' said about Mister James Mull."

Longarm frowned. "What are you talking about, Jasper?"

"I'm talking about Mister James Mull of Brownsville, the high muckymuck for the Customs down in this part of the country. You gone and got him ringed in on yore deal. Well, that figures to cost you another hunnert dollars."

Longarm shook his head slowly, but his mind was working fast. It wasn't hard to figure how Jasper knew about Mull. Raoul had told his brother Raymond and Raymond had told Jasper. It was good news in a way. It meant that Mull was actually coming to Laredo, that he was actually part of the scheme and not just some bluff that Caster was going to try to run. But it wouldn't do to let Jasper know how far things had progressed. "Jasper," he said, "where you getting your information? For all I know, you're trying to do me out of more money. What makes you so sure that Mister Mull is involved?"

Jasper began nodding his head. "That's all right, how I know. The thing is, I know. People tell me things because they want me to know. Sometimes so I'll talk and get word around, and sometimes when they don't want me to talk. Fact of the business is I know the difference. They don't want it knowed about Mull. He's coming in on the Q.T. Telegram is gonna get sent to him saying a certain thing and he be gettin' on the train and come straight here. Now, about my money—"

"Wait a minute. You said whoever knowed about Mull didn't want it talked around. Yet here you are talking to me, telling me. That ain't a very good reference."

Jasper was sitting straight up in his chair, his back not even touching the back of the seat, just sitting upright on the front half. "Well," he said, "what's telling you? You already knowed. In fact was you caused Mister Mull to come down. And I'll tell you something for nothing—Mister Caster ain't overly happy about it. Nosir."

"That what Raoul said?"

Jasper looked prim. "I don't never say who I heard from. But that ain't got nothing to do with my money."

It occurred to Longarm that he hadn't the slightest idea what James Mull looked like, and he very much doubted that Austin Davis did, either. And Caster had said that Mull was not going to be present at the time of the final transaction. That was going to make him a little hard to arrest. But if they had someone who could identify him when he stepped down off the train, then Austin Davis could keep close tabs on the man and they'd be able to lay hands on him when the time came. But Longarm didn't want to tell Jasper that he didn't know Mull. He didn't want him to see that he was in a valuable position. For all Jasper knew, Mull was known to Longarm or would be seeing him as soon as he got off the train. "Hell, Jasper," he said offhandedly, "Mull ain't worth no hundred dollars to me. I don't need no introduction to him. You want to try and rob me, go and get yourself a gun."

Jasper frowned. "That ain't the way I figure it at all. If I hadn't made you known to Mister Caster, then Mister Mull would not be coming down here. You paid for one and are getting two. An honest man would see that."

Longarm picked up his beer and sipped at it thoughtfully. After a moment he said, "Well, I don't want to cheat you, Jasper, and I don't want folks thinking that I have. But I can't see paying no more than fifty dollars for Mull. You got to admit I done most of that on my own. Hell, do you even know James Mull? I bet you never laid eyes on the man."

Jasper looked outraged. "Why, damned if that be so!" he said heatedly. "I've met up with him twenty times. I—" He paused. "Well, maybe not that many, but I damn shore know the man. Real skinny kind of feller like Raymond, though he ain't built nowhere the way Raymond is. Tall and skinny. An' always wears a suit with a vest. And a derby hat. Dresses like a real big shot."

Longarm yawned. "Well," he said, "I'll give you

fifty for him. You reckon that to be fair? He wouldn't even be coming it weren't for me."

Jasper turned the matter over in his mind. "Well," he said finally, "I would reckon him being the boss of Mister Caster, he'd fetch a better price. Say seventy-five."

Now Longarm frowned. "Seventy-five? For a man I caused to be fetched? Hell, Jasper, I'm beginning to think this town is full of thieves. If I give you the seventy five it has got to be with the understanding that you don't tell nobody about this little talk we had. I don't want it getting around that I'm such an easy touch."

Jasper looked insulted. "Say, maybe you didn't hear me when I said folks tell me things when they don't want them getting around. I can keep a secret better than any man alive."

"You'll tell Raymond. He's your partner. You'll tell him."

"Raymond ain't my partner in everything," Jasper said staunchly. "Just some little business we got."

"Yeah, you'll tell Raymond and Raymond will tell Raoul and Raoul will tell Caster. And Caster will jump my ass and say the deal is off because I let the cat out of the bag. Ain't nobody supposed to know that Mull is coming."

"Well, they won't hear it from me," Jasper assured him. "No, sir."

Longarm pursed his lips and appeared to be thinking. "Tell you what," he said. "I'll give you the seventy-five, but I ain't going to give it to you until Mull actually steps down off the train."

Jasper started to protest. "Now, what's that got to do with me? I ain't got no say about him actually coming or not."

"If Mull doesn't come, Jasper, then I ain't getting two for one, am I?"

Jasper thought about it for a moment, frowning, working it around until it finally made sense to him. "No, I mean yeah," he said uncertainly. "I reckon you're right. But how am I gonna get my money? You'll be with Caster."

"Tell you what—My foreman, the man who's gathering the cattle for me, he'll be in town in the next couple of days. Soon as he gets here, Mull is supposed to come. Raoul San Diego will more than likely be the one that sends the telegram. You'll be in the know about that, won't you?"

Jasper looked uncertain, but he said, "I reckon I would. I can make it my bid'ness to be in the know."

"Then there you have it. I'll send my foreman along with you to the depot. You point out Mull to him and he'll have instructions to hand you the money."

Jasper peered closely at Longarm. "You wouldn't be trying to trick me, would you?"

Longarm gave him a patient look. "Jasper, I know who your friends are. A pair of brothers who are supposed to be worse than the smallpox. I don't figure to get myself in bad with them over a matter of seventy-five dollars. I ain't a gunfighter a neither is the man gathering the cattle. We're just trying to do some business."

The doubt vanished from Jasper White's face. "Well, so long as you understand how matters stand." He stood up. "When are yore cattle due in?"

Longarm shrugged. "Any day now. The sooner the better, so far as I'm concerned."

"Well, our business is finished. I point out Mister

James Mull, and yore man gives me seventy-five dollars. Is that right?''

"You better point out the right one," Longarm warned. "The man you described could be a ribbon salesman calling on general merchandise stores. I ain't paying no money for a ribbon drummer.''

Jasper was insulted. "Long," he said, "I ain't never cheated nobody on my facts and I ain't goin' to start with you, even if I do think you tried to pull a fast one on me. Nosir. If Mister Mull is on that train, he will be pointed out to yore foreman.''

Longarm shrugged and picked up his beer. "Then we got a deal, Mister White." He raised his mug and watched Jasper nod curtly and walk out of the bar. After the man was gone Longarm called for another large whiskey, and then he sat back and began trying to figure out how they were going to succeed in carrying off an operation that was becoming more and more complicated. One thing he did need to do was get over to a bank and make arrangements for them to receive funds in his name. He didn't know where he was going to get such funds, or more to the point, *how* he was going to get such funds, but he did know that arrangements had be made to receive them the money. But it was Saturday, and the clock on the wall behind the bar showed it to be half past noon. After finding out from the bartender that the local banks definitely closed at twelve noon, Longarm relaxed. That was one thing, at least, he didn't have to worry about today. The banks were closed and he couldn't do a thing about that. Matters would simply have to wait until Monday. He picked up his new whiskey and began sipping at it reflectively. Then a thought hit him. "What's the biggest bank in town?" he asked the bartender.

The bartender shrugged. "First National of Laredo, I reckon. At least they claim to be."

Longarm got up quickly, leaving two dollars on the table. "Is there still a train going north this afternoon?" he asked.

"Yeah, San Antonio Express. But it leaves at one o'clock. You ain't got much time."

"Oh, I ain't going," Longarm said. "Just seeing a friend off."

He hurried out of the bar and began walking as fast as he could toward the depot. Once again he was breaking his vow against walking, but he didn't see what he could do about it.

Chapter 7

It was a long hard trip. Longarm had to ride the train over a hundred miles before they got to a town that had a telegraph office, Hondo; a little village that existed because it had once been an important jumping-off place for herds that were trailing to the far north. Now it made its living off the railroad and such businesses and ranching as were in its vicinity.

But then, once Longarm had got the telegram off to Billy Vail with instructions about the money, he realized he'd have been better off going on to San Antonio because he was stuck in Hondo until the next southbound train came through, out of San Antonio, and that wasn't due until two in the morning. At least in San Antonio there would have been some first-rate bars and a chance at a real poker game. His disgust almost knew no bounds when he finally found a game being played in a place that was half saloon and half feed store. The game was a nickle ante, quarter limit. He barely managed to choke out ''No, thanks,'' when he'd been invited to sit in.

In the end he'd taken a room at a rickety hotel and,

armed with a bottle of whiskey had spent the time until two A.M. drinking and dozing and feeling bitter. He was bitter because, by rights, such a job should have been handled by Austin Davis. It was a chore for the junior member of the team. But Longarm had been afraid to wait until Davis showed up. There might not have been enough time to send him off on the train to a telegraph station and time for the money to be sent. Caster was too impatient, and Longarm had no intention of giving him any excuse to slip out of the noose, especially now that he knew James Mull was coming. He had telegraphed Billy to have five thousand dollars sent by wire to the First National Bank of Laredo, to be held for C. Long. He had not used his first name because of the nagging fear that someone would recognize it. Unlikely as that was, he didn't see any point in taking a chance.

He got back to the Hamilton Hotel just as the sun was threatening to rise, a little before six. He had breakfast in the hotel dining room and then went to his room, armed himself with a few stiff drinks, and got into bed. On top of everything else his bad tooth, seemingly aggravated by the jolting and banging of the train, had ached the whole time he was in Hondo. It was a little quieter now, but he had every intention, once he'd had a nap, of finding an apothecary open on Sunday and getting himself a supply of laudanum or morphine or anything he could find that would give him some rest from the pain.

He slept until early afternoon and then got up, slowly and sleepily, and sat on the side of the bed and yawned. He was grumpy and felt ill-tempered. He hated it when his sleep pattern got all turned around. Now, more than likely, he wouldn't be able to sleep in the night ahead and it would take him a week to get back on schedule.

After he'd had a drink or two and smoked a cigarillo, he got up, feeling creaky, and took a kind of half-bath out of of the wash basin, then shaved and put on a fresh set of clothes. After that he went into the dining room and talked a waiter into getting him something to eat, even though it was long past time for serving the midday meal. The waiter managed to get him a steak and potatoes and some stewed peaches. Longarm had that with coffee and, after paying his check, gave the waiter two dollars, one for himself and one for the cook. He did not ordinarily throw money around like that, but he fully intended charging it to the U.S. Marshal Service as expenses, and Billy Vail be damned.

Sunday afternoons were when the gay blades of the town and the eligible señoritas promenaded around the plaza, the girls walking in one direction, the men in the other. Longarm wandered out to watch the young men strut and the girls try to flirt without getting caught by their severe-looking chaperones.

The Laredo plaza was a big one for a town of its size. Almost a hundred yards long and half as wide, it had a bandstand and a fountain in the middle, with benches and chairs scattered about and a pleasant sprinkling of oak, elm, and even a magnolia here and there. It was paved with flagstone and offered a nice view of the river and the International Bridge. From its center Longarm could almost see Caster's office. Wondering where Austin Davis was, he sure as hell hoped he was getting close.

He finally took refuge under a magnolia in the northeast corner of the plaza, right at the edge. He had seen the woman named Dulcima walking at the far end, and he had retreated to the hotel side to be well out of her way. The last thing he wanted or needed was for Raoul San Diego to come gunning for him over his woman.

But she did make a striking figure, even at a distance, walking along the south side of the plaza, about midway, clad in a pink dress of some shiny material that Longarm reckoned to be silk. She was carrying a closed pink parasol over her shoulder, and her gown was of a length that now and then allowed Longarm to catch a glimpse of her trim ankles beneath the ruffled hem. But it wasn't her ankles that drew his eyes so much as the swell of her breasts and her small waist that fed into the flare of her hips. Dulcima was, indeed, a very tasty-looking woman.

He kept watching her as she reached the eastern end of the plaza and abruptly turned north. She was no more than sixty yards off, and it appeared to Longarm that she was headed directly for him. But, of course, he knew that was nonsense. She was just walking the third leg of her promonade, and would turn back west when she got to the corner. Besides, he was in the shade of the magnolia and he doubted she could see him very well from out in the bright sunshine.

She kept walking. When she got to the point when she should have turned west, she kept straight on, walking directly toward him. Suddenly Longarm was in a panic, wondering if he'd offended her in some way by eyeing her so closely. But, hell, every other man in the plaza was doing the same thing, and that was the reason she was here, to be looked at. The other women promenading were declaring themselves to be elgible, but everyone in town knew that Dulcima wasn't up for grabs—not unless a man wanted to lose his hands.

But she was coming straight toward him, a small smile playing over her full red lips. Ten feet away, she took the parasol off her shoulder and swung it carelessly by its handle. It seemed to Longarm that the nearer she got, the more erect and inviting her carriage became. He was thinking of bolting, turning and walking away, when she said, still a yard or so away, "You like to look at Dulcima, I theenk."

She had a pleasant, musical voice with a slight Spanish accent, but it took the words a moment to register on Longarm's brain. Finally he managed to stammer, "Uh, ma'am—uh, what was that?"

Now she was standing right in front of him, and once again he was very conscious of the square-cut bodice of her dress and the way her golden-hued breasts swelled out at him. Holding the pink parasol in one hand, she tapped it in the palm of the other and said, "I theenk you like to look at Dulcima, no? I theenk your eyes follow me all over the place, no?" Then she laughed lightly and ran her moist, pink tongue over her lips.

The sight excited Longarm so that he could feel his jeans getting a little tight. Trying not to stammer, he said, "Why, ma'am, I didn't mean no offense. You are wearing such a stylish outfit that it naturally took my eye." He took off his hat and ducked his head in a kind of bow. "I hope you didn't take it unkindly. I shore meant no harm."

With sparkling eyes and lips curved in a smile that was very close to a laugh, she took one hand off the parasol and shook her finger close to Longarm's face. "Oh, no no no. Now the señor tells the lie. You like my outfit. Ha ha ha. I know what you like and it ees not the dress Dulcima ees wearing. No no no. You tell me what you were looking at, hokay?''

Longarm blushed; he couldn't help himself. ''Wh-wh-why,'' he stammered, ''I reckon the color and style of your clothes just seemed to catch my eye, ma'am. I can't think of nothing else.''

She put her head back and laughed, causing her long, silky hair to cascade almost to her waist. ''I theenk you are the liar, señor. I know what you were watching.'' She moved the slightest bit closer to him and said, ''I theenk you were admiring Dulcima's breasts and her legs and the part of her maybe you like the best.''

It caught Longarm so off balance that he stepped back as if a flaming torch had been thrust at him. Instinctively his eyes flitted around the plaza, the image of Raoul San Diego in his mind. That would be all he needed—to have to kill Caster's gunman right before the deal was to be completed. And there was Raymond, his brother. The Tejano Cafe wasn't that far away. He glanced in that direction, but there was no sign of the small Mexican. And, of course, there was always Jasper. He could be anywhere. But as far as that went, anyone standing around the plaza could see him talking to Dulcima and make a beeline to tell Raoul San Diego. Longarm swallowed and tried to fight the blush off his face. ''Ma'am,'' he said earnestly, ''I don't reckon you ought to talk like that. I understand you are already attached to another gentleman of the town. A rather well-known gentleman. I'd as soon not get crosswise with him.''

''Raoul?'' She laughed. ''I doan theenk a man like you is afraid of Raoul. I have been watching you, señor. I have seen you several of the times and I say to myself, 'Dulcima, thees is a handsome man. Very strong-looking. Very ha'some in a big, rough way.' I say to

134

myself that such a man would make the kind of love a woman like me would like. What you theenk of that?''

Longarm could feel himself starting to sweat under his hat. "Ma'am—" he began.

"You call me Dulcima. You know what that means in English?"

He said helplessly, "Kind of."

"It means sweet." She stepped up close to him, so close he could smell the musk of her body. "You taste me, you never find nothing so sweet. You weel see."

He took off his hat and used that as an excuse to step a little further away from her. "Ma'am," he said, "I got to tell you that I ain't got the slightest doubt that you are a mighty tasty dish. But the thing is, I ain't one to go poaching on another man's territory. Right now you are on Señor San Diego's range, and that kind of makes it wrong to talk the way we're talking now."

She smiled. "I theenk you lie again. I theenk you doan care who a woman belongs to if you want her. No, you lie." She shrugged. "I doan tell. Do you tell?"

"Ma'am," Longarm said, "I think you ought to look around. Every eye in this plaza is on us. I don't reckon it is going to take long for word to get back to your Raoul. And I don't reckon he is going to be too happy."

She snapped her fingers. "What do I care what he theenks! He ees my man so long as I weesh. But I have other men. What he going to do, keel them all? I doan theenk so."

Longarm gave a little laugh. "It's just this one I'm worried about. Me."

"Bah!" Dulcima said. She locked her eyes with his. "You lie. Look down at my breasts and tell me you doan lie."

Longarm looked, instead, over her shoulder to see how much attention they were attracting. In his retreat he'd managed to keep himself hidden from the hotel porch, where a number of spectators were seated in wicker chairs. There wasn't much behind him, but he could see a number of people to the south who appeared to be taking a considerable interest in their conversation. "No ma'am," he told her. "I don't reckon I'm going to do that. At least not out here on the street."

She laughed, her voice tinkling like a bell. "You blush like a boy, but I doan theenk you do other theengs like a boy. I theenk you make love a *mucho hombre*."

Longarm swallowed and tried again. "Ma'am, I reckon we ought to call off this here little talk. Or save it for some place a little less public. I can't up and walk away from you. Wouldn't be the gentlemanly thing to do. So I wonder if you wouldn't mind just kind of sashaying on along."

"Do you know where I leeve?"

"I can't say I do."

"I have the beeg house on the leetle hill east of town down by the river. Anyone can tell you where Dulcima leeve."

He shifted his gaze from over her shoulder to her face. "Yeah," he said. "Along with Mister Raoul San Diego."

"Bah!" she said. "He leeve there when I say hokay. It ees *my* house. It ees *my* hacienda. You come see me and we weel talk and maybe then you weel want to look. No?"

"Ma'am," Longarm said, "I assure you that if circumstances were different I'd follow you home so fast you'd need a race horse to beat me there."

"Ha-ha! So, I theenk you like Dulcima a leetle."

"It ain't hard," he admitted.

"Maybe not now, but I make it so. Ha-ha?"

Longarm said weakly, "Yeah, ha-ha. Ma'am, you are making me mighty uncomfortable I shore wish you'd finish up your walk."

"Not unteel you call me Dulcima."

He let out his breath. "All right. Whatever you say. Dulcima, would you please let me out of this corner before you get me killed."

She gave him an amused look. "You talk of being afraid. How come I doan theenk you are afraid? What is the reason for that? Huh?"

"I reckon you just never seen enough scared men."

She laughed and twirled her parasol. "I go now. But you better come see me queek or I come see you at the hotel." She laughed again when he gave her a quick glance. "Oh, yes. I know where you stay. Thees place does not get many han'some mens, so Dulcima keep her eye open all the time. I see you the first day and I see you seeing me, so I say myself, 'Dulcima, there ees a good cheeken for your pot.' So you see, eet has already been decided. I go now. *Adios.*"

She gave him one last smile with her sensual mouth, then turned and walked off, twirling her parasol. Longarm followed her with his eyes, thinking she made near as pretty a picture from the rear as from any other angle. But damnit if word got back to San Diego, there could be big trouble and he didn't know a way to avoid it. If he had to, he'd kill the man, but that would more than likely make Caster that much harder to deal with. One thing for certain, he wasn't going anywhere near her house, not until the deal was done and all parties were

137

either dead or in custody. With his heart still beating a little rapidly, Longarm turned and walked back to the hotel. As he stepped up on the porch, he wondered if it was his imagination or did several of the railbirds give him more than just a casual eye.

He stayed close to the Hamilton the balance of that night, eating in the hotel dining room and drinking in the hotel bar. A little after nine a halfway decent poker game started up, though it was a limit game and five dollars at that. But it was something to do and his luck was just short of hot, so he managed to win about eighty dollars by midnight, when he decided to make it an early night and turn in. One of the gamblers made a remark about him quitting winners, and Longarm turned to stare at him. He hadn't heard anything that foolish in a long time. "Why don't you gents wise this fellow up?" he said to the rest of the players. Then he addressed the disgruntled man. "That's the point to the game, fellow. The object is to win. It's like coming out of a gunfight alive. You understand? Maybe nobody told you before and that's the reason you keep losing. You don't know no better."

The gambler, a sharp-faced little ferret of a man who looked like a storekeeper, replied, "Maybe not, feller. But I know better'n to hold a conversation with Raoul San Diego's woman right in the big middle of town."

Another of the players said sharply, "Keep your mouth shut, Hurley."

Longarm gave Hurley a long look. "And," he said, "another thing you don't seem to know is when to mind your own business."

The man who had spoken sharply looked up at Longarm. "He don't mean nothing, mister. He just runs off at the mouth sometimes. He didn't mean to be butting into your business. No offense meant.''

Longarm stared at Hurley for a long moment. The little man kept his attention fixed on his cards. Finally Longarm let his breath out slowly, then he reached in his pocket, fished out a five-dollar gold piece, and flung it on the table. ''No offense taken,'' he said. ''You gents have a drink on me.''

He had given the little storekeeper a hard look, but as he turned away and headed out of the bar, his heart was beating a little faster. If his encounter with Dulcima could be remarked upon so readily by a stranger in a bar, then heaven only knew how far the news had traveled around the town. Longarm had little doubt that unless Caster had sent him off on another errand, Raoul San Diego already knew about the long conversation that had taken place under the magnolia tree. And if not Raoul, then his brother, and if not his brother, then certainly Jasper White, and if Jasper White knew, it was a cinch that Raoul would know as soon as word could be carried to him. As he walked to his room Longarm resolved that he would have to regard Raoul San Diego in the same way he would a rattlesnake. Expect him to strike at any instant. He would have to walk a very devilish tightrope, watching San Diego with one eye, while keeping the other one on Caster and Mull. What he'd first expected to be a pretty straightforward piece of business—catching and arresting a corrupt official—was rapidly getting more and more complicated. He wished to hell that Austin Davis would get back with the cattle and they could complete the deal and get the hell out of Laredo before somebody got killed.

He had breakfast the next morning in the dining room

and then sat around the lobby, watching the various characters come and go, until the banks opened. At nine o'clock he walked the two blocks to the First National Bank of Laredo, which was up from the river and in the center of town. As luck would have it, there was an apothecary in the same block, and with his tooth acting up again, Longarm swerved in at the door and asked for laudanum. The young man behind the counter took his money and handed over a small glass-stoppered bottle containing a milky white liquid. When the clerk asked if he'd ever taken laudanum before, Longarm hesitated. "Well, yeah, but it's been a spell. I got shot accidentally once. Broke a bone and it hurt considerable."

"What are you taking it for this time?"

Longarm pointed toward his mouth. "Toothache."

"Why don't you go to a dentist? We got some good ones in town. A few even speak English."

"Right now I ain't got the time."

"Well," the clerk said, "I don't reckon I need to warn you about the laudanum. Don't take any whiskey with it. It's powerful stuff—and it might make you a little groggy if you take too much."

"How much is too much?"

"Don't take over half a teaspoonful. Teaspoonful at the most. Was I you, I'd try and work it up around the gums where the tooth is hurting. I wouldn't swallow any more than I had to." Just as Longarm was leaving, the clerk called after him, "And don't do no dangerous work while you're taking it. It kind of slows you down."

Longarm stopped and looked back, his mind suddenly on Raoul San Diego. "What do you mean by dangerous work?"

"Oh, anything. I wouldn't work wild cattle or ride a bucking horse."

Longarm started to say, What about a gunfight? but he kept the words to himself and just nodded and went on out the door and then next door to the bank. He put the little bottle in his shirt pocket and buttoned the flap. He'd been planning on taking a quick dose, but as careful as the apothecary had said he ought to be, he figured he'd wait until he was back in his room at the hotel.

The matter at the bank did not take long. It was a routine transaction for a bank in cattle country. There was nothing unusual about it except for the fact that he was using only his initial, and the bank, to Longarm's surprise, charged him a fifty-dollar fee. Longarm was a little irritated by the transaction fee, and told the bank manager as much. But the manager, a sleek-looking portly man, assured him it was the custom and had been for some time. That had shut him up, since transferring cattle money was not in his normal line of business. Privately, Longarm thought, it was the custom, all right, but only in Laredo, since it was in line with the border practice of helping themselves to your socks once they'd stolen your boots. He'd very nearly come to grief when the manager had asked what bank would be wiring the money. For a moment he'd fumbled and hemmed and hawed before saying, "Well, it's my new partner. I reckon he'll be using his bank. Thing is I don't know which bank that might be. He does business with several. But I'd reckon it will be one in Colorado."

He'd ducked the business about not using a first name by simply declaring, "Never cared for it, so I don't use it much. 'Long' suits most folks well enough. Does me."

Then he'd paid the manager fifty dollars out of his own pocket and gone back to the hotel. The toothache had come back full force and he was hurrying to get to his room so he could use some of the laudanum. It seemed as if there hadn't been a moment in the last month that he hadn't been hurting.

But as Longarm hurried through the hotel lobby, it seemed to him that a lot of eyes were following him and that more than one man lowered his newspaper to cast a look his way. He could almost hear them whispering to each other. "That there is the feller was talking to Dulcima yesterday. Yessir, right out there on the plaza. Big as life. Damn near had his head down in her tits. Seen it myself. Wonder when San Diego is coming to settle his hash? Wouldn't care to be in his boots. But anybody foolish enough to carry on like that, and I mean right there in front of the preacher and ever'body, near about deserves what he gets."

He let himself into his room and sat down on the side of the bed, took his hat off and then unbuttoned his shirt pocket and took out the little bottle filled with the milky liquid. He removed the glass stopper and smelled it. It didn't smell like much of anything. He held the bottle out at arm's length. It looked harmless enough, but the apothecary had cautioned him as if he were dealing with nitroglycerine. And maybe he was. If San Diego came around, all he'd have to be was about a heartbeat too slow and there wouldn't be any more heartbeats.

But the toothache was pounding by now, and he decided, the hell with it. What were the chances of San Diego coming around in the next few hours? Damned slim, he thought. And if he didn't get some relief from the pain, he was liable to get to yelling. Not having a teaspoon to measure it out with, he tried to imagine how much half a teaspoonful might be. Maybe just as much as would go on the tip of his tongue. Not much more than that.

He drew the bottle from his lips and put it down, resting his arm on his knee. Hell, he was scared to take the damn stuff. Sure as shooting, the minute he took a swig, there'd come a knock on his door and it would be Raoul San Diego wanting to know what the hell was going on with Dulcima. And when that moment came, he had to be at his best. It was a hell of a quandary. He reached over and set the still-open bottle on the bedside table, laying the stopper beside it. Maybe, he thought, he ought to just pour it out and put temptation out of his way, especially with his toothache screaming down the clouds. For a good few minutes he sat there staring at the little bottle, letting the ache in his tooth wash over him like a wave. The apothecary had said something about rubbing some on the gum around the tooth. Hell, that couldn't do much harm. He reached over, got the bottle, and held it for a moment in his left hand. Finally he put his index finger over the mouth of the bottle and tipped it over. There was a little of the white liquid on the ball of his finger. As quickly as he could, he reached up into his mouth, trying to find the exact place where the pain was coming from.

It wasn't as easy as he'd thought. He scraped a little of the laudanum off on his lip trying to manuever his finger into his mouth. Then he had to feel for the right spot, and that used up quite a bit more of the laudanum. By the time he'd located the bad tooth, there seemed to be nothing left on his finger.

He took his finger out of his mouth and waited. After

a moment or two he felt his lip going a little numb. Then part of his mouth seemed to be numbing up also, but not the right part. Damn, he thought, the stuff was strong as hell. He didn't remember it having such an effect. But then he'd been hurting so bad the last time he used it he hadn't noticed much of anything. Now he not only had his toothache to worry about, there was this new element that he didn't know what to make of. He set the bottle back on the night stand and sat still for a moment, wondering if he'd done any harm to himself. Suddenly, like he hadn't planned it, he made a quick move with his right hand toward the butt of his revolver. He sat, and was very still for a second. Then he did it again, and then again a few seconds later. "Damn!" he said aloud. He couldn't tell if he was slower or not. He made an abrupt turn toward the door, leading with his left eye, seeing how fast the door came into view. "Damnit!" he said, "damnit damnit!"

And damn that sonofabitch Austin Davis. If the man was back, he could take care of Longarm, like a partner ought to, and Longarm could drink some of that pain-killer and get a little relief. As it was, he was scared to take it and scared he wouldn't be able to keep from taking it. What he ought to do, he thought, was get himself lodged in the jail by punching a deputy sheriff. That way at least he could down a good dose of the stuff and get some rest from the pain. But, Laredo being what it was, they'd probably just fine him the money in his pocket and put him back out on the street. He sat there thinking and hurting and getting angrier by the moment. It was one hell of a mess, to find himself practically hiding out in his hotel room, avoiding some cheap nickel-plated gunslinger and having to live with a toothache because he couldn't afford to mess up an arrest of corrupt officials that some damn junior marshal he didn't even like was hoping to bring off to make himself look good. And that same damn junior marshal didn't even have the decency to show up when he was needed. Longarm was thoroughly disgusted. He wasn't worried about being able to handle San Diego, laudanum or not. The problem was he couldn't risk any trouble with the man until the trap was sprung. He couldn't think of a time he'd ever got himself into a more ridiculous situation and, damnit, it was all Austin Davis' fault. He hadn't as yet figured out how, or why, but the sonofabitch ought to be around when he was needed. Davis could take on San Diego and it wouldn't cause an upset in the plans. Davis was supposedly the stock contractor Longarm had hired to bring up cattle to the border, and what he did once he'd delivered the cattle had nothing to do with Longarm. Hell, Davis could pick a fight with Raoul San Diego and kill him and it wouldn't make no difference to the plan Longarm had set up. He could say, and act quite righteous about it, that he couldn't be held responsible for what some tequila-crazy border stomper got up to. He'd hired the man to deliver cattle and he was quits with him after that. He was damn sorry about Mister Caster's number one man, but that kind of thing could happen any time to anybody.

Except Davis wasn't in Laredo and Longarm had no clear idea when he would show, and there was only a few more days, less than that really, to deliver the money to Caster—or worse, to put it in San Diego's hands. That, Longarm thought, ought to be some meeting. That is if they didn't have another one before that. He shook his head and sighed and reached over and got the whiskey bottle. The apothecary had said not to mix the two, so once he set in on the whiskey, the laudanum was out the window for the time being. He took the cork out of the bottle and tilted it up and rolled some into his mouth. Then he leaned his head to the side so the whiskey could get over and drown the sore tooth. It was a damned slow process and one that Longarm knew from experience wouldn't keep on working but for now it was all he had.

He could have taken the laudanum. He wasn't afraid of San Diego. He didn't figure it would be much trouble to kill the Mexican gunman. He'd observed that men who went around with hard faces and tried to put a look in their eyes that said they were dangerous, were, as a rule, not as badass or tough as they acted. He even felt confident that Austin Davis could take San Diego in anything even resembling a fair fight. But that wasn't the point. He couldn't afford to kill San Diego until the right time. Until then he had to handle him, and that was considerably tougher than just gunning the sonofabitch down.

Longarm shook his head. Things had come to a sorry pass when a man of his experience and resources was forced to hide out in his hotel room to avoid some tinhorn shooter. Who also happened to have a woman who looked to Longarm like about the most delicious pie he'd ever eaten. Lord, could he do with some of that! And maybe it might be available once all the cards had fallen out. But, for the time being, he reckoned he needed to stay as far away from Miss Dulcima as possible. He swallowed the whiskey he'd been holding in his mouth and reached for the bottle again. Meanwhile three dollars worth of painkiller was going to waste sitting on a bedside table.

Chapter 8

It was early afternoon Tuesday, just after lunch, when Austin Davis finally showed up at the hotel. By chance Longarm was waiting around in the lobby when Davis, dusty and looking tired and trail-worn, came walking in. Davis had come in the door heading for the desk, but he swerved when he saw Longarm, and headed his way. Keeping a straight face and speaking loud enough for the onlookers to hear, he said, "Mister Long? Mister Long? Is that you?"

Longarm gave him a look warning him not to get cute. "Yes, Mister Davis," he said. "Something wrong with your eyes? It hasn't been that long since you've seen me."

"I reckon it is," Davis replied, "because you're clean and your clothes are clean. I haven't seen anybody cleaned up in about a month."

"I didn't realize you had been gone that long, Mister Davis." Longarm put out his hand as Davis came up, and they shook. "Have a successful trip, I hope?"

"I got your cattle. Right at a thousand head. We'll

have to get a head count, but it won't miss what you ordered by ten cows. Lord, I'm mighty glad to be back in civilization. I want a bath and some hot food and a barbershop shave.''

Longarm was studying him closely, trying to get the information across to Davis that they needed to talk, and soon. ''Then I reckon you ought to get you a room and maybe a bath. Where is the herd?''

Austin Davis was returning his look. Longarm could tell from his face that he knew something had changed since he'd left. Davis said, ''They're being held just across the river. Few miles east. I was able to rent a pasture for a couple of days. The cattle are in good shape. Yeah, I'll get a room and have a bath. You staying here?''

''Yeah,'' Longarm said, giving Davis his room number. ''I've got to run over to the bank for a minute, but I'll be back shortly. Why don't you knock on my door soon as you get fixed up.''

''I'll do that, Mister Long. I'll be as quick as I can and then we'll get down to business. Glad to hear you're going to the bank.''

Longarm could see that the loafers in the lobby had lost interest in them. But he said, for the benefit of anyone listening, ''Yeah, I reckon I owe you some money.''

''Soon enough for that.''

''All right,'' Longarm said as he stepped toward the door, ''I'll see you quick as you can get yourself shaped up.''

He went out the door, thinking of all he had to tell Austin Davis and hoping the deputy would understand how delicate the situation was. But Longarm was feeling better than he had in days. He'd suffered with his tooth all through the previous day and into the night. But then, when it had come eleven o'clock and time for bed, he'd given in and taken a dose of the laudanum. The effect had been miraculous and he had gotten an excellent night's sleep and awakened for the first time in a week without the toothache dragging him to the edge of consciousness. It had done wonders for his frame of mind. He didn't know how long the relief would last, but he was going to enjoy it while he could. He knew it was just a temporary condition of his mind but, right then, he felt he would rather have the absence of pain than a woman.

As luck would have it, the money had come. He directed the bank to hold it on deposit for him and to have it ready in big bills.

Coming out of the bank, he saw Jasper White standing across the street, seeming to look his way. Longarm raised his hand in salutation, but White made no response. Longarm wandered if Jasper was following him, either on orders from Caster or San Diego or just on his own hook. It didn't matter. Whatever Longarm would be doing in the immediate future wasn't anything he cared if Jasper saw. He and Austin Davis would act and talk in public just as if they were, indeed, a stock gatherer and a contractor.

He went back to the hotel and went directly to his room. There was a small round table at one end of the room and he pulled it out a little, drew up two chairs, and set out a bottle of whiskey, a jug of water, and two glasses. After making sure the door was unlatched, he lit a cigarillo, sat down at the table, and poured himself a drink of the Maryland whiskey that was so smooth it was a jailable offense in that state for anyone caught gulping it down. He took a small drink and let it slide down his throat. It was a real pleasure to be able to drink again like a normal man without first watering the whiskey down with spit while he swished it around to comfort the damn tooth. He sat, smoking and drinking, letting the whole scheme revolve through his mind as he went over it step by step. It seemed pretty good to him, although he doubted that Austin Davis would think so. But then, James Mull had been just a "maybe" in Davis's plan, with no sure way to rope him in.

Longarm had been sitting like that for close on to half an hour when there was a tapping at the door. He swiveled slightly to his right so his holster would be clear and he'd be facing toward the door. He expected it was Austin Davis, but he hadn't stayed alive as long as he had by not allowing for the occasional surprise. "Come in," he said. The door swung open and it was indeed Austin Davis, looking considerably cleaner and better dressed than when Longarm had last seen him. "Shut the door behind you and come have a drink," Longarm said. "I'm sorry to say all I got is whiskey. No sody pop."

"Then I reckon whiskey will have to do," Davis said, "though I shore hope my old mother don't hear I've gone bad."

Longarm poured out a drink for both of them, and they made a toast to good horses and bad women, and drank down a satisfying amount of the smooth liquor. "Well?" Davis asked after a short pause.

"A well is a hole in the ground," Longarm replied.

Austin Davis waved his hand. "Yeah, yeah. Turn it sideways and you got a tunnel. You know what I mean."

"No, I don't."

"Well, what the hell has happened? Have you managed to really foul my deal up?"

"Your deal?" Longarm looked at him mildly. "When did we go to giving out title on arrests? I'll have to wire Billy Vail about that one. Never had it come up before."

Davis gave him a sour look. "You know what I mean. Tell me."

Longarm talked for a quarter of an hour, laying out the proposition as he saw it and relating everything that had happened or been said with the exception of his conversation with Dulcima. When he was through he sat back, drew on his cigarillo and looked at his partner. "Well?" he said.

Davis looked thoughtful for a moment. "It sounds pretty good," he said guardedly. "Though I think you took one hell of a risk going after Mull straight out like that. They might have thought it was fishy. Still might as far as that goes. And what makes you think Jasper White won't tell Caster about the deal you made with him? By the way, I did just like you. I got to Caster through Jasper White." He laughed a little. "Though I didn't give him but twenty dollars. Reckon he thinks you looked easy."

Longarm shrugged. "Forget about that. You say you think I took a risk. I did, and it might still be a risk. They might be sucking me in. I don't know. But I started out on this job taking risks and it ain't let up yet. A marshal's job is about risks. That's what we do. And I didn't see where it would have done a bit of good putting the iron on Caster without taking down his boss.

151

Caster is like a .44 cartridge, easily replaced with another one.''

Davis rubbed his chin. "I guess . . ." he said slowly. "I just hadn't run it out this way in my mind. I had figured to get Caster in hand and then have him ring Mull in.''

"Implicate Mull? How?"

"Why, on his say-so. What else?"

Longarm laughed. "That would last about five minutes in a court of law. As long as you're getting him to implicate Mull, why stop there? Hell, get him to point a finger at the President of the United States. That old dog won't hunt, Austin. Mull has got to implicate himself. He has got to be involved. And you were talking about Jasper White playing me for a sucker—Do you know what James Mull looks like? Do you?"

Austin Davis slowly shook his head. "No. Reckon I don't.''

"So whether it's a risk or not, I got to use Jasper White and the only way I had of getting him to help me was with money. I'll take it away from him when I'm done and offer him a jail cell if he complains, but for the time being, I have to play the cards I was dealt. Caster has made it clear I ain't ever going to set eyes on Mull. What would you have done?"

Davis shrugged and took a drink of whiskey. "I reckon what you did. I just might not have thought it up is all.''

Longarm gave him a long look. "Be careful, Austin,'' he said. "You come damn near to paying me a compliment. You want to be leery of that.''

Davis smiled faintly. "Sorry. It slipped out.'' It was clear to Longarm that the junior deputy had his mind busy trying to take in all the new information. Davis studied the floor for a moment, then looked up at Longarm. "And you say you got the bribe money right here?"

"In the bank, ready to go."

"Well," Davis said, "that means I don't have to wire that cattleman's association. Of course I hadn't counted on you going as far as you did. I'd told them I figured to get the cattle through for three dollars, maybe two a head." He paused and took a moment to light a small cigar. "I still feel like we're riding over icy ground. This thing is going to be touchy as hell to bring off."

Longarm drummed his fingers on the tabletop. "Yeah," he said, "it's going to be dicey." He hesitated. It was about time to tell Austin Davis something he wasn't going to want to hear. Longarm blew out a breath and looked at a far corner of the room. Then said, "And on account of that, you can't be here. As soon as you move the cattle across the bridge I want you to head back for Mexico." He detached his gaze from the corner and looked around at Davis.

His partner was staring at him, not blinking. Finally he said slowly, "What?"

Longarm sighed. "Yeah, you heard right. I want you to get clear of the area. It can't be done with both of us. If you were a legitimate stock gatherer, you'd see the cattle into the quarantine pens and then you'd be on your way once you were paid off by me, the man that contracted with you to get the cattle in the first place. What would go on between me and Caster wouldn't be none of your concern. And if you hang around, it ain't going to seem natural. Your business with me is done."

Austin Davis started slowly, but his voice rose with

heat as he spoke. "Now you wait just a damn minute! You talking about what old dog won't hunt? Well, that old dog just drug out from under the porch not only won't hunt, that sonofabitch can't move! This here is my deal, Longarm, and you ain't going to cut me out of it. I got some little time invested in this proposition and I ain't going to go sit with the Sunday school class while you get to preach."

Longarm sighed. He truly felt sorry for Austin Davis, and not just a little guilty. He wished then that he hadn't made such a big commotion about coming to the border to work with the man. This was going to make it seem like he'd cut him out just out of meanness. "Austin," he said, "it can't be any other way. I've thought and thought on this, dreading having to tell you, but I can't see no other way. You were talking about fish—well, it would seem fishy as hell, us just doing some business, for you to be around. Oh, hell, I don't mean you got to take straight off for Mexico. They would expect you to stay on this side for a while, drinking and whoring and whatnot. But I cannot see any way that you can be present when I put the iron on Caster and Mull. It wouldn't make any sense."

Austin Davis was staring at him stiffly. "I suppose it makes sense for you to come down here and take over the job?"

Longarm shook his head. "Nobody is coming down here and taking over the job. Damnit, Austin, you'll get just as much credit doing it this way as if you actually done the arresting yourself. You and I will both write the report and we'll put it anyway you want. I know you got time in on this and so does Billy Vail. You'll get the recognition you got coming. Ain't nobody going to cheat you.''

''You sonofabitch,'' Davis said with cold heat. ''Who the hell cares about credit or recognition? Maybe that's the way your mind runs, but mine don't.'' He leaned forward. ''I want to catch the sonofabitches and I want to see their eyes when I do. *I* want to put the iron on them. And you ain't going to stop me, short of getting word here from Billy Vail. Or are you pulling rank on me right here and now?''

''I ain't pulling any rank, Austin. All I got on you is a little more time behind the badge. And I ain't trying to shove you aside. I'm just saying the way I see it.''

Davis's face had colored slightly. With an edge in his voice he said, ''Well, it ain't the way I see it, and this is a proposition that *I've* got a little more time on than you. And, mister, you ain't shooting the birds I've flushed. You take all the credit you want. Write the damn report anyway you want. You be the hero or whatever. I don't care nothing about that, but I took some guff off of Caster and I want it to be known to him who it is putting him behind a wall.''

Longarm felt the short hairs on his neck bristle at Davis' hard words. With an effort he controlled his temper. He said, as evenly as he could, ''Well, you know, you kind of flushed your birds a little quick. That is, if you were intending on doing any shooting. Caster told me that the man who was gathering my stock come at him with a proposition about rising the price of the bribe and splitting the money. He told me I had better keep an eye on you.''

Davis flushed. The anger went out of his face and he looked down at his half empty glass of whiskey.

"Damn!" he said. "I never thought that would come back to haunt me."

Longarm leaned back in his chair and fiddled with his glass. "You reckon how it would look if I had you along after what you proposed to Caster? I'd look like a rare jackass. Talk about smelling fish. Caster is jumpy as it is. I get the impression that he and Mull are fixing to wind the business up. I think that's the reason he's raising his prices. I can't back it up, but that's the feeling I get."

Davis looked away. "Well," he said with a sigh, "I reckon I ain't got no kick coming. I had my reason for doing what I done. I made that proposition to Caster early on in the game in hopes of getting his confidence. I figured that if I appeared to be crooked, he'd be that much more willing to trust me. Birds of a feather."

Longarm nodded. "Yeah," he said, "I can see that. And if you'd been playing a lone hand or had known what your man was up to, it might have worked. But you can see how it is now."

Davis nodded slowly and sighed. "Yeah, I reckon I can." He looked away. "Damn, Longarm, I can't just walk away from this business now. I got too much in it. Hell, got to be something I can do."

"It appears to me you've done a pretty good piece of work already. Hell, all I'm doing is sweeping up your shavings. You done the whittling."

"Yeah, but you're going to need somebody to watch your back. I know you've run across this Raoul San Diego and his brother too. But that is a couple of bad hombres. You say you got to hand the money over to Raoul. Or Caster said you do. Ain't a damn thing to keep him from popping you off once he's got his hands on the cash.''

Longarm smiled slowly. "I think it won't take no cash to get Mister San Diego hot at me. I got a real good idea he already is."

"What are you talking about?"

As briefly as he could, Longarm told Davis about how Dulcima had approached him on the plaza. As he talked, Davis's eyes got wider and his mouth dropped open. "The hell you say!" he exclaimed.

Longarm nodded. "Right out there in front of the mayor and his horse and anybody who happened to come by. And she went on for about five minutes, with me backing up inch by inch and begging for her to leave me the hell alone."

"Dulcima! Hot damn. Ain't that about the most mouthwatering piece you ever run across? I'd like to have been in your shoes."

"Yeah? And what would you have done?"

"I'd of had her in this hotel room and out of that dress before the dust could settle on the tracks we'd of left behind."

"And what about Raoul San Diego? What would you have done about him?"

"I wouldn't have shot holes in him if he hadn't bothered us."

"I don't think he'd of left you alone. I think you'd of had to turn him into Swiss cheese."

"Well, that could have been arranged. Man don't get many chances at a woman like her."

"Uh-huh. And how you reckon you would have stood in with Mister Caster after you'd killed his number one man and main gunhand? How you reckon he'd of taken that part of the business?"

Davis looked at the glowing end of the cigarillo he was smoking. "Probably not right kindly," he said. "In fact he might not have wanted to do no more business with me." He shook his head slowly from side to side. "Guess you were thinking ahead of me on that one, Longarm."

"Listen, I holed up in this hotel for two days to keep from running into the sonofabitch and having trouble. You reckon I liked that?"

"No, but I don't see how you could have known for sure he'd been told."

"I couldn't. But I couldn't take the chance of getting in a fight with San Diego. I knew half the town had seen us talking, and if I know anything about a puffed-up Mexican, I know they will kill you over a woman, or honor, or any combination of the two faster than they will holler if you steal their horse. And if word had got back to him about the little social me and his señorita was having, he'd *have* to do something."

"He ain't but half Mex."

"Well, I hear he's right-handed and the Mex half is on that side, same as his *pistole*. Whatever he is, I didn't figure to take the chance. Not after all the work you done put in."

The junior deputy lifted his head and gave Longarm a mocking smile. "All the work *I* put in? Somebody is shoveling bullshit around here and it ain't me. All my work, and you're sending me to the barn. Come on, Longarm, that thought never crossed your mind.

"I give you my word that that is what I was thinking."

Davis gave a little laugh. "And you said that the woman called you handsome?"

"That is exactly what the lady said. Her very word."

Davis put his head back and laughed out loud. "I'll never believe another word you say, Longarm. If Dulcima said that, then that means the woman is near blind—and I never seen nobody leading her around."

Longarm leaned back and folded his arms. "I did not intend to tell you about all that for the very way that you are now acting. I told you what happened. You can believe it or not."

Davis reached out for the whiskey bottle and poured more of the amber liquid in both their glasses. "Right now," he said, "I ain't real interested in that. What I got my mind on is what I can do here at the tail end of the business. I'm the one throwed the loop, I'd shore like to be there to see what it snares."

Longarm held his hands out helplessly. "Hell, Austin, I've laid it out for you. How in hell am I supposed to explain you being around?"

"That ain't fair, Longarm," Davis said quietly.

Longarm stared at him. "Fair? Fair? You sound like some schoolboy. The only thing I know about fair is that every county has one, but that ain't until fall. Fair. You are in the wrong business you looking for fair. We got a job and we do it fair or not. You *savvy*?"

"How'd you like it if the shoe was on the other foot?"

"I wouldn't. I'd be mad as hell. But I'd do what had to be done to get the job done."

Davis looked away and shook his head. "Sheeeeet!" he said in a long, peeling burst. "Damnit damnit damnit!"

"I'm sorry, Austin—I don't see no other way for it."

Davis shrugged. "It can't be helped. What you say makes sense. When you want me to clear out?"

"Well, not right away. You still got to move those cattle from the Mexican side over here to the quarantine pens. I reckon that would be in the morning. Can you manage that by then?"

"I don't see why not. We're holding them close-herded on some good grass."

"What kind of shape are they in?"

Davis glanced at him. "What the hell do you care? These ain't your cattle, Longarm. Remember?"

Longarm laughed slightly. "Guess I got carried away." He lifted his glass to his lips and took a drink. "I guess the next step is for me to go see Caster and let him know the cattle have arrived. We're going to have an argument. He's going to want me to give him the money right now, and I ain't willing to do it before the cattle are in his pens."

"He ain't going to want the money before then."

"Why not?"

"Because. Once he's got your cattle in his pens, he knows damn good and well that you have to pay him."

"I reckon you're right," Longarm agreed. "I hadn't thought of that." He lifted his glass and finished the rest of the whiskey. He stood up. "I reckon I better get on over and see him."

"You better watch out for San Diego. Either one of them. I hear that little one who acts like a dandy is meaner than his brother. Raymond? Is that his name? I hear he's a back-alley bushwhacker. Uses a shotgun."

"Right now I ain't too worried about either one of the San Diego brothers. I figure Caster don't want nothing to happen to me until he's got my cash in his hands. Say, I got the feeling that the cafe owner, Raymond, and Jasper White are on some kind of dodge. Are they smuggling?''

Davis shook his head. "I don't know for sure. But if it's illegal, they're doing it. I heard they were smuggling gold. But then I also heard they were smuggling peons up to big cities like Chicago and New York City to work as street cleaners at two bits a day. You can get nearly any kind of gossip around this town that you're looking for. I ain't really been concentrating on them.''

"I reckon I better get," Longarm said. He put on his hat and walked across the room. With his hand on the knob he stopped and said, "By the way, what did you have to pay for those cattle? Jay Caster might ask. And if they *were* my cattle, I'd know.''

"Right close to seven dollars a head, depending on the final count. I spent six thousand nine hundred and some odd dollars for the herd, buying it in different lots, first one place and then the other. By the time I'm through, I'll have spent about seventy-five hundred of the coastal cattlemen's money.''

"Are the cattle worth it?''

Davis shook his head. "Not within a mile. They won't bring them in like they are now, and they sure as hell ain't going to want to pay to take them through regular quarantine. The only thing they can do is turn them back and sell them in Mexico. They'll lose two or three dollars a head doing that.''

"It appears they're buying justice pretty dearly.''

Davis disagreed. "Not when you figure it costs them a fortune when they lose a herd of beef worth thirty dollars a head to Mexican tick fever. We get this operation shut down, or run clean, and it will have been worth the price. Though I do think it is a poor comment on the state of government when a citizen has to go out and pay to have the law enforced.''

Longarm smiled thinly. "You mean you don't think it's fair, Austin?''

"Go to hell, Longarm. Just go straight to hell. I hope that half-breed blows a hole through you that a small horse could get his head into. Just get on out of here. Go collect your glory. Go set it up so you look like the hero.''

"Now you can go to hell, Mister Davis." Longarm started for the door.

"Wait a minute," Davis said, putting up his hand. "You never said if you'd figured out how Caster gets one herd through in a week's time. After coding them with that paint. Paint looks mighty permanent to me. How does he get red paint to turn to green?''

"I never even tried to find out. I told you all I'd been doing. How he does it is a question we can ask him once we got him in jail.''

"Oh? You mean I'm going to get to see him behind bars?''

Longarm gave him a sour look and stepped out into the hall, pulling the door to behind him. Davis had said that he'd taken some guff off of Caster and hadn't liked it. Well, so had he. He hadn't mentioned it because there'd been other things to say, but he was going to take some personal satisfaction in putting the spurs to the smart-mouthed Caster. Saying he was an officer of the law. Yeah, he was an officer of the law all right, an outlaw officer.

•   •   •

Jay Caster was wearing sleeve garters. He was seated behind his desk with some kind of a ledger in front of him and a nub pen in his hand. Once again Longarm took a seat unbidden. Caster looked at him silently for a long time, slowly chewing his plug of tobacco. Finally he leaned over and spit in the bucket by his desk, hitched up his sleeves so as to protect his cuffs from the ink on the pages of the ledger, and then went back to his work, all the while not saying a word to Longarm.

Longarm crossed his legs and put his hat on his knee, got out a cigarillo and lit it. His tooth was starting to ache again, though very mildly. He put that down to the upset Austin Davis had caused him. He looked at Caster. The man was wearing a white shirt with a stiff collar and a foulard tie. A gray suit coat was hung over the back of his chair. Longarm figured he had business later that day. Maybe James Mull was coming in to ask after matters. That seemed doubtful, but one thing Longarm didn't doubt: he wasn't going to sit there all day and watch Jay Caster scribble figures in a book. He cleared his throat. Caster didn't look up. "Uh, Mister Caster," Longarm began, "I reckon you ought to know that I—"

Without glancing up, Caster said, "Hold it, will you? This is important and I got to get it right."

Longarm subsided, but it put him on slow boil. He sat there smoking and watching Caster. He could bide his time. Hell, if he had to, he could wait on this son-ofabitch a week, a month, six months if he had to. But, in the end, Jay Caster would be doing something else besides making marks in a ledger.

Finally Caster put his pen down and, after carefully blotting his last entry, closed the ledger. He sat back in his chair, raised his arms over his head, and stretched and yawned. Then he put his arms down, reached in his desk drawer, and pulled out a bottle of whiskey. A glass followed and Caster poured himself out a drink. He made no move to offer one to Longarm. He corked the bottle, put it back in the drawer, then lifted the glass and drank off half of it. After that he belched and put a wooden toothpick in his mouth. Finally he looked at Longarm. "Whata you want, Long?"

Your hide nailed to the barn door, Longarm wanted to tell him. Instead he fiddled with his hat for a moment, then said, "I reckoned to let you know that the money I wired for has come in."

"You got it with you?"

Longarm pulled his head back. "Walk around with five thousand dollars in this town? Not very damn likely. No, it's at the bank. Besides, I thought I wasn't supposed to give you the money."

"You ain't. What about yore cattle?"

"Them too. My cattle gatherer come in just after noon. He's holding the herd in Mexico, down by the river."

"How many?"

"A thousand head, give or take a dozen. Won't know until we count them into your pens."

"You ain't paid him yet?"

Longarm shook his head. "I ain't likely to pay him until I see what I got. Would you?"

Caster ignored the question. "You brace him about that proposition he made to me?"

"About raising the price and him taking a piece of the money?"

"Him cheating you. Yeah. You ask him about that?"

"Mister Caster, I don't know how you do business,

but I've found it's a good idea to keep matters friendly until you get what you want. Right now he's still got the cattle. Besides, what you told me didn't come as no surprise. I told you I knowed the man before. I wouldn't be the first one he's tried to cheat and I won't be the last."

"You seem to take it pretty well. You scairt of the man?"

Longarm frowned. "I don't look at it like that. It's business. I've said I'm not a gunhand, and I'm not. I don't know whether he is or not. Frankly I don't intend to find out. Now, tell me how you want to do it about the cattle and the money. Can we bring the cattle over in the morning?"

Caster looked thoughtful for a moment, then nodded slowly. "Yep. I reckon you can. I'll send a man across to Mexico to meet yore contractor and clear the way to bring the cattle over the bridge."

"What about the money? You want it the same time? I want to get shut of it as quick as I can once I pull it out of the bank."

Caster showed his brown-stained teeth. "My, my," he said. "Ain't you the jumpy one. You must be scairt of yore own shadow."

Longarm stared at him and didn't say anything. He did think, however, that Jay Caster was nearly as big a fool as he'd ever met. He certainly had a fool's mouth.

"Don't worry about the money," the customs man said. "When I've got yore cattle in my pens we'll make arrangements about the money. Now go on and get out of here. I've got serious work to do."

Longarm stood up slowly, trying to keep it fixed in his mind that he was a cattle buyer making a crooked deal and worrying about it. "Excuse me," he said, "but what about Mister Mull? Is he going to be there when the money changes hands?"

Caster suddenly slammed the palm of his hand down on the top of the desk. His eyes got small in his fleshy face. "Listen, Long," he shouted. "When in the hell you going to learn to tend to yore own bid'ness? Maybe you'd like to keep them cattle in Mexico. That can be arranged if you keep on with that mouth of yours."

Longarm swallowed and reminded himself that his day was coming, one way or the other. "Well," he said, "I figure this *is* my business, Mister Caster. After what I've paid for these cattle and what I've got to pay you and Mister Mull, I got to be able to drive them through the coastal plains and you know what that depends on. I got to have Mister Mull's seal and signature on them road papers."

"You been told, I don't know how many times, that you ain't going to see Mull. Get that clear in yore head."

"Just take your word?"

"That's the way it is, Long. Now get out of here."

But before Longarm could walk the length of the long office, Caster called to him . "How much you pay for them cattle, anyway?"

Longarm didn't bother to think. "A little over eight dollars a head."

Caster laughed. It was a malicious sound. "He done it to you again, that drover you hired. I bet he never give more than seven dollars for a single head and more likely less than that. But he'll have him a bunch of bills of sale and you'll have to pay him off on that." Caster shook his head and spit in the bucket. "I'd like to do bid'ness with you, Long, as long as yore money lasts.

Which I'd reckon ain't going to be very long as dumb as you are.''

"You think he cheated me?''

"Oh, hell, feller, of course he cheated you. And will probably cheat you again before it's all over. Next time you want some cattle gathered, you need to get in touch with Raymond San Diego over at the Tejano Cafe. He's the brother to the man works for me, Raoul San Diego.''

"The one I'm supposed to give the money to.''

"That's right, Long. Now, have yore cattle at the bridge as early as you can tomorrow morning.''

Longarm left Caster's office in a very thoughtful mood. He and Austin Davis both wanted a piece of Caster to take home for a keepsake, but the man was being mighty leery and careful. As far as Longarm was concerned, if they didn't get Mull the operation would have been a failure. He couldn't visualize exactly how the final action would play out, but there had to be some way to get Caster and Mull in the same place with both their hands in the cookie jar. And meanwhile, there was Raoul San Diego to think about. Longarm had gone to Caster's halfway expecting the man to be there. He wondered what he'd do if San Diego did create a ruckus before the job could be completed. He reckoned he'd just have to do a good imitation of a man crawfishing and begging pardon and making excuses. San Diego was one more reason it was best to have Austin Davis out of the way. Longarm didn't believe the young deputy had the control to take dirt off a man. He'd kill him first. Well, at least Caster had done him the favor of driving another wedge, supposedly, between himself and Davis. So long as Caster thought he was dealing with a fool, so much less on guard he'd be.

Longarm's room was empty, though he noticed that the half-full bottle of Maryland whiskey was missing. For a man who expressed no particular preference for the hard-to-get stuff, Austin Davis seemed to guzzle it at every opportunity. He made fun of Longarm for not drinking the local whiskey, but he never passed up a glass of the Maryland corn squeezings. Longarm went on down the hall to Davis' room. The door was ajar, and Longarm felt a brief twinge of worry, but when he pushed the door all the way open he found Davis sitting cross-legged in his stocking feet in the middle of his bed, playing solitaire with a greasy deck of cards. He looked up as Longarm came in. "You get all the doings done?"

Longarm found a wooden chair, turned it backwards, and straddled it so he was facing his partner. "Yeah, I reckon so. You know, you said you'd taken some guff off Caster. I'm willing to bet he ain't talked to you nowhere near as corn-mouthed as he has me. The sonofabitch has done everything but call me an idiot. He says you're cheating me on the price paid for the cattle, that you've got some phony bills of sale, and that if I believe you for more than the time of day with the town clock to check you by, I'm the biggest ignoramus in the county."

Davis chuckled quietly. "I'm glad to see I ain't getting all his business out of that particular store." He jerked his head toward the table beside the bed. "Help yourself to some of your whiskey. Is it kind of getting under your skin having him talk to you like a school-boy?"

"I'm not partial to it, I'll say that. But I'm taking it with the expectation of better days to come."

"That's what I done." Davis gave him a look. "But

168

I guess them better days won't come for me."

Longarm shot him a glance and got up and poured himself a glass of whiskey out of his own bottle. "Cattle have got to be brought over as soon as possible. I reckon that means you roll out mighty early."

"What about the bribe?"

"I don't know. Caster said he'd tell me in the morning. I reckon I'm to hand the money over to Raoul San Diego. Twenty-five hundred. Half of it."

"And you give him the other half when he turns the cattle loose, is that it?"

"So far. But he may change his mind. He's acting mighty skittish." Longarm thought a moment, then said, "Austin, I've been forgetting something. Jasper White is supposed to point out Mull to somebody when he steps off the train. I ain't sure that can be me. Maybe you better stick around."

"You mean I can come to my own party now?" Davis said sarcastically.

"Hold up, now. I ain't saying you can be in on the transaction, the business when Caster and Mull go one step too far."

Davis put a black queen on a red king. "Let's see how it goes. I'll do whatever you think is right. Though I'm damned if I can see how you're going to get Mull and Caster hemmed up in the same corner. Not from the way you say Caster is acting about it."

Longarm had been thinking about something. "You know," he said, "Jasper is supposed to point out Mull, but he could point out anyone getting off that train. Could be a drummer or a banker for all we'd know."

Davis paused with the deck in his hand, looking down at the cards laid out before him. "That's true," he agreed. "But what are you going to do about it?"

Longarm rubbed his jaw. "Maybe you ought to take a quick train ride to Brownsville and take a look at Mister Mull. Just go up there and then turn straight around and get on back."

"Me see him without him seeing me?"

"Something like that."

Davis shrugged and put a red six on a black seven. "I don't see why not. Soon as I get the cattle crossed and counted out and penned. You reckon I ought to try and give you a phony count? Give Caster some more ammunition that I'm a crook."

"I don't know." Longarm rubbed his jaw again. "Let's don't complicate this damn mess anymore than we have to. It already looks like a set of mule harness the kids have gotten hold of. Snarled up and tangled."

"Your tooth bothering you again?"

Longarm grimaced. "It flares up from time to time. I got some laudanum in my room, but that stuff makes you kind of goofy. Raoul San Diego has already got enough advantage on his side with me not knowing what he's liable to pull. I'd just as soon have my wits about me."

"How you see it falling out?"

Longarm shook his head. "I ain't got the slightest idea, to tell you the truth. I'm just drawing all the cards the dealer will give me and waiting to see who raises the pot."

"But he's definitely going to put the cattle through in a week?"

Longarm sighed and stood up. "That's what he said." He turned to face Davis and pointed his finger. "One thing I forgot. Caster said today that the next time I wanted any cattle gathered in Mexico I'd do well to contact Raoul's brother, Raymond San Diego. Him, and probably Jasper, are mixed up in this deal in some way. Beats the hell out of me exactly how. But I think we ought to be damn careful about them from now on."

Davis gave him a look. "I have been. Wasn't me hired Jasper to spot Mull when he gets off the train. I reckon that one might come back to haunt you."

Longarm gave him a look. "I'm going out and get some supper," was all he said. "I reckon it's best we not be seen socializing together."

"That your way of getting out of playing me poker?"

"Yeah, Austin. Of course. You just go right on believing that." Longarm let himself out of the room and walked on down the hall toward the lobby.

Chapter 9

The final count came to 981 head of cattle that Austin Davis had brought across the bridge and delivered into the quarantine pens at the customs station.

Jay Caster said, "It's still five thousand."

He and Longarm were sitting horseback at the far end of the pens, watching the cattle as they were herded in by the *vaqueros* hired by Austin Davis and the hands who worked for the customs inspector. Longarm just shrugged at Caster's words. "Why not?" he said wearily. "Hell, what's another ninety-five dollars."

Just then Austin Davis rode up and spoke to Longarm. "Mister Long, I don't understand it. I swear they was a thousand and eight head of cattle. I got the sales vouchers to prove it. Somebody must have cut them twenty-seven head out when I had them on the grass over in Mexico."

"Yeah," Longarm said. He deliberately did not look at Davis, looking instead at the herd. "I'm sure that's what happened." His voice was flat and toneless.

"Well, I can't explain it no other way," Davis went

on. "But I guarantee you that I laid out the money for one thousand and fifteen head and got here with that one thousand and eight. I don't know what happened to them last nineteen. I told you we lost seven head on the trail and you said that was to be expected."

Longarm shook his head slowly. He was trying to play the part of an honest man stoically accepting his fate at the hands of swindlers and thieves. "Yeah, yeah," he said. "Them things happen."

"Well," Davis offered, "I'm willing to split the difference with you. Let's just say you owe me for nine hundred and ninety head. How's that sound? Poor as I am, I'll take the loss on them other ten head."

Longarm kept looking past Austin Davis. "We'll worry about that when we settle up," he said. "Right now I wish you'd get back to the cattle and see that they get settled in. It appears to me that I'm in danger of losing more than just nineteen head to some rough handling. I see a dozen steers fighting, and them damn hired hands in the pens act like they never saw cattle before."

"Well, it's not my boys," Austin Davis said. He gave Caster an accusing look. "They been gentling that herd right along like they was made out of glass."

"Then how about getting on back and supervising the work." Now Longarm looked at Davis. "Your job ain't over, you know. You're getting paid to get them in the pens in one piece."

Davis replied in a huffy voice, "I ain't responsible for the work done by folks that don't work for me. No, sir. And I ain't to be held accountable for it either."

But he reined his horse around before Longarm could speak again, and loped off toward the pens where the cattle were being corralled.

Longarm hadn't realized how extensive the network of big, wooden-railed pens was. Each would hold about 200 head of cattle and they stretched from a quarter mile of the bridge to the east, at least, he calculated, another quarter of a mile and they were at least that wide. He figured he was looking at somewhere between six and eight thousand head of cattle, crowded in as thick as a busy anthill. He'd seen the stockyards in Chicago, which weren't a hell of a lot bigger and handled herds of cattle from all over. Of course they did a much faster turnover than the quarantine pens. They'd get cattle in that would be shipped out within forty-eight hours. But still it was a lot of cattle and he said so to Jay Caster.

Caster seemed amused. "Oh, I don't know," he said. "Sounds to me like you ought to be worrying about the cattle you're missing. And them phony bills of sale your contractor is going to hand you."

Longarm didn't answer. He was too busy watching the cattle being marked. As each head went single file through a short chute formed by two fences, a worker would slap a daub of paint on the cow's side. In this case it was red paint, to designate cattle that had just arrived. Jay Caster had told him that in thirty days the paint would have just about worn off as the cattle rubbed up against each other. "That's when the get a coat of white to show they're in their second thirty days," he'd said. "After that they get slapped with green and that's the end of the line."

Longarm had wanted to know how his cattle were going to be released in a week if they were still marked with the red paint. Caster had glared at him. "That's something you ain't ever going to know."

"Well, I ain't setting out on the trail with a bunch of

red-marked cattle. I'm sure those ranchers along the coast know all about that."

"Yore cattle won't have no red on them. You better learn to keep that mouth of yours shut, Long. Especially when it's got a question in it."

Watching the herd intently as it was strung out to be driven into the pens, Longarm had been trying to pick out individual cattle that had some easily distinguishable mark, like an odd color pattern or a twisted or broken horn. Thus far he had spotted five and was trying to keep them in his head while he'd been talked at by Jay Caster and then by Austin Davis. He wanted to remember the marked cattle so he could come back the next day and see if his herd had been worked forward in the milling sprawl of cattle that made up the pens. It seemed like an impossible thing to do, but maybe Caster had some method Longarm couldn't even imagine. He had to keep reminding himself that he knew a great deal more about cattle thieves than he did cattle. He was a deputy marshal, not a cattle broker.

The mocking tone was still in his voice, the customs man said, "You that easy to run over, feller? Hell, that drover is cheating you blind. He got something on you? He take care of your wife for you when you ain't there?" Caster laughed.

Longarm looked around at him. "I ain't married." he said stiffly. "But then that ain't none of *your* business. You keep telling me what ain't none of my business, I reckon it's time I started making you aware of when you get to crowding me."

Caster let out a hoot. "Aw now, *Mister* Long," he said, "it be a little late to start getting tough. You ain't got the reputation for it."

"I reckon you ought to quit worrying about who else is cheating me and just concentrate on your own gouging. You seem to be doing a pretty fair job."

Caster laughed again. "Oh, I ain't through. When you think I'm finished, I'm going to have Raoul San Diego grab you up by yore ankles and hang you upside down and shake out any loose change we might of missed."

"Let's get that business over with," Longarm said, still stiffly. "You want twenty-five hundred dollars as payment in half. You said you want me to give it to this San Diego. All right, I'm ready. Where is he and how do I get there? Or is this the wrong time? You got my cattle. I'd like to start in buying them out of those pens."

Caster shrugged. "Then go see San Diego."

"Raoul?"

Caster looked at him curiously. "You heered me speak of another one?"

"There are two of them. For all I know, they both work for you."

Caster said flatly, "You'll find San Diego about two miles east of town. That's *Raoul* San Diego. He stays at a hacienda out that way. Big house. Middle part is two-story. It sits up on the only hill anywhere near the river. You can't miss it. At least you ought not to miss it."

It sounded disturbingly similar to the place where Dulcima said she lived. "Is that his place?" Longarm said, with a little hesitation in his voice.

"What the hell do you care? No, as it happens it ain't. Belongs to a woman that he stays with. But it might as well be his."

"His woman wouldn't happen to be somebody named Dulcima, would it?"

Caster grinned, his teeth outlined in tobacco juice.

"So you been watching her, have you? She likes to sashay around the plaza and get all the boys on the prod showing them what they can't have. Yeah, I can tell by the look on yore face you seen her. Probably had yore tongue hangin' out like the rest of them."

Longarm shook his head. "It ain't that. Yes, I've seen the lady. Even spoke to her. But from what I heard about this Raoul, he might not take kindly to being disturbed at home. Couldn't I give him the money in your office or somewhere else?"

"In my office? Say, are you a little slow? I don't want no connection to that money. Do you get it? Now turn yore horse around and go and find San Diego. It's not half past nine yet. He's probably still in bed. Get going and you're sure to catch him. He don't get up and get around until late in the day. Spends most of his nights playing with that woman, I expect. Can't say that I blame him."

"All right," Longarm said. "But I want to have a word with that drover first. Then I'll stop at the bank and then head out."

"You better make it snappy. San Diego ain't going to want you trying to pass him a wad of money in a crowded place. You better catch him to home."

Longarm nodded and touched his horse with his spurs. He rode down past the end line of cattle pens, where Austin Davis was directing several *vaqueros* in getting a knot of steers bedded down. He turned in the saddle as Longarm rode up. "How's the big boss up yonder? He sent you for his lunch yet?"

Longarm pulled his horse up beside Davis. "Any minute I reckon. But right now he wants me to deliver the twenty-five hundred to San Diego. And guess where?

To Dulcima's house. That is liable to get a little tick-lish."

"Damn!" Davis said. "You reckon that's wise? A woman like her will give you away to San Diego just to amuse herself. She'll think you'll crawfish."

Longarm grimaced. "I may have to," he said. He looked over the younger man's shoulder. "I swear," he said, "I have had to swallow more manure on this job than any I can remember. Remind me to thank you for that sometime."

"You ain't the only one got the taste of shit in his mouth. I don't think you ought to go up to her house. Can't you hand him the money someplace else?"

Longarm shook his head. "No. Caster has got his mind set on me doing it this way. He may have heard about me and Dulcima having that little talk on the square and this appeals to his sense of humor. I've been acting the part of the businessman who don't see no profit in fighting. Maybe he's got it in mind for San Diego to throw a good scare into me."

Davis looked thoughtful. "Or he could be setting you up. It might not be in fun. You think on that? I noticed you haven't been wearing a cutaway holster like you usually do."

"Didn't seem to fit the part of the cattleman. But I got the cutaway in my saddlebags. No, I don't think he's trying to get me killed. I still owe him too much money."

"Yeah, but he's got your cattle. Who claims them if you get killed? He don't know they belong to the South Texas coastal plains ranchers association. Or whatever it is."

Longarm shrugged. "Well, it can't be helped. I'll just

have to try and talk my way out of any trouble I get into. I don't want to kill San Diego, but I reckon you can guess what choice I'll make if it comes to it."

"I reckon I better bird-dog you."

Longarm rubbed his jaw. His tooth had picked a hell of a time to start gnawing at him again. He shook his head. "I reckon you better not, Austin. Caster liable to see you and there'd be hell to pay and not much way to explain it. Besides, San Diego might spot you."

"I can look like a tree when I've a mind to. No, I won't get too close. Besides, you ain't paid me off. Most natural thing in the world is for me not to want to let you out of my sight."

Longarm grimaced. "Well, do what you think is best." He gave Davis a crooked smile. "After all, this is your scheme."

"You pick the damndest times to remember it."

"Don't I?" Longarm wheeled his horse around. "I'll see you."

He rode back into town, making a quick stop at the bank, and then started out a little road that led to the east and down toward the river. The twenty-five hundred was in his saddlebags in big bills, twenties and over.

A half mile out of town he could clearly see the house sitting up on a solitary hill in the featureless terrain. It was painted a startling white, made even more so by the drab brown of the surrounding countryside. Longarm kicked his horse up into a slow lope, eager to have the chance to see Dulcima again even though he knew it might be a dangerous encounter and certainly one that could not lead to anything. But he was also curious to have a closer look at, and perhaps a few words with, the cold and venomous-appearing Raoul San Diego. He wasn't worried about his ability to handle the man, not so long as he didn't turn his back.

He rounded a grove of mesquite trees, and the road rose up straight toward the house. Now he could see that it was fairly big, with three or four rooms on the bottom story and then, in the middle, a second story perched atop the bottom like a child's building block. As he rode closer, he could see that the lower story had small, casementlike windows and that the house was constructed of half lumber and half concrete or adobe. There were a few small outbuildings behind the house and a small corral, but it was clear the place was a town house that had wound up in the country. Nowhere was there a sign of any ranching or other working activity.

A porch ran the entire length of the lower story, with a roof that jutted out from the body of the house and a floor raised about six inches off the ground, made of heavy lumber planks. There were several tables and quite a few chairs scattered around on the porch. The roof of the porch, just like the roof of the house, was constructed of the red clay tiles found on houses of quality all over Mexico and along the border.

When Longarm was within a hundred yards of the place, the road dipped off to the left and a little driveway continued on toward the house. He veered to his right, pulling his horse down to a walk. It was time to start getting cautious. He looked back, thinking he might see some sign of Austin Davis tailing him, but the country was too thick with brush and groves of mesquite and stunted post oak. Austin Davis could have been within shouting range and Longarm wouldn't have seen him. Besides, he wasn't even sure that Davis was coming.

There was a hitching rail right in front of the porch,

and he stopped his horse just short of it and sat the saddle for a moment, studying the house, especially the windows and the upper story. As he'd neared the place, he'd seen a few women working around the back, but they appeared to be intent on the wash and a kitchen garden. There had been a couple of horses in the corral, but they'd looked as if they been there for some time. Both had been standing three-legged, resting one leg, their heads down, baking in the sun. Other than that, Longarm had seen no movement about the place. If Raoul San Diego was at home, he was either still in bed or not at all curious about who might be approaching. Neither he nor anyone else had appeared in any of the windows. For that matter, Longarm wondered if Dulcima was around. He didn't know what the custom was at this particular house, but if he'd lived here, with the reputation that Raoul San Diego had, one of the women working out back had better have come in and announced that someone was approaching or she'd have been out of a job. Yet none of the servants had paid Longarm the slightest attention, and, he figured, if he could see them, they could see him.

He climbed slowly out of the saddle and took a second to loosen his revolver in the much bigger, cutaway holster he was wearing. Then he tied his horse to the rail, took three strides and stepped up on the porch.

The front door was a large, wooden affair without a screen. It was ornate, and Longarm took it to be mahogany or some other exotic wood. He lifted the brass knocker and gave a light tap or two on the door. He waited a moment and no one came. He lifted the knocker again and was about to bang harder, when the door was suddenly pulled wide open. For a second he couldn't see into the dim interior. He knew someone was standing right in front of him, and he could tell it was a woman by the shape and the faint scent of perfume, but he couldn't see clearly. "I've come to see Raoul San Diego," he said. "I've got business."

"That ees right. You have beesness, but your beesness ees with me."

Then Longarm's eyes adjusted and he could clearly see that it was Dulcima. For a moment he was so startled by the way she was dressed that he opened his mouth but couldn't think of a thing to say. She stood before him, in her bare feet, with a serape around her neck. It was highly colored and gay, with tassels, and it came down to just below her knees. It covered her breasts and the left and right of her front, but it was open in the middle revealing her nude body. He could see the shining blackness of her thick pubic hair, could see the faintly dusky silk of her inner thighs, the faint rise of her belly with its small navel. He swallowed and stammered out something and was about to step back, when, with a quick motion, she took the serape off over head and flipped it around his neck. The next thing he knew she was pulling him into the house as neatly as a roped calf. He said, still stammering, "Dulcima, wha—What the hell, uh, are you doing?"

"You have come to see me," she said. "No?"

He stared at her. He couldn't help himself. She was one of those small-boned small-waisted women with outsized breasts. Hers were as big as grapefruits, each crowned by a nipple as big as a strawberry and as brown as a ripe fig. He didn't think he'd ever seen a woman's body so lavish and luscious, so inviting, so made for love. "Dulcima," he said hoarsely, "you trying to get me killed? I'm standing under San Diego's roof and his woman is standing in front of me naked."

She had come to a stop after pulling him into the middle of a big tiled room. She let go of the serape so that it fell around his sides. "Bah," she said. "I am not hees woman and theese ees not hees roof. This ees my house."

Longarm was having trouble with his breathing and his jeans had gotten far too tight. He knew he should look away, but he couldn't keep his eyes off her. They roved between her big, erect breasts and the fascinating, glistening patch of hair that grew at the apex of her legs. Wanting to back away, he said, "Listen, what is going on here? Where is San Diego?"

She shrugged. "He has gone across the river. He does hees business there. So he say to me. I doan care where he ees. I like you the first time I see you. I theek we go make love now."

He reached up and quickly took the serape from around his neck and returned it to hers. "I think I better get the hell out of here," he said, "while I still can. I got a feeling San Diego is liable to come walking in any second with a gun in each fist."

Dulcima cocked her head and looked at him. "Why you want to make theese kind of talk? You are not escared of Raoul. I doan theenk you are escared of anybody. Why you talk like that? Who you trying to fool? You doan fool Dulcima."

He looked around. The room they were in was big and furnished with heavy Mexican furniture. A door to his right obviously led to some kind of dining room and on into a kitchen. The door to his left was closed. A staircase along the right-hand wall led up to a small landing on the second floor. "Who is in this house?" he asked her.

She reached out and took his hand and pulled it to her, laying it between her breasts and holding it there with both her hands. "There ees nobody in theese house except for us. *Mi mozos*, my servants, are working outside. I have been watching for you since theese morning."

He looked at her, feeling the almost electric heat of her body through his hand. "You couldn't have known I was coming out here."

"I look for you every morning. Since we talk in the plaza, I knew you would come."

"But I came to see San Diego."

"Fah on San Diego!" She stamped her bare foot on the smooth tiles. "I throw heem out! He does not leeve at theese place no more."

"I thought you said he was gone to Mexico?"

"He ees gone to Mexico. Fah! He ees not here. What you care where ees theese man named Raoul San Diego? He look like a man, he act like a man, but he not really a man. He fool all the people, but he no fool Dulcima." She grasped Longarm's wrist with both hands and started walking backwards, pulling him along, toward the stairs. "You come with Dulcima. I much want to play with all of your body."

He went reluctantly. His breath was coming rapidly and he was aroused so that his heart was going fast enough for him to feel it. But he was suspicious and worried that it might be a trap of some kind. "What do you want with me, Dulcima?" he asked. "You could have your pick of the men in town. Hell, in the county. Maybe in the whole state."

She held his eyes with hers. She was on the first step and stepping backwards for the second. "I theenk you are *mucho hombre*. Much man. I am never wrong about theese theengs. You come with Dulcima and we will feel good."

He glanced behind him, but she was already a third of the way up the stairs and he was about to mount the second step. He looked at her soft, warm, inviting body and thought that if she was the cheese he was one mouse that was ready to be caught.

He followed her up the stairs to the small landing at the top. She had turned her back to him, but was still holding his hand with one of hers. Her round, firm buttocks, were as sensual as her breasts; the sight of them made his breath catch. There was only one door on the landing, a big, dark wooden one that was almost a match to the front door. She opened it, shoving it wide, and he could see past her enough to tell it was a large bedroom with another room leading off to his right. She led him over the threshold and then turned to shut the door. He looked to see if it had a latch or a sliding bolt, but there was just the knob. He was going to ask her if there wasn't some way to lock it, but she didn't give him time. She led him straight to the biggest bed he'd ever seen, then turned and started unbuttoning his shirt. Longarm could feel his legs beginning to tremble. He unbuckled his gun belt, being careful not to dislodge the derringer hidden in the concave buckle, and then lowered the rig slowly to the floor, bending over so that his lips and hers naturally came together. Her mouth was already opening as he bent his head over her. He could feel the sudden flush of her warmth on his mouth and then the sensual darting and stabbing of her tongue. Her arms were around his neck and he raised her up, lifting her off her feet. She was smaller and lighter than she had seemed that day in the plaza. Her feet dangled as she held on with just her arms around his neck. Finally he eased her back to the floor, took her around the waist, and lifted her onto the bed, laying her across it. The bed covering was white, accentuating her musky darkness. For half a moment he just looked at her lying there, legs open and inviting, breasts heaving with passion, lips parted as she looked at him with her big, luminous eyes.

In frantic haste he ripped his shirt off, then sat down on the side of the bed and yanked his boots off and then his jeans. Austin Davis had made fun of his not wearing underwear. Well, here was a good example of the usefulness of such a practice.

Behind him she said, "*Arriba arriba. Pronto!*" Hurry hurry hurry.

He turned quickly, and crept across the bed to her on his hands and knees. As he went between her legs, they came up to encircle him around the chest. Longarm feared it would make her too far away for his penis to reach and penetrate her, but then she did something with her hips as her arms encircled his neck, and he almost cried out as he felt himself slide into her hot, throbbing body. He stayed on his hands and knees as her mouth came up and her tongue went inside his mouth to complete the circle. Holding him around the neck, she thrust herself into him rhythmically, over and over, faster and faster her breath coming in gasps.

Now she was biting him on the lips and the cheek and the ears. Longarm was trying to hold back, give her time, but the heat she'd generated in him with the first sight of her in nothing but the serape, had fanned into a flame that he could not turn down. He lifted his right arm and cradled her back in his big hand. He knew he would collapse on her when he exploded.

And then her mouth was back on his, her hips still pulsating into his groin. Longarm could feel the firmness and heat of her buttocks as they slapped into him. But he could also feel the power of his own, final passion rising. He knew he could not hold back for another half a moment. And then came a low, keening sound from deep in Dulcima's throat. She began to gasp, and then the gasp became a soft wail that grew and grew until her wet lips and tongue were all over his face and her hips were working faster than he would have thought possible. Her lips left his face and she put her head back, arching her neck and her body, and he could feel the quiver run all through her as she began to scream and to dig her fingers into his back, clawing at him.

And then he knew no more, for he exploded in a cascade of pent-up fever and excitement and release. Some giant wind seemed to be tumbling him end over end across a misty plain. He was a tumbleweed swept up in a tornado. The world went black as he was buffeted and toppled over again and again.

Then it was over and, gasping, trying to hold his weight off Dulcima's tender body, he collapsed as his arms gave way and his legs betrayed him. He fell full length on her, feeling her softness, her arms around him and her hands in her hair, but not being aware of much else.

After a moment he felt her squirm slightly beneath him and he knew his dead weight was probably suffocating her. As gently as he could, he slid off her, toward the edge of the bed, and rolled over on his back. For the moment he was as satisfied as he reckoned he'd ever been in his life. Even his aching tooth was at peace. For a long moment he lay with his eyes closed, letting his body sink into the cushiony softness of the bedclothes. He could feel her moving around beside him, but he had no intention of opening his eyes until he recovered. The sight of her body was sure to arouse him all over again, and he didn't want to start anything that he wouldn't be able to finish. But then he felt her soft little hand on his hard belly, felt that hand work its way down until she was stroking his member. His emotions began to stir. He opened his eyes and looked up at her. She had propped a couple of pillows behind her back so that she was almost sitting up, making it easier to reach him. As he lay still, she squirmed around and leaned over and he could feel her smooth, hot tongue working its way down his belly, kissing and licking and leaving streaks of heat in its wake. He groaned, feeling himself coming erect. Then he felt her slip him inside her mouth, and it was like being dipped in a churning bucket of hot liquid. He could feel his member stretching its head to touch the back of her throat, feel her taking so much of him inside her, he wouldn't have thought it possible. His groans were coming faster and faster as she worked her mouth over his throbbing penis. Then she suddenly stopped. His eyes fluttered open. She was sitting straight up on the bed, and staring toward the door. Her eyes had gone wide, and her face was suffused with fear. Longarm didn't hear anything, only felt a presence. He did not hesitate. Without thought or plan he pushed Dulcima hard with his right hand shoving her toward the far side of the bed. In the same instant he rolled to his left, rolled off the bed and landed on the floor, his hand frantically

189

seeking his revolver. In the instant he pushed her and started his roll he was aware of a thud againt the wall, the back wall, and the crack of a gunshot.

But now he was on the floor, and the butt of his revolver was in his hand. He cocked the hammer as he raised it to aim at the figure in the wide-open door. He did not bother trying to jerk the gun out of the big cut away holster. There was no time. The figure at the door, having missed him in the bed, was now turning his gun toward him on the floor. Knowing his first shot was going to have to count, Longarm fired an instant before a second crack from the intruder's gun resounded.

Chapter 10

He saw his bullet take Raoul San Diego square in the chest. The force of the slug knocked the man backwards just enough so that his second shot was jerked up and went harmlessly over Longarm's head.

But Longarm was leaving nothing to chance. As San Diego was falling, Longarm cocked his revolver and fired again. The second slug took the gunman in the side of the chest, sending him sprawling to his left, the gun falling from his lifeless fingers.

After a long moment Longarm slowly raised himself to his knees, his ears still ringing with the sound of the gunshots echoing in the room. He had finally shaken the holster and belt off the revolver and it was naked in his hand. He could see San Diego's boots and most of his left leg, but the rest of his body was hidden from view. He looked to his right, toward where Dulcima had last been. She'd gone off the bed on the other side, but now, she too, was up on her knees staring toward the bedroom door. Longarm watched her, not sure of what her reaction would be to him shooting her lover. She had been critical of San Diego and said she didn't care, but that was when he was still alive. Now she slowly turned to look at Longarm, saying, with just a slight tremble in her voice, "Yeah, you chure escared of heem. Yes, I theenk I was right about you." She gestured toward the door. "He make the beeg mistake. He should have been escared of you, not you heem."

Longarm listened to her, not saying anything.

She pointed toward the wall. About a foot and a half up from the head of the bed, Longarm could see where San Diego's first bullet had plowed into the whitewashed masonary, burying itself in the soft concrete and leaving what looked to be a big black eye in the white plaster.

"I doan know who he chooting at," Dulcima said, "you or me. I theenk maybe he doan care, but I theenk you save my life when you push me so hard that I fly off the bed."

Longarm looked at her, standing there naked. Nothing stirred in him, which he could well understand. "He got home a little faster than you said, didn't he?"

She shrugged and put out her hands philosophically. "He comes, he goes. I doan always know. But, yes, he come back faster. I tol' heem I didn't want heem to come back, but he come back anyway. Beeg surprise for me."

He still looked at her. "Yeah, I guess you were surprised." He swung his eyes to where the slug had hit the wall and to where she had been sitting on the bed just before San Diego had fired. The trajectory of the bullet had been too high to have hit Longarm, because he'd been lying flat on his back. But it would have caught her neatly right between her lovely breasts. "Still," he said, "we could have locked the door. Might have saved us a surprise. And his life.''

Dulcima crawled slowly back up onto the bed. ''I was een too much of the hurry. I din't theenk of the door. Maybe you din't theenk of it also.''

He shrugged and sat down on the bed and started pulling on his jeans. Behind him he heard her say, ''Why for you get dressed? We jus' start, no?''

He looked around at her. ''There's a dead man out there just beyond the door. I killed him. You really think I feel like making love right now?'' He stood up, walked past the foot of the bed, and crossed to the door. There he could see the remains of Raoul San Diego. He lay halfway down the stairs with just his boots and part of his left leg on the small landing. Longarm knew he didn't have to go down and touch him to make sure he was dead. There was not a great deal of blood. The first slug had taken him so flush in the chest that Longarm reckoned the second shot had been wasted. But it was reflex and he had gotten it off so closely on the heels of the first that San Diego hadn't fallen very far before the second bullet twisted him to his left, taking what life remained in him. Longarm looked down and shook his head and sighed. He had escaped San Diego's bullet, but he still had a hell of a mess on his hands. The very thing he'd tried to avoid had happened; he'd killed Caster's go-between and gunhand. And Caster wasn't going to like that. As he walked back into the bedroom, Longarm debated his options. There didn't seem to be many, unless he could somehow persuade Dulcima to help him drop San Diego's body in the Rio Grande and then to forget what she'd seen and be ready to swear the man had left her and gone to Mexico and that was that.

But he had the uneasy feeling that the volatile and

voluptuous Dulcima would not be willing to go along with the idea. It was clear that she wasn't very upset about San Diego getting killed. And maybe she really had been through with him. But she didn't seem to Longarm like a woman who could keep a secret, or even wanted to. He had an idea she would want him to cut the man's ears off and go parading around town with them like he'd seen a matador do in a corrida he'd once been to in Mexico City. That would be more her style. He went over to the bed and looked at her, trying to think of how to broach the subject. Just as he was about to open his mouth, he heard a sound from downstairs. He instantly put his finger to his lips, warning Dulcima to be quiet. But she said, "That ees just one of my servants coming een. Maybe they hear the chooting."

And that was another problem; the servants. If they got a look at Raoul San Diego, there would be no way at all to keep the news of his death from reaching Caster's ears. Or, worse his brother's.

Longarm turned toward the door, still signaling Dulcima to be quiet. He'd stuck his revolver in the waistband of his jeans, and he drew it out and softly pull back the hammer as he moved to the door. He stood just inside the bedroom, mostly covered by the left side of the door frame. He could see the landing and most of the way down the stairs. He could hear a voice, either speaking to someone or calling something out in low tones. Longarm stepped through the doorway, crossed the landing, and plastered himself up against the wall next to the stairs. He peeked around the corner, his revolver at the ready. He could see down into the main room at the foot of the stairs. He heard the voice again and, just as he recognized the words, Austin Davis suddenly stepped into view, his revolver in his hand. He moved slowly, looking around, calling out, "Mister Long? Mister Long?"

Longarm relaxed and shoved his gun back in his waistband. "Austin, up here," he said, "Here, at the top of the stairs." He stepped out, standing over San Diego's body.

Davis looked up, relief on his face. "Longarm, wh—"

"Watch that."

"Mister Long, what the hell are you doing? I heard gunshots." Then Davis came near enough to the stairs to see the body. "Who the hell you got there? Looks like he come in second in a two-man race."

"Never mind. Get up here. We got some figuring out to do."

Longarm watched as his partner came slowly up the stairs, staring at the body. Halfway up, he cocked his head around so he could see into the face of the dead man. "Hell, that's Raoul himself," he said. "Had a gun in his hand. There it is. And he's got two holes in him that he didn't have before." Davis glanced up at Longarm. "This your work?"

Longarm nodded. He stepped to the door of the bedroom to give Davis room to come up. "He didn't give me no choice," he explained to Davis. "He come through the door shooting I'm lucky he either missed me or wasn't shooting for me."

Davis got to the landing and looked down at San Diego. "I thought you didn't want to kill him."

"Damnit, Austin, of course I didn't want to kill him. I told you he didn't give me no choice. Hell, I wasn't going to take a bullet myself or let him shoot somebody else. No, I didn't want to shoot him. Right now I'm trying to figure out what to do. Caster ain't going to like this one little bit.''

The young deputy was standing just back from the door. ''You said shoot somebody else?'' he asked. ''What else? Who else? And, by the way, what the hell are you doing up here? This his office, or something?'' And with that, he stepped in front of Longarm and into the doorway. The move caught Longarm off guard and all he could do was turn with Davis so as to see what Davis did.

Dulcima was standing on the far side of the bed, near the foot. She had put on some sort of thin silk robe that barely came below her knees—but she had not bothered to close it, much less tie the wide sash. She was standing there, her feet a little apart, all of her left breast showing and some of her right, and her lustrous pubic hairs shining against her pale tan skin.

Austin Davis stopped short at the sight of her. ''GREAT HORNED FROGS!'' he exclaimed, and his mouth fell open. Almost involuntarily he took a step backwards, as if he had intruded upon a private scene.

Longarm moved into the room, saying, a trifle sharply, ''Dulcima, cover yourself!''

''Why? He look like a beeg boy who has seen eet before.''

''Damnit, just cover yourself! This is a mess.''

Austin Davis turned to him.''I see who else you was talking about. That is some kind of an 'else'. What happened, San Diego catch you stealing his cookies?''

Longarm gave him a weary look. ''How long you figure you'll have to go on about this before we can get down to the real problem? I mean, how much talk you got to make about it? I can understand you can't just let it go for what it appears like."

Davis shrugged, then turned and glanced at Dulcima. She had closed the robe, but the thin material did very little to hide her nakedness. He said, to Longarm, "I don't *have* to say nothing. But it's kind of hard not to. I don't reckon the second man on the scene after somebody had just struck gold could keep his mouth shut either." He nodded his head toward Dulcima. "I call that *oro puro*. And if you dipped your biscuit in that gravy, all I can say is that I wish it had been me and you'd had a feather up your ass and we'd have both been tickled."

Longarm sighed. "All right, all right. Get it out of your system."

Davis grinned. "I'm just jealous. You come out here to deliver a man some money and instead you wind up taking some of his pie. You got my admiration. I'd call that some pretty slick work."

"Listen," Longarm said as patiently as he could, "I come out here like I was supposed to. Dulcima said he'd gone to Mexico, and one thing led to another and we ended up here in the bed without our clothes on. Next thing I know I seen a look on her face that told me somebody else had come to the party. I had my back to the door at the time, but I didn't bother to look. I rolled off the bed and come up shooting. I got to tell you I was blind lucky, because I hadn't left my revolver in a handy place. I'd been too busy at the time. But I somehow landed with it near my hand and I fired through the holster." He pointed toward the back wall. "You can see yonder he got one off that missed one of us by a cat's whisker. I don't know who he meant to kill."

Davis shook his head, and let out a low whistle as he looked at the bullet hole. "I'd say you got double lucky, partner. I take it you weren't exactly set up for action at the time."

"Not that kind," Longarm said dryly.

Davis glanced at Dulcima. She was sitting on the bed, examining her fingernails, not seeming to pay the two men any mind. Davis jerked his head toward the door. "Let's go take another look at the situation outside," he said.

"What?"

Davis jerked his head again and then stepped through the doorway. Longarm followed him. Davis drew the door to, but didn't latch it. He walked past Longarm and went halfway down the stairs, motioning his partner to follow. "C'mon down here."

Longarm descended the few steps. "What?"

"I don't think we ought to be talking in front of her."

Longarm frowned. "Why not?"

"Because I don't think you're going to be telling Caster about San Diego."

"What have you got in mind? He's a little large to hide. And I don't see how we can bury him, with Dulcima's hired hands working out in the back. I'm sure they didn't mistake them gunshots for firecrackers."

"I would imagine they hear gunshots around here all the time."

"You got some kind of idea how we can not tell Caster anything?"

Austin Davis nodded slowly. "Maybe."

"Who the hell am I supposed to have given the money to?"

"How about you gave it to San Diego and the last

time you saw him he was striking out for Mexico with the girlfriend right by his side."

Longarm turned and glanced at the closed door, "You talking about taking his body across the river?"

Davis nodded. "Yeah. I don't know no place around here to get rid of him without risk of being seen or him being found too soon. I got some friends about twenty-five, thirty miles south of here ought to be willing to do me a favor."

"Mexicans?"

"Yeah. Ranchers. In fact I bought some of that herd from them. Not many, about a hundred head. But the way I see it is you've got to be able to tell Caster that you gave San Diego the money and you don't know what happened to him after that."

"Why do I have to have given him the money? How come I can't say I couldn't find him?"

"Because Caster ain't going to take the money from you," Davis explained, "and I doubt if he's got another go-between lined up. And that would just delay matters. Right now that ain't what we need. On account of her. Dulcima."

"What about her?"

Austin Davis pushed his hat up. "Well, I figure she's got to go to Mexico with me. Either that or we got to shut her mouth some other way. She seen you kill San Diego. You willing to bet your hide she won't go and tell Caster or tell somebody so word gets back to him?"

Longarm looked at the door again. When he turned back to Davis, he said, "No, I reckon not. But seems to me you are making plans mighty fast here. You sure you're thinking good?"

Davis gave him a small smile. "At least I'm thinking

with the right head. I'd say you been through a rodeo here just lately.''

''What if the lady don't want to go to Mexico? She's got this nice house here. What makes you think she'll be willing to go off with you to some damn small rancho where they're still eating tortillas and beans out of the same pot?''

''I'm counting on you to talk her into it. You seem to have a way with her.''

Longarm looked at the bedroom door once again. ''I wouldn't be counting on that. That's a lady got a mind of her own.''

''Hell, she can't say no to a big, handsome man like you.''

Longarm gave him a look. ''What say we let that kind of talk slide for a better time? I know I'm fair game right now, but save it.'' He reached up to reposition his hat and realized that he only thing he was wearing was a pair of jeans and a revolver. ''I don't know, Austin, you are carrying me kind of fast right now.''

''What the hell you want to do? You want to go and tell Caster you were slipping San Diego's girlfriend a little of ol' Slick Willy and he come in and didn't like it and you killed him? Reckon how he'd take that?''

Longarm shook his head. ''Damn. This is messy. Hell, I don't much care for doing things in this manner.''

''You shot that robber in San Antonio that come out of an alley at you. You went to the sheriff about that and damn near ruined the job. You want some more?''

Longarm shrugged. ''I reckon you're right. We can't let San Diego's body be found before we make the arrest. And I don't reckon we can let Dulcima run around loose. I think it would amuse her to tell folks about these two men having a gunfight over her." He scratched his head. "But how the hell we going to work it?"

"Ask her to go with me to Mexico. Make up some story."

"And if she won't go?"

Davis shrugged. "Then I reckon she'll have to be hogtied and taken."

Longarm gave a dry laugh. "That ain't a job *I* want."

"Well, you're the boss. You tell me a better way."

"Damn!" Longarm said. He looked down at the body sprawled on the stairs. "Why did the sonofabitch come in when he did? Damnit!"

"Why? You wasn't finished?"

Longarm gave him a sour look. "That ain't the point, Austin. Damnit, if you don't take the worst side of a situation, I never saw anybody who did. I mean if he hadn't come in like that, if I could have met him under different circumstances, I might not have had to kill him."

"How about if you hadn't been up here in the bedroom with his woman and both of you with your clothes off? Or I guess that was in the line of duty."

"Oh, go to hell, Austin," Longarm said. He stood there on the stairs trying to think of a better plan than the one Davis had proposed. There wasn't one. Until the job was finished he couldn't let it be discovered that he'd killed San Diego, and he couldn't leave Dulcima running around loose to talk to the wrong people. But he had no idea how he was going to get her cooperation. "Well, let me go in and talk to her," he said at last.

"Don't you reckon I better come with you?"

"Well, hang back."

Longarm was surprised to find that Dulcima had

201

dressed while they had been talking. She put on a pair of blue velvet *charro* pants that flared at the bottom over her small, polished boots; little silver conchos ran up the outside seam of each pants leg. A frilly white shirt with a little black string tie completed the outfit. If anything, the clothes made her look even more desirable. Behind him Longarm could hear Austin Davis let out his breath in appreciation. Dulcima turned from a chest in the corner when they came in. "Dulcima," Longarm said, "I need to ask you a little favor."

She looked amused. "You choot Raoul and now you are escared bad thin happen to you from his friends and his brother. So chou want to feex eet so nobody know. What chou want to do?"

"Well, what we thought . . ." Longarm pointed behind him. "This is Mister Davis here. He works for me. Mister Davis thought we ought to take San Diego's body across the river and into Mexico—quite a ways into Mexico. He's got some friends there that will help."

She peered around Longarm and gave Austin Davis a critical look. "He's hokay," she said. "What you want me to do?"

"Have you got a buckboard here?"

"Chure. What you theenk?"

"Can the women who work for you get it hitched up?"

"Of course. Or the buggy. Or the carriage. What you theenk I pay them for?"

Longarm cleared his throat. "Uh, we don't want them knowing about Mister San Diego. In fact we don't want anybody knowing about San Diego. So I need you to tell them to hitch up the carriage or the buckboard and bring it around front. Don't give them no explanation."

"Buckboard would be better," Davis put in. "Crossing the river. And a team of horses. Not just one."

Longarm looked questioningly at Dulcima. "Can they handle that?"

She tossed her head, making her shiny black hair fly. "Chure. What you theenk?"

"Then I'd appreciate it if you would go and tell them to hitch a buckboard up and bring it around to the front. And tell them when they are done to get back to their work."

He assumed she would go out the door they'd come in, and down the stairs past the body of San Diego, but she surprised him by crossing the room and opening another door that he'd thought led to a bathroom, or the like. She disappeared, and in a few seconds they heard her downstairs, yelling to the servants.

"That is one hell of a good-looking woman," Davis said. "I ain't going to mind taking her to Mexico one little bit." He had been looking toward the door where she'd vanished, but now he turned to Longarm. "How long you figure I ought to keep her over there?"

Longarm shrugged. "I don't know. Depends on how willingly she goes. Caster has the got the cattle for a week. I'd guess five days. The thing is I might need you here. This has changed a good deal of our plans."

"I reckon you realize I can't go down to Brownsville now and take a gander at James Mull."

Longarm grimaced. "Damnit," he said. "I think this may be the most complicated job I ever went on. Hell, I wish it had been Caster and Mull that had come through the door. At least the business would be settled."

Dulcima came back in. "They do eet pretty queek,"

she said. "They leave eet in the front. I tol' them to put the canvas cover een the wagon. I doan theenk you want that peoples chood see Raoul."

Longarm thanked her, and then he said, "Dulcima, I need you to go along to Mexico with Mister Davis."

Her eyes suddenly narrowed. "Yes? Why you need that?"

Longarm cleared his throat. "Well, he don't speak Spanish so good. He might ask you to interpret for him."

She stared at him for a moement and then laughed her tinkling little laugh. "You make the lie, señor. You want me to go to Mexico because you know peoples will be coming to ask for Raoul and you are escared what I say. No?"

Longarm shrugged and looked around at Austin Davis.

Austin came forward. "Listen," he told her, "We'll have a good time. My friends got big hacienda. Maybe we'll go on to Monterrey. How does that sound?"

She gave him an amused look and then stepped back as if to make a lengthier appraisal. She surveyed him from boots to hat for a long enough time that Davis began to look uncomfortable. Finally she shrugged. "Hokay." Then she held up a finger and shook it at Davis. "But you no touch me. I do the touching. You unnerstan'?"

Davis gave Longarm a puzzled look. Longarm laughed, and explained, "The lady is telling you she'll do the choosing. If and when she does."

"Yes," Dulcima said. "That ees the way I always do. And when I am finish, I am finish." She looked at Longarm. "I doan theenk he is *muy macho* like you."

Longarm could not keep from smiling as Davis said, "Ma'm, I'd like a chance to prove that."

She shrugged. "How long we be gone?"

Longarm gave Austin Davis a quick look. He said, "Two or three days."

Dulcima turned toward the clothes chest in the corner. "I must pack a valise."

Longarm started toward the door. "Let's get out of here, Austin. Give the lady some privacy."

Once on the landing, he said, "You know, you and Raoul wear the same kind of hat and the same color."

"It's common along the border," Davis told him. "That's why they call it a border hat."

"Yeah, but you're also about the same size, except you're maybe ten, fifteen pounds heavier, mostly in the shoulders and chest. Why don't you wear his vest?"

"What are you getting at?"

"I'm thinking maybe you ought to cross at the International Bridge."

Davis screwed up his face in concern. "Are you crazy? I don't look like that Mex."

"Not up close, no. I don't mean for you to stop and visit. Is his horse outside?"

"There was two horses tied out there. I guess one of them is his. Yeah, I—reckon it is. Big black saddle. Got enough silver on it to feed a family for a year."

"All right, that's my point. Folks will see the saddle and they'll see Dulcima, because that is what will take their eyes. You keep the brim of your hat down low and kind of scrunch up on that buckboard seat and just brisk right on over that bridge, and more than one person will think it's San Diego."

Davis looked thoughtful for a moment. "Well," he

said, "I can see where it will help your case when you tell Caster that the last you saw of Raoul was him taking off with Dulcima and your twenty-five hundred dollars. But what if somebody hails us?"

"Don't look up and don't stop. In that half mile or so where you're liable to run into someone just keep your head down and the horses in a good trot or lope. Tell Dulcima to do the waving if any waving has got to be done."

"What if I see his brother, Raymond? The Tejano Cafe ain't that far from the bridge."

Longarm shrugged. "I don't know. Hope like hell you don't, I guess. I'll be following you, so I'll know how it goes. Hell, Austin, it will strengthen my story."

"Hell, why not," Davis said. "How long you want me gone?"

"Well . . ." Longarm looked down the stairs, thinking. "I don't know. I don't know when Caster will release the cattle. He said a week. You reckon you can keep her over there for a week? We can't arrest Caster until he turns the cattle loose. He ain't done nothing illegal until then."

"I don't know if I can keep her there or not, short of, like I said, hogtieing her. But, Longarm, I'll be back for the arrests. Don't forget now that I can't go to Brownsville and look Mull over."

Longarm grimaced. "I hate to not know about Mull. Like I said, this is the most snarled up, complicated damn job I was ever on in my life. I had an easier time of it when I was courting five women at the same time in Denver one year. And killing San Diego has just snarled it up more. Hell! I had counted on us knowing Mull when we seen him."

"I still don't think you can depend on Jasper White."

"I ain't got no intention of depending on Jasper White. We'll just have to think of something else." He scratched his head, realizing he still hadn't put his hat on. "Though I don't know what, right now. You really think I ought to tell Caster that I gave San Diego the money?"

"I give you my reasons for that, but you do like you want on the matter."

"We better get back in there with Miss Dulcima. I didn't know there was an outside door before."

"You scared she'll run off?"

"Listen, Austin—The lady is now your problem."

"I don't know how I'm going to keep her over there a week. I'm serious, Longarm. She acts like a woman who bores easy."

"You can't let her back here."

"You want me to shoot her in the leg?"

Longarm shook his head. "I don't know what to tell you. Like you say, this is your barn dance. She gets back over here, it could burn the barn down."

"Oh, *now* it's my party. I see how you think, Longarm, and I don't much like it."

"If you see you're going to be settled in one place for a few days, wire me where I can wire you. I'll try and let you know what's happening. But you better get a move on."

Longarm pulled up a quarter of a mile short and watched as Austin Davis, with Dulcima seated beside him and the body of Raoul San Diego in the back, drove to the main southbound road, took a left, and then drove the remaining three or four hundred yards to the bridge.

Austin had the matched team going at a good high trot and, with his horse and San Diego's tied to the back of the buckboard, struck the bridge and then crossed it in a matter of a few minutes. The last Longarm could see of the buckboard was a thin trail of dust as it headed into Nuevo Laredo on the Mexico side. As near as he could tell, no one had shown any interest except for what might naturally be expected at the sight of a flying buckboard with a beautiful woman up front and a pair of good-looking horses, one with a silver-mounted saddle. Davis's route had taken him within fifty yards of the Tejano Cafe, but Longarm hadn't seen Raoul's brother or Jasper White or anyone for that matter who seemed overly interested. He was satisfied that anyone who had seen the wagon and the pair on the driver's seat would have thought it was who it was supposed to be.

He looked across toward where the customs office was, but decided it wasn't the right time to see Jay Caster. Instead he wheeled his horse around and loped him slowly back to the hotel livery. There he untied his saddlebags, turned his horse over to a stableboy, and then walked back to the hotel, the saddlebags over his shoulder. He didn't know what to do with the twenty-five hundred that was in the saddlebags. It was too bulky to carry around on his person and he sure as hell wasn't going to take it back to the bank, in case Caster had a spy there. He couldn't ask the clerk to put it in the safe for the same reason, so in the end he heaved up the mattress on the bed in his room, cut a slit in the bottom with his pocketknife, stuffed the money in, and then re-made the bed, making it look as if he'd laid down for an afternoon nap.

After that he went down to the dining room for a late

lunch. It was already after one o'clock. His tooth wasn't acting up, for which he was grateful, but he was careful to eat mostly soft food and nothing too hot or cold.

After his meal of chicken and dumplings, sliced tomatoes, and caramel pudding, Longarm returned to his room, took off his hat, and lay down on the bed, staring at the ceiling. He was of two minds about going over to see Caster, wondering if maybe he ought to wait and see if Caster sent for him when San Diego didn't show up to deliver the money. In the end he decided that the best course was just to lay low and wait. He figured a little stewing might do Caster some good.

In the evening he went quietly down to the quarantine pens just before dark and moved from corral to corral, looking over the cattle and trying to figure out how Caster jumped one herd in front of the others. Nothing came to his attention. The paint on the cattle's sides was as it should be, in that it corresponded with their progress toward the end set of pens, the green area where they were to be released. He did notice that his cattle, or the cattle that were supposed to belong to him, appeared to be in good flesh and were being well taken care of. They were also all wearing that red splotch of paint. He was able to locate two of the five cattle he'd chosen to watch with either an odd color pattern or cockeyed horns. He was sure the other three were there also. They just didn't come to eye in the gathering twilight and with all the cattle milling about. In fact, of the two he'd managed to spot it seemed as if the red paint was not quite as bright as on some other of the cattle. Of course that could have been the light, but Longarm guessed it was due more to the animals rubbing up against each other.

As he was riding back to the hotel, he thought about Austin Davis and Dulcima, wondering how they were getting on and whether or not Dulcima had gotten interested in Davis yet. Then he frowned, thinking about Davis. The young deputy had hit him a pretty good shot after they'd loaded Raoul San Diego in the bed of the buckboard and covered him over with a piece of canvas so he looked like luggage. As Davis finished cutting off a piece of rope they'd used to secure the canvas, he'd said, "Well just tell me one thing, Mister Long . . . If the lady is so preferential toward you, how come she didn't ask why it wasn't you taking her over to Mexico? She ain't supposed to know you've got to be here to deal with Caster. Not unless you told her, which I don't think you'd do."

It had stumped Longarm, leaving him temporarily speechless. Davis had been all too right. How come Dulcima hadn't asked, at least once, why he, Longarm, couldn't take her over?

But she hadn't. Longarm considered it down right insulting. Worse, he knew he'd never hear the end of it from Austin Davis.

Chapter 11

In the morning, word was sent to Longarm at the hotel that Jay Caster wanted to see him. He let an hour pass and then fetched his horse from the livery stable and rode slowly over to the customs office. Caster was sitting behind his desk with a slight frown on his face. You'd have had to have been looking for it, for the frown to be noticeable. But Longarm had been looking. "You see Raoul yesterday?" the customs inspector asked.

"Oh, yes. Sure did." Longarm eased himself into a chair. He looked at Caster expectantly, as if waiting for him to go on.

Caster wrinkled his brow. "It go all right?"

Longarm nodded. "Yeah. Why shouldn't it have?"

Caster leaned over and spit in his bucket. "What time you see him?"

"Oh, little after mid-morning. Can't say to the minute, but I'd reckon sometime between ten-thirty and eleven."

"See him out at that house?"

"Yeah. Just like you told me." Longarm took off his

hat and leaned forward. "Why? Is something wrong?"

Caster didn't answer. Instead he spit again. "Was she there?"

"Who?"

"Who, hell! Dulcima."

Longarm acted as if he was giving it some thought. "I think so. Yes, I caught a glimpse of her off that big room downstairs. Toward the kitchen, I guess you'd say. And maybe she came out and went upstairs. I wasn't noticing. But I wasn't there that long. I just give the money to San Diego and he give it a quick count. Then we had a little argument about a receipt."

Caster looked up quickly. "You asked him for a receipt?"

"Hell, yes. That's a wad of money I was passing him."

"What'd he say about the receipt?"

"Said for me to go to hell. Not in those words, but it came to the same thing. Mostly he just give me a look like I'd been eating loco weed."

"What then?"

"Nothing. I got on my horse and left. You'd told me to give him the twenty-five hundred, so I did. When it was clear he wouldn't give me anything in writing saying he got it, I give up and come on back to town. Say, what is this all about? Is something wrong?"

Caster gave him an irritable look. "There you go, asking questions again. This is none of yore affair."

Longarm leaned forward again. "The hell it ain't. I got twenty-five hundred dollars invested here. I reckon that gives me the right to ask a few questions about what's going on."

Caster waved his arm dismissively. "Ain't nothing

going on. Now get up and get on out of here.''

That afternoon Raymond San Diego came to see Longarm. He found him in the hotel bar having a solitary drink at a back table. Longarm watched the dapper little man as he picked his way between the tables. He was wearing a light tan linen suit with a starched white shirt and a brown foulard tie. He was, Longarm reckoned, about the neatest man outside of the banking profession that he'd ever seen. As San Diego approached, Longarm looked him over carefully for a weapon. Austin Davis had said he carried a pistol under his coat, but Longarm couldn't figure out where.

San Diego came straight to the table and stopped, looking down and not saying a word. Longarm nodded his head. ''Howdy. Whyn't you set down and have a drink?''

San Diego ignored the invitation. ''When you see my brother?'' he said.

Longarm gave him a slow look, trying to give the impression of a man who is just slightly offended. ''Well,'' he said, ''I can't see where that would be any of your business, Señor San Diego. But if you want to know, why don't you ask your brother yourself?''

''Caster say you saw him yesterday morning at the hacienda.''

Longarm nodded. ''If you're getting your information from Mister Caster, then you ain't got nothing to talk to me about. I told him all I knew about the situation. Now, how about you answer me a question? Something going on with your brother? Has he gotten out of pocket?''

Raymond San Diego was still staring down at him. ''I hear you have a long talk with hees woman, Dulcima.''

213

Longarm shook his head. "I don't talk about a lady's business, Señor San Diego. I had a conversation, a mighty short conversation, with her, out yonder on the plaza. That took place in front of half the town. If that's what you are referring to."

"You doan see her again?"

Longarm tried to look irritated. "Look here," he said, "what is all this? I'm a cattle broker in town trying to do a little business. My dealings are my own and I don't give a minute's thought to the business of others. You and Mister Caster are both starting to make me think something ain't quite right with your brother, and that is fixing to make me nervous. Why are you walking in here and asking me questions about him? You ain't never done that before. Now what is going on?"

Abruptly, and without another word, Raymond San Diego turned on his heel and marched out of the bar. Longarm watched him go, laughing to himself. It appeared that Raymond's disappearance had them churning around. Longarm was almost willing to bet that someone had seen Austin Davis and Dulcima cross the bridge, the day before, and word had got back to either Caster or Raymond that Raoul had been seen leaving for Mexico. Presumably with twenty-five hundred dollars that didn't belong to him. What would be coming next? Obviously, Caster had asked Raymond about Raoul, told him what he knew, and Raymond had started his own line of inquiry. Longarm imagined that Austin Davis would enjoy the confusion. He hoped, however, that that was all Austin Davis was enjoying. As far as Longarm was concerned, he hadn't more than got started on Dulcima and he damn sure didn't want somebody else stirring around and leaving tracks in his pie.

With the new information provided by Raymond's visit Longarm considered going over and bracing Caster and asking what in the hell was going on with Raoul. But finally he decided to let the pot just simmer along.

It was late the next afternoon before Longarm got another summons from Jay Caster. Longarm reflected that Austin Davis had been gone better than forty-eight hours and there had been no word from him. It was bothersome trying to play the hand without knowing whether he could count on help from the other lawman. But then, that was the way it was. It was another reason Longarm preferred to work alone. If you never had any help, then you never expected any. Still, he would have liked to hear from Davis. The man wasn't all that bad, though the situation he was in, with Dulcima, wasn't the kind Longarm believed he could be trusted with. The woman required a man with a special kind of strength and Longarm didn't think Austin, as good an opinion as he had of himself where the ladies were concerned, measured up.

Before Longarm could even sit down, Jay Caster said, "I'm turning yore cattle out tomorrow. You better have some drovers there to handle them unless you want them scattered all over hell and back."

Longarm cocked his head questioningly. "You mean I'm ready for the trail. You ain't going to make me wait a week?"

Caster snorted. "Hell no, I don't mean that. I mean yore cows are going back to Mexico. The deal is off. Get the hell out of here."

"Wait a minute, wait a minute!" Longarm said heatedly. "What the hell are you talking about, the deal is

215

off? Like hell it is. I paid you twenty-five hundred dollars and you ain't pulling no plug on me!''

Caster leaned back in his chair and looked at Longarm from a long way off. ''Let's me and you get one thing straight,'' he said. ''You ain't paid me a dime. And you go around saying you did and I'll have yore ass in court.''

Longarm stood up and leaned over Caster's desk. ''I give the money to your man, Raoul,'' he said, ''and you know damn good and well I did. Look here, Caster, you can't pull this on me. You ain't got the right! By what right do you plan to turn my cattle out?''

Caster yawned, then leaned over and spit in the bucket. He wiped the back of his hand across his mouth. ''Yore cattle are showing signs of tick fever. Law says I got to turn 'em back to Mexico.''

Longarm tried to sound angry. ''Don't give me that, Caster. Hell, them cattle ain't been in your pens but three days. They ain't had time to show no signs of tick fever!''

''They do to me. And I'm the one makes the rules. You don't like it, go to Brownsville and talk to the boss, James Mull.''

Longarm was silent for a long moment. Then he said, ''Look, what the hell is this all about? We had a deal.''

''Not that I know about.''

''Damnit, Caster, you can't do this. You'll ruin me. I've got near eight thousand dollars in those cattle. Plus that twenty-five hundred I give San Diego. I can't take a loss like that. That's better than ten thousand.''

''That ain't my lookout. Sell 'em back in Mexico.''

Longarm made a disgusted sound. ''Hell, you know I'd be lucky to get four dollars a head back there. Especially if word got around I'd been turned back at the border.''

"Drive 'em a couple of hundred miles into the interior.''

"Then I'd get three a head and be out the cost of a long drive.'' Longarm paused to stare at Caster, then demanded once again, "Mister Caster, what is all this about? I've done what you asked, right along. What the hell caused this switch? At least you could tell me that much.''

Caster seemed to be thinking. Finally he heaved his shoulders and said, "I reckon I could give you that much. The short and long of it is it was that damn woman. Raoul never was no good once he got his nose in under her skirt.''

Longarm pretended he didn't understand. "That woman?'' he said, in a puzzled voice. "I don't get it. What woman you talking about?''

Caster gave him a sour look. "That damn Mexican woman he took up with when she moved here about a year ago. Bought that big house up on that hill. Claimed she was Spanish, Castillian Spanish. Sheeet! She was a high-dressing Mexican whore was what she was. And Raoul was a man you could depend on. But once he got wrapped up in her gown tail all he did was worry about her fooling around on him. Most jealous sonofabitch I ever saw. Wasn't good for a damn thing after that.''

Longarm let him finish and then said slowly, "Mister Caster, what has this got to do with our deal? I mean, I know the woman you speak of and I could see where she would be a temptation, but what has all this got to do with me?''

Caster snorted. "Hell, ain't you heard? Ever'body

else in town knows. Where the hell you been hiding? Raoul San Diego took off for Mexico better'n two days ago with that woman up on the buckboard seat with him. And I would reckon yore twenty-five hundred dollars was in his pocket.''

"*My* twenty-five hundred!" Longarm blurted. "Not very damn likely. That was *your* money. You told me to give it to him and I did. If he stole the money, he stole it from you. What makes you think he's gone?''

"Hell, he drove right across the bridge. A half a dozen people saw them. And as for it being my money, well, we don't agree about that. It never came into my hands. So the money is lost. I don't see where we can do no business. Not the kind you want to do with James Mull.''

Longarm sat back down and glared at Caster. "Mister Caster,'' he said again, "you can't do this to me. I can't afford this kind of loss. I'm not as well financed as I used to be. I've got to be able to drive those cattle to Galveston.''

Caster shrugged and looked bored. "That ain't my lookout. Now that Raoul has took half the money, that only leaves twenty-five hundred. The last half of that five grand. I guarantee you that Mull ain't going to do it for twelve-fifty, which would be half of the money left. And I ain't going to give him the balance of what you'd pay and leave myself out in the cold. I don't do nothing for free. So I reckon you better get yoreself some drovers and be ready to drive yore cattle back to Mexico. They sure as hell can't stay on this side of the river.''

Longarm sat a moment, frowning. Then, in a hesitant tone, he said, "Look, Mister Caster, I got to salvage what I can out of this. I ain't going to waste no breath arguing the right or wrong of your position. I can't *make* you do anything. But what if I was to come up with another twenty-five hundred? What about that? Would that do the trick?''

Caster looked interested for a moment and then he pulled a face. ''I might. But you ain't got that kind of money here and I can't wait for you to go and wire for some more. This thing has got to get done in the next couple of days. This whole mess has called too much attention to me. Too many people knew that Raoul worked for me.''

Longarm leaned forward, playing the eager business-man. ''I could have it quick. I could get it off that fellow that brought my cattle up. He just got some advance money to finance him to go down to Mexico and round up another herd. He'd let me have it.''

Caster thought about it. ''You right sure about that? You sure you ain't playing for time, hoping Raoul will show back up with yore money? If you're doing that, you're a bigger fool than I thought. Raoul ain't coming back. Even his own brother says that.''

''I can get another twenty-five hundred dollars. I can have it for you tomorrow.''

''You understand that still would leave you owing another twenty-five hundred when you get yore trail papers.''

Longarm nodded. ''Yes, sir. I do. I know that means I will have laid out seven thousand five hundred dollars, but I got to salvage what I can. Of course that means for certain I got to have the papers signed and sealed by Mister Mull. My only chance is to drive to Galveston.''

Caster spit and looked off in the distance. Then, with a hint of hesitation in his voice, he said, ''I reckon that

219

will still work. Mister Mull don't know about Raoul yet. And I'd just as soon he didn't know. I was going to tell him you'd backed out on the deal. But if you're willing to make up the extra money . . ."

"I am, I am."

Caster shrugged. "Well, maybe we can still do business."

"Who you want me to pay this sum to? Raymond? Jasper White?"

Caster looked pained. "Go on back to yore hotel now. I got to think on this. When I've figured it out, I'll let you know."

"Can you lay your hands on that money right now?" Caster said.

Longarm sank into the chair in front of Caster's desk. "Just have to go to the bank. Ten minutes. You want me to bring it here?"

"No. And don't bother making yoreself comfortable in that seat. You ain't going to be here that long. Go to the bank and then go straight back to yore hotel. Lift up the mattress on yore bed and put it just in under the edge. Have it in some kind of sack."

"How about one of them little canvas sacks the bank has?"

Caster gave an irritated motion with his head. "The hell with what kind of sack it is. Just a sack. Put the money there and then close the door to yore room. But don't lock it. Then go stand in the lobby. Better yet, go in the bar and have a drink. Wait ten minutes before you go back to your room."

Longarm stood up. "You going to pick it up?"

"Sonofabitch!" Caster burst out. "Won't you never

220

learn? Just do what you're told. And you better get you some drovers. I'm turning your cattle loose mid-morning, tomorrow. So be sure you have that other twenty-five hundred ready.''

"You're turning them loose for me to drive north?''

"That's what I said, ain't it?''

"What about Mister Mull?''

"You just never mind about Mister Mull.''

"But I'm paying for—''

"I know what you're paying for and you'll get it. Now get the hell out of here and see to yore end. Remember, don't waste no time.''

Longarm stopped off at the bank and picked up the remaining twenty-five hundred dollars on deposit there. He did it in case Caster had someone following him. He had them put it in a small canvas sack that had the name of the bank printed on it. He figured the other twenty-five hundred stashed inside his mattress was safe enough. He felt almost certain that Caster intended to pick up the money himself, but he still didn't know about Mull and he was not about to trust Jasper White to make an identification for him.

Then, just as he was stepping up on the porch of the Hamilton Hotel, an idea struck him. The daytime desk clerk was a smart young man and eagerly accommodating. Longarm risked the few moments it took him to speak with the clerk. "Look here,'' he said, "there's a man might be coming in today or tomorrow. Old friend of mine. I'd like to surprise him. Name is James Mull. He didn't say, but I got an idea he might be staying at this hotel. Wonder if you'd tip me a wink if he checks in, without letting him know. He played a little joke on me last time and I'd like to get him back.'' He slid a five-dollar gold piece across the desk.

"Why, yessir, Mister Long." The clerk said. "I can shore handle that." He put the five dollars in his pocket with a deft move. "As a matter of fact Mister Mull stays with us quite often. But I won't let him know you asked after him."

Longarm gave the clerk a wink and moved off toward his room. He couldn't imagine such a simple solution hadn't occurred to him before. The Hamilton was easily the best hotel in Laredo and certainly the most respectable. It was also near the customs office. Unless Mull was going to wait at the depot between trains or hang out in a saloon, he was going to need a hotel room. It would have to be the Hamilton.

Caster had let Longarm sweat for two days before he'd sent for him to give him instructions about the money and let him know he'd go through with the deal. Longarm wasn't sure if that was because Caster had had to clear the situation with Mull or if he was just being suspicious and careful. But it didn't matter, not now when it appeared he was going through with it. And Longarm liked the fact that Caster himself would be handling the money. He hadn't admitted to it, but Longarm greatly doubted that there'd be anyone else going into his room.

He let himself in, went straight to the bed, and slipped the canvas sack in between the mattress and the coil springs. He was on the point of leaving when he noticed that the window curtains were pulled back and the window itself was halfway up. His room was on the ground floor, at the back of the hotel. Looking out his window, you could see a pasture, and beyond that, part of the town. But anyone walking behind the hotel could see in through the ground-floor windows, and Longarm didn't think that Jay Caster would want to be seen in a hotel room fetching out twenty-five hundred dollars from somebody else's mattress. He put the sash down even though a nice breeze was blowing through, and then pulled the curtains to. After that he took a quick look around, let himself out, and walked down the hall and across the lobby to the bar. He didn't see Caster, but then he didn't expect to.

As he sat down at a table his mind turned to Austin Davis. Austin had been gone four days and once again Longarm wondered how he was doing with Dulcima. Either he'd won her over or she'd killed him. She didn't seem like a woman who went in for halfway measures. Longarm sat there, sipping at a whiskey and dreading the thought of going to see Raymond San Diego. But he would need eight or ten *vaqueros* the next morning when Caster turned his cattle loose, and Caster had suggested San Diego as someone who could round him up a crew. Of course Longarm had no intention of trailing the herd north, but he had to keep on acting like he was.

He took his time finishing his drink, then got up, paid his score, and went back to his room. He could see that the bedclothes and spread had been disturbed and, when he looked under the mattress, the canvas sack of cash was gone. Turning around, he sat down on the bed and rummaged around in his pocket until he found a cigarillo and a match. When he got the cigarillo lit and drawing he sat there, blowing out clouds of blue smoke, giving the whole proposition a good thinking over. As far as he was concerned, Caster, had taken the bait. Now all that remained was to gather him and Mull up in the same sack and the job was done.

That afternoon he rode over to the quarantine pens and looked across the sprawling mass of cattle. As best he could tell, his cattle had not been moved. It was difficult, however, since he had only the five head he'd marked in his mind to watch for. They did not brand cattle in Mexico, which made the job a good deal harder, but Longarm couldn't see any changes. Perhaps Caster and his crew did their work by a falling moon. If so, they had to work at a pretty good clip to get nearly a thousand cattle up to the release pens, which were almost a quarter of a mile away. He still couldn't figure out how they did it, but that part really made no difference. Caster would tell him when the time was right, if he was still curious about the matter.

When he got back to the hotel he went into the dining room and made a supper of beef stew and chocolate cake. He was still being careful of his bad tooth, which so far had not been bothering him. He intended to return the favor by not eating anything that would irritate it. Coming out of the dining room, he started to make for the bar, which was just off the lobby, but when he realized it was too early to find a poker game, he veered off, crossed the lobby, and headed down the first-floor hall to his room. He used his key on the door, which was unusual because most places he stayed the key wasn't much use, since the lock seldom worked. But the Hamilton was different. Using his key was also unusual because Longarm seldom locked his door, seldom having anything in his room worth stealing. But now he had twenty-five hundred dollars in the mattress and he guessed that was worth stealing. He swung the door open and there was Austin Davis stretched out on the bed with a glass of Longarm's whiskey resting on his stomach. He looked tired and grimy, but he held up a hand in greeting.

Longarm shut the door behind him. "How the hell did you get in here?" he said.

Davis waved vaguely behind him. "Came in through the window. Them sashes ain't nothing to raise up and open. Ain't got no lock on them."

"How'd you know which window?"

Davis sat up, swung his legs around, and sat on the side of the bed. He yawned. "I knew your room number, so all I had to do was count down from the lobby. Wasn't hard."

"Huh," Longarm said. He walked to the bedside table, poured himself half a glass of the Maryland whiskey, noting the bottle had taken a pretty good beating since he'd last seen it, then pulled up a chair, turned it front to back, and sat down astraddle. He took a drink of whiskey. "What," he said, "are you doing back here? I'm glad as hell you are, but what happened?"

Austin Davis's face fell. He grimaced. "She ran out on me, Longarm. Got away. Last night. I don't know what time 'cause I didn't wake up. But when I did, she was gone. I nearly killed two horses getting back here. I ain't been, here long."

"Hmmmm," Longarm said, and took another sip of his drink. "I take it you rushed back because you figure she don't mean us no good. Is that it?"

Davis shook his head. "I don't know. But I figured you ought to know. I mean, she did slip off. Took Raoul's horse, the best I can figure. I know she bribed a couple of the peons working on my friends' hacienda to help her saddle up and get away. We determined that much."

"How was she to you?"

The young deputy wrinkled his brow in thought. "Kind of calculating I'd say. She asked me a bunch of questions about you, but I just stuck to my part as a cattle contractor. Told her you was a cattle broker, and that was all I knowed. That you was dealing with Caster and your business with him had brought you out to see Raoul. Said it was damn unfortunate about him, but them things happened."

"What'd she say to that?"

Davis shook his head. "Not much of anything. If she was feeling any loss about Raoul, she kept it damn well hidden from me. It took us two days to get to these folks' place. They knew I was a deputy marshal, but I tipped them not to let on and I'm sure they didn't. I got rid of the body along the way, though Dulcima never knew about it. We spent the first night in a little hotel, and I slipped out when it was good and dark and found a canyon in some wild country and buried Raoul at the bottom of it."

Longarm rubbed the back of his neck. "I don't know a hell of a lot about the woman," he said, "except she is strong-willed as hell and wants her way. Did you do any good with her?"

Davis shook his head again. "No. And it was a damn big disappointment. But you remember she'd said she'd do the touching if it come to it. So I waited and it never happened. We slept in separate rooms, though they was side by side and had a connecting door. I slept mighty light and kept a check on her through the night. That's how I come to find out she was gone as soon as I did. I reckon it was around two in the morning. Hell, it was *this* morning. So I've come forty miles just about as fast as you can without being on a train. You reckon she means to make trouble for us here?''

Longarm took a drink and looked thoughtful. ''I'm not sure,'' he said. ''Women are a strange breed and she's one of the strangest I ever run across. Maybe it took her a few days, but it might have occurred to her I killed her lover right there in her house and that was a slap to her. If she takes it that way, then yes, I got to figure she means trouble. And then her slipping off like that. Got to be something in it.''

''Then how come she never put up no struggle about it? Why didn't she fight me more?''

''Maybe figuring to lull you to sleep. Maybe she figured if she put up a fight, we'd of throwed her in a sack and taken her anyway. But that ain't the important part. The important part is how fast can she get back here?''

''Ain't any way she could have come by horseback and beat or even come close to my time. I'm saying I rode *hard*. Other way is to head about fifteen miles west to a little town where the rail line to Nuevo Laredo stops. If she done that, the train would get her into town sometime early tomorrow morning. But how could she know?''

Longarm shrugged. ''That's a mighty resourceful lady. She bribed the peons to help her, she might have got the information out of them. And she could have found a guide that would have helped her. I would imagine she had plenty of cash on her.'' He stood up and walked over to the table to pour himself more whiskey. Austin Davis held out his glass and Longarm filled that. Then he turned and went back to his chair. ''But I better tell you where we are,'' he said. ''We got some plans to make.''

227

Item by item, Longarm related everything that had transpired. "So it looks like tomorrow morning is the time. Either we catch our rabbit—or rabbits—then, or they're going to get away. As a matter of fact, much as I hated to do it, I was going over to ask Raymond San Diego to get me up a crew of *vaqueros* to handle the cattle when they're released. But now, with Dulcima a wild card in the game, I don't reckon I care for that idea over much."

"Don't worry about it," Davis told his partner. "I'll go down to a saloon later on and hire us a crew in nothing flat. There's a couple of places where the *vaqueros* hang out. In fact, I think most of the bunch I hired to go into Mexico are still in town. I'll offer them three dollars a day for a short drive and get more takers than I can use. But it does sound like Caster is getting jittery. Now, I'm supposed to have loaned you that extra twenty-five hundred?"

"Yeah. You just got some money in to pick up another herd in Mexico."

Davis ran a hand through his dark hair. "Boy, I'll tell you the truth—this is one job I'll be glad to get shut of. It's like handling day-old fish—they're slippery and they smell to high heaven."

Longarm looked at him sharply. "*You*? Damnit, Austin, you ever involve me in anything like this again and I'll move to Canada."

"Oh, by the way," Davis added, "I found out what Raymond San Diego and Jasper White been smuggling. Raoul, too. And Caster."

"What?"

Davis grinned slyly. "Cattle."

"Cattle? Into the U.S.? Hell, we already knew that."

228

Austin Davis shook his head. "No, into Mexico."

"Mexico?"

"Yeah. When I was telling these friends about Raoul and Raymond they asked me if the San Diegos had a gringo friend, and then they described Jasper White. You said that Caster saw signs of tick fever in your cattle? Well, he sees that in about ten percent of all herds. Either that or about that many die. Only that ain't the case. Them cattle are being herded back to Mexico. These friends of mine have bought many a one from the San Diego brothers and Jasper White. Paid around four dollars a head. And then turned around and sold them to contractors like me for six and seven dollars. A very nice little business. One of them, Jose Quinto, said there was one old yellow steer that he personally bought and sold at least four times."

Longarm just shook his head. "You'd think one crooked sideline would be enough for Caster. No wonder he got nervous when Raoul disappeared. He knew all of Caster's secrets."

"How are we going to play it tomorrow?"

Longarm shrugged. "Fast and loose I would reckon. Bareback. All I can say is just keep one eye on me and be ready to jump one way or the other." He held up his hand as Davis opened his mouth to speak. "I know. They're your birds by right and I'll make damn sure you're in at the kill. One thing—I'm going to insist that Caster release the cattle before he gets any more money. I don't know how we're going to swap the money for the trail papers, but you get as close as you dare to that."

Davis looked tired. "Well," he said, "I hope we get lucky. This has been a long trail. I guess I better get a room and a bath."

Longarm stood up. "Let me get out of here first. I'll probably stay out a while tonight, maybe get in a poker game. I reckon you'll be busy with hiring *vaqueros*."

It was a little after ten o'clock that night when Longarm came back into the hotel. He went to the desk to collect his key and was surprised to see the day clerk on duty. The young man said he was pulling a double shift. "The night man had some business. At least that is what he say. I theenk maybe the monkey business."

Longarm nodded and turned away. He'd gone only a few steps when the clerk called to him, and turned back. "Oh, by the way," the young man said, "Señor Mull has checked in."

Longarm felt his excitement rise. "Yeah?" he said.

"Yes. He is in room one ten. That is four doors down from where you are."

Longarm nodded, trying to conceal a smile. "Thanks, amigo. Be sure and not let on you told me and I'll see you get taken care of."

The clerk waved his hand. "Oh, no, no. You have already been most generous, Señor Long."

"We'll see," Longarm said. He was smiling to himself as he walked down the hall. If he got the chance, he was going to be especially generous to Mister James Mull. He was going to see that he got a lot of years in a small place to think about his sins.

Chapter 12

Longarm sat his horse just by the release gate where the cattle were coming out of the last quarantine pen. On the other side, Austin Davis was on horseback with a tally sheet in his hand. Which seemed unnecessary, since Jay Caster had already told him he would be getting 940 cattle. The rest, Longarm thought wryly, were probably already on their way to Mexico. Caster had said they'd died, and Longarm didn't doubt that it could have happened. The cattle that were coming by him were poor and looked like they'd lost considerable flesh. They didn't look at all like the cattle he'd observed the night before and the night before that. Also, some of them seemed to have brands, and Longarm found that fairly interesting since they were supposedly all from Mexico. But if he asked, he was sure that Caster would tell him that his contractor, Austin Davis, had probably bought some stolen U.S. cattle that had been taken to Mexico, and that was none of Caster's doing. The customs inspector had an answer for everything.

Then Longarm saw what he'd been looking for. All

of the cattle were splotched with green paint, though it looked old and faded. And now he caught sight of one of his "key" cows, a brindle-colored steer with a twisted horn. He had a big splotch of bright green paint on his side, but a little trace of the original red was showing. As the steer exited the pen Longarm rode alongside the animal and leaned down and wiped his fingers across the smear of red that was showing. He straightened back up and looked at the red substance on his fingers. With his thumb he rubbed it back and forth and then smiled slightly. He said, half aloud, "So that's how he does it."

Just then he saw Caster riding toward him and he quickly wiped his fingers on his jeans. The red stain came off easily. He turned his horse to meet the customs official.

"You 'bout ready to wind this up?" Caster asked sourly. "I want you and them damn cattle out of town quick as possible."

Longarm looked over the pens. There appeared to be about a hundred cattle yet to go. "Let's let them get clear of the corral and in the hands of my drovers. I want word from Davis on the tally."

"The tally is going to be whatever it is," Caster bristled. "And you better not have no ideas of that Davis tagging along with us. I don't like that feller's looks."

Longarm smiled. "I'll tell him you said that. I'll be ready in just a moment, Mister Caster. This ought not to take long."

"You got the money?"

Longarm turned in the saddle and slapped his saddle-bags. "Got it right in here." Though the money, in fact, was still in his mattress. "You ain't told me how you

232

want me to get it to you. Or who? Raymond San Diego?''

''In a moment we will ride to the hotel. I'll tell you then.''

Longarm glanced around at Caster. It was hard to tell, since the man was so unfriendly at his best, but this morning there seemed to be a special edge to him. Then again, Longarm reflected, maybe he was just imagining it, worried as he was about Dulcima making it back and telling the interested parties what had really happened to Raoul.

He could see Austin Davis watching them across the stream of cattle, and Longarm dipped his hat brim just a fraction to let his partner know that things were still going along all right. Actually they were better than that. He now knew what he was going to arrest Caster for, and in fact, could have arrested him at that second. But he had the feeling that another fish was going to swim into his net, so he planned on being patient.

Then the last of the cattle were out of the corral, and the drovers Austin Davis had hired, fell in on the sides and behind the herd and started moving them toward the east. They'd take them in that direction until they were around the town and then turn them north. Austin Davis went along with them, casting a glance back toward Longarm. He would accompany the herd only until he saw Longarm and Caster making a definite move in one direction. Then he would cut back and find a position in which to place himself for the final moment.

''You ready to go now?'' Caster asked.

''Yeah. I reckon that's about it.''

''Then head for the hotel. I'll ride along beside you.''

Caster didn't speak again until they were both in front

233

of the hotel. He dismounted and stood by his horse. "Take yore saddlebags and go to yore room," he instructed Longarm. "Leave the money laying on top of your bed. Then walk out, leaving the door unlocked."

"What about my papers?"

"Damnit, keep your mouth shut. You come out of that room, wait fifteen minutes, and then go back in there. Yore papers will be laying on the bed. But don't be hanging around in the hall. Go in the bar or stay back in the lobby."

"Just like that? I'm supposed to lay some more money down without having seen a damn thing? Why should I trust you?"

"Don't, then," Caster said coldly. "I don't give a damn. See how far you get with those cattle."

Longarm grimaced. "I don't seem to have much choice."

"No, you don't. And don't be in no rush to come out of yore room once you've got yore papers. Give it another quarter of an hour. Have yourself a drink to celebrate."

"And these are Brownsville papers? Mull is going to sign and seal them?"

Caster gave him a disgusted look. "Long, I will be damn glad to see you out of town. You ain't worth the money. I told you about Mull and it is still the same. Now get in that hotel and do like I told you."

Longarm untied his saddlebags and slung them over his shoulder, thinking he would be glad to see Caster in jail. He couldn't remember when he'd taken such a dislike to a quarry in all his career. Mostly he looked at it as business, but the mouth on Caster had began to personally irritate him.

He walked into the hotel and to the desk, picked up his key and went down the hall to his room and unlocked the door. Just before he went in he glanced down four doors to room 110. If things went the way he had them figured, Mister James Mull was sitting in there waiting to get a chunk of money in return for his signature.

Longarm stepped into his room and closed the door behind him. He pitched the saddlebags on the bed, then went to the window and made sure it was closed. Then he carefully drew the curtains so that some casual passerby couldn't see what was going to be on the bed. He took a sack out of his saddlebags, an empty sack he'd gotten from the bank. Then he lifted up the mattress and held it in place with his shoulder while he removed the money and put it in the sack. When he was through he let the mattress down, smoothed the covers, and placed the sack squarely in the center of the bed. He was done. He took one last look around and then exited the room, carefully closing the door behind him but not locking it.

He walked down the hall and went into the lobby, going to the far side and shielding himself behind one of the big square support columns that rose to the ceiling. He could just see the front door. A moment passed and then another. He was starting to get jumpy. Was Caster not going to go for the cheese in the trap? Had he been forewarned by Dulcima?

Caster walked into the hotel. He looked left and right and seemed to study the faces in the lobby, but he did it quickly. Without any further hesitation he walked down the hall toward the rooms at that end, just as if he were going about official business. Longarm watched him until he disappeared. As quickly as he could, Longarm slipped over to the hall and peeked around it. He was just in time to see Caster open the door to his room and slip inside. He shut the door behind himself.

Longarm did not pause. He loosened the gun in his holster; he was now wearing his cutaway model. He walked quickly down the hall and stopped opposite his own door.

At first he stood across the hallway, his back against the wall. But after a moment had passed he decided he didn't care what anyone might think of him standing in front of a room door. Stepping across the hallway, he stationed himself right in front of his room. He stood there, staring intently at the doorknob, waiting for it to turn. He had been waiting for this moment for what seemed like weeks, maybe months, days for certain. In his mind he ran through all the insults Caster had paid him, all the sneering remarks, all the condescension. Oh yes, he owed Mister Caster more than Mister Caster knew.

Caster had been dressed in his customary vested suit with a small tie. While they were watching the herd Longarm had taken some pains to note that he'd also been wearing a small revolver high up on his waist. The gun had appeared to be a short-barreled .38 caliber. It was strictly a belly gun, to be used at close quarters.

Longarm was gradually tensing up as he watched for the knob to turn. It seemed like half an hour had passed. Several people had come and gone down the hall. They had glanced curiously at Longarm, but hadn't said anything.

And then he saw the knob start to turn. He raised his head to eye-level so he'd be looking directly into the customs inspector's face when the door came open. The door opened slowly. Caster's left shoulder came into view and then his chest and then his face. Longarm took only time enough to register the surprised look on Caster's face before he pushed forward, knocking the door aside, and grabbing both lapels of his coat. With a heave of his shoulders he shoved the man a yard back into the room, then swung him around to the right and smashed him as hard as he could into the wall by the door. Caster let out a whoosh of air, but he tried feebly to strike at Longarm with the sack he was holding in his hand. Longarm let go of Caster's right lapel, doubled his free hand into a fist, and then drove it hard into Caster's stomach. The customs official went pale, his eyes opened wide, and a moan oozed out of his mouth. He would have doubled over, but Longarm was holding him upright. Without losing a moment, Longarm reached out with his right hand, grabbed the door, and slammed it shut. Then he put his forearm under Caster's chin, pressing it against his neck, and straightened the man up on his tiptoes against the wall. Caster's face went from white to beet-red as Longarm attempted to strangle him. His mouth worked like a fish's but no sound came out. Longarm saw him drop the cash sack and try to bring his right hand in toward his belt. "I reckon not, Mister Caster." he said, knocking his hand away. Reaching in under Caster's coat with his left hand, Longarm found the little revolver, jerked it out of its holster, and threw it behind him on the bed. Then, because he felt like it, he made a fist with his left hand and slugged Caster in that side of the stomach. Caster's face contorted with pain and he waved his arms uselessly trying to beat at Longarm's back. He was making little gurgling sounds.

"Now," Longarm said, "how do you like this, you sonofabitch? Why don't you pay me an insult now?

237

Can't talk? Something got your tongue? You say you're strangling? You say you can't breathe? Right sorry to hear that, Mister Caster. You make it a habit of bad-mouthing U.S. deputy marshals, do you?" Longarm saw Caster's eyes grow even wider. "Aw hell, Caster, don't tell me you didn't know I was a federal marshal. Hell, I figure you went to all that trouble to tell me how dumb I was and what a hayseed, and how there wasn't no way you could be caught, just on account of you knowed I was a U.S. deputy marshal." He forced his forearm up even tighter against Caster's throat, lifting up against his chin so that he was almost pulling the man off his feet.

But something was nagging at Longarm, something he'd seen when he first charged into the room. Something wasn't right, but he couldn't bring it to mind. He was going to have to turn around and look the place over, but first he needed to park Caster somewhere he couldn't cause trouble. Longarm suddenly grasped Caster by the shirt front, releasing his forearm hold as he did. For a second Caster gasped for air, but he had little time to savor the relief. Longarm swung him around with his left arm so that he was pointing toward the far side wall, set him up, and then hit him square in the face with his big, heavy, right fist. He drove through the blow, putting his shoulder into it. He had meant to catch Caster on the jaw, perhaps breaking it, but Caster's head had wobbled at the last instant and Longarm's fist had taken him in the mouth. But Longarm had the satisfaction, as Caster dropped like a sack of meal, of feeling some teeth break. Caster went down, sprawling on his back. He was not unconscious, but he was so stunned that it would be a long moment before he could get up.

Longarm turned away to look at the room, shaking his hand. He saw a little blood on his knuckles and knew that one of Caster's teeth had cut him. "Damn you, Jay Caster," he said. "You've bit me. When are you going to quit doing me harm? Hell, I'd rather be bit by a mad dog."

He took a step toward the center of the room and glanced around. Then he saw what had bothered him, what had caught in his mind's eye. The window he'd made sure was closed and the curtains he'd pulled together so no one could see in from outside were wide open. Longarm glanced toward Caster. The man was still down, but he was starting to stir around. "You sonofa-bitch," Longarm said, "What have you been up to at that window? Did you drop something out of it?" He walked over to the window and stuck his head out. He could see the ground below. It was clear of anything suspicious. He pulled his head in and shut the window and drew the curtains. "Caster, what the hell you been up to?"

Longarm walked over to the spot where Caster had dropped the sack of money. He picked it up and looked inside. It appeared to be intact. He glanced at Caster, who had hoisted himself up on his elbows and was shaking his head. His mouth was bloody. "I don't know what you were up to, Caster, but it better not make me angry. I'm already a little put out with you. Especially now that I see I've injured myself on your teeth." He hooked the sack down on his belt.

He stopped beside the bedside table and picked up the half-full bottle of Maryland whiskey, drew the cork, and poured a little on his hand. It stung. He said, "Now look what you've caused me to do," he said. "Waste good whiskey pouring it on the floor. What else are you going to do to me, Caster? I swear, I don't believe I ever met a man had less respect for a United States marshal than you.'' He finished with the whiskey by taking a good pull from the bottle. It felt good going down, warming his stomach. He corked the bottle and set it back on the table, shaking his right hand in the air. Then he walked around the bed and looked at Caster. He had made it to a sitting position, but his eyes still looked dazed. He raised a hand to his mouth and touched it and then looked at the blood on his fingers. ''I guess you didn't know I've had a toothache this whole week,'' Longarm said, ''and you never said one word in sympathy about it. Well, I reckon you'll know how I felt now. By the way, where the hell are my papers? Just because I'm a federal marshal don't mean you can cheat me out of what I paid for. But I guess they're down in Mister Mull's room.'' Caster glanced up in surprise. ''Yeah, I knew about him. But listen, you have got to get up. You can't lay around in here all day. We got to get this situation wrapped up. Hell, wasn't you in a hurry a while ago? Well, what has changed? C'mon, man, you've got to get on your feet. What happened, you take a little too much wine with lunch? Here, let me help you.'' He leaned over, grasped Caster by the shirt and coat, and jerked him to his feet. The sound of cloth tearing was loud in the room. Most of Caster's collar came off.

''Aw, hell,'' Longarm said. ''Did you tear your shirt? Damn, I feel bad about that. But we've got to move along.'' He gave Caster a shove toward the door. The customs official stumbled, but recovered his balance and leaned against the wall. Longarm came up behind him, reached around and opened the door, then shoved him out into the hall. Caster came to a stop, his hand to his mouth. Longarm shoved him forward. "Room one ten," he said. "That's where my papers are, right? You were going to give me my papers, weren't you? I reckon you were. Hell, I paid enough for them. You were going to come out, go down and get the papers from Mull, leave them in my room, and then—And then what, Caster? What did you open that damn window for?"

He shoved Caster down the hall until he came to rest in front of room 110. "What say we drop in on your partner, Mister James Mull? Reckon he'll have pie and coffee ready for us? Let's don't bother to knock." He pushed Caster aside, raised his leg, and smashed the door open with his boot heel. As soon as the door flew back, Longarm grabbed Caster and threw him bodily into the room. The man stumbled and staggered, but didn't go down.

Longarm stepped through the doorway. The room was bigger than his. There were two windows on the back wall, about six feet apart. One of them was partly open. A light breeze was fluttering the curtains. Longarm looked to his left. There was a divan against the wall and a small table in the middle of the room. The bed was to the right. A man at the table, clad in a black split-tail coat, had risen to his feet. He was wearing a starched shirt and a string tie. Longarm said, "I reckon you'd be Mister James Mull. Well, you got something belongs to me."

The Brownsville customs officer stared at Longarm, speechless, and then shifted his gaze to Caster. "Wha—" he stammered. "What, what in hell is going on, Jay?"

Longarm said, "You'll find out soon enough, Mister Mull." Mull was tall and thin and younger than Longarm had expected him to be. There were a few papers on the table along with an inkwell and a nub pen. Longarm glanced at the table and then at James Mull. Caster was leaning against the bed, his hand still to his mouth. "Mister Mull," Longarm said, "if you're carrying a gun, you better be damn good with it or be prepared to eat it raw."

Mull's eyes got round. He looked over at Caster. "Jay! What is this?"

Caster just shook his head.

Longarm picked up one of the papers from the table and scanned it hurriedly. Then he looked back at James Mull. "My name is Custis Long," he said. "I'm a United States deputy marshal. Mister Mull, you are now under arrest for malfeasance in office. I am holding an official document here, a quarantine release certifying that a herd of mine, nine hundred plus cattle, have cleared quarantine in Brownsville, Texas and are cleared for the trail. Hell, Mister Mull, you should have paid more attention in geography class. This ain't Brownsville, this is Laredo. I ought to add a charge of being just plain stupid. Hell, you're dumber than Caster, far as that goes. But he'll do more time, I'm glad to say. You'll like it in prison, Jay."

Caster said, in muffled tones, "You haven't got a thing on me. I haven't signed nothing. I'm not guilty of any malfeasance in office."

Longarm laughed. "Damn, I wish my partner was here. Name of Austin Davis. He's the cattle contractor you thought was so dumb and crooked, Jay. He'd enjoy this. Hell, I ain't arresting you for malfeasance; I'm arresting you for cattle theft. Those cattle you turned over to me this morning weren't my cattle. And they damn

242

sure weren't yours to give away. That's theft, Jay, cattle theft, and it carries a mighty handy little penalty.''

Caster took his hand away from his mouth and stared malevolently at Longarm. ''You sorry bastard,'' he said in a hard tone.

''Now, that's no way to talk, Mister Caster. Hell, I'm doing you a favor sending you to prison. I had promised myself, after you had stuffed me full of your bad mouth, the pleasure of beating you to death. But I swore on oath to uphold the law and I don't reckon I can—''

Longarm stopped. The twin eyes of a double-barreled twelve gauge shotgun had suddenly come thrusting through the window. The barrels were pointed straight at him. His hand had involuntarily flicked toward the revolver at his side, but then he relaxed. You couldn't outdraw an aimed scatter gun at ten-foot range. His first thought was that it was Austin Davis, playing a prank, paying his partner back for making the arrests without him present.

But then an arm and hand, a left arm and hand, came thrusting through the window to sweep the curtains back. Longarm felt himself go cold. Framed in the window were the head and shoulders of Raymond San Diego. Longarm wouldn't have thought he was tall enough to reach the window. Inanely he wondered what the man was standing on. He was conscious of how shiny black Raymond's hair was, almost as shiny as the barrels of the shotgun.

Sighting down the barrel of the big gun, speaking to Longarm, San Diego said, ''You keel my brother. Now I going to keel you.''

His voice steady in spite of the shaking inside of him, Longarm said, ''Whoever said that is a liar. Dulcima

243

killed your brother. I was there when it happened. Then she run off to Mexico with a boyfriend of hers.'' It made no sense, but he was caught dead. All it would take was a slight pressure on the trigger of the shotgun to blow a good portion of him out in the hall. He went on, talking wildly, ''It was Caster's idea. This man here. He wanted Raoul out of the way so he could get a bigger cut of the money y'all made smuggling cattle back into Mexico.'' He heard Caster draw a sharp breath, but he kept on talking. ''Raymond, I'm not your enemy. You got it all wrong.''

For answer San Diego raised the shotgun slightly so that Longarm was staring down the twin holes that looked as big as dinner plates. ''You lie,'' he said ''I keel you. You gentlemens step back.''

In another instant he was going to pull the trigger. Then, from behind him, Longarm heard a word said so softly that he thought he must have imagined it. Then the word came again, this time a little more distinctly. ''Drop.''

He let his legs collapse and hurled his shoulders sideways at the floor. As he fell he heard the sharp report of a revolver and then the boom of the shotgun. The noise filled the room and echoed and echoed.

As Longarm went down, he could see Raymond San Diego distinctly. Halfway to the floor, he saw a red mark suddenly appear on the little man's forehead, right in the middle. Suddenly Raymond fell backward, the shotgun tilting up, the double load blasting up and into the ceiling. For a moment Longarm lay on the floor, deafened by the shotgun blast. Finally he turned his head toward the door and said, ''You damn well took your time.''

"I figured you wanted a chance to get out of it by yourself," Austin Davis said. "I know I would have."

That night they were having a drink in Longarm's room. They had trusted the local sheriff to keep Mull and Caster caged overnight, but they were taking them to San Antonio the next day, not trusting the local authorities to keep such prisoners until they could be sent before a federal judge. Longarm said thoughtfully, "That was a pretty good shot you made."

"Pretty good?" Austin Davis was indignant. "Dead center in the forehead? An offhand shot with a partner's life hanging in the balance? Pretty good? What the hell do you call a good shot?"

Longarm shrugged. "All right, it was a hell of a shot, a damned good shot. You saved my life." He sighed. "And I'll probably never hear the end of it."

Davis shook his head. "Not from me." He paused. "Of course I think it might want to make you cut down a little on that talk about being a better poker player than me. And better with the ladies."

"All right, all right. Damnit."

They were quiet for a few moments, each busy with his drink and his own thoughts. Finally Davis said, "I got to admit that was a mighty slick way that Caster had. He gave you cattle that had been in quarantine ninety days. And if you hadn't noticed how poor they was, nobody would have ever been the wiser."

"Except for the paint he supposedly used on the few cattle that stuck out. Odd-colored ones and them as had funny horns. Them he painted with that limestone water."

"Colored limestone water. Chalk. Wipe right off."

"It was slick all right."

Longarm sighed again. "I never been so tired of a job in all my life. I wish we were through."

Davis looked surprised. "Through? Ain't we? Outside of escorting them two to San Antonio, what is left?"

"Her."

"Who?"

"Dulcima. Who'd you think? She damn near got me killed. You know that was planned. Caster had told me to stay in my room at least fifteen minutes after I went in there to get my papers. He didn't know I knew about Mull. And he had the window all set for Raymond to blow me in two. If I hadn't broke in there, if I hadn't known about Mull already being in the hotel, I'd have been a sitting duck. It was just bad luck that San Diego went to scouting around. Though I would guess he knew which room was Mull's. As did you. And no thanks to Jasper White. If I see that bastard, I'm going to beat the hell out of him. Unless I can think of some reason to put him in jail."

"Yeah, I agree about Jasper, but why don't you leave the damn woman alone? Hell, let's be done with this mess and get on back and have a good time somewhere."

Longarm frowned. "Hell, Austin, she done her best to get me killed."

"Yeah, but you'd have a hell of a time making such a charge stick. Especially on a woman that good-looking. Something bad will happen to her eventually anyway."

"Well, it makes me angry," Longarm said stubbornly, "I'd like to give her a good scare, anyway."

"Hell, Longarm, all she did to you was try to do what you done to her."

Longarm glanced at Davis. After a moment, he said, "Yeah, I reckon you're right." Then he smiled. "But I bet I had a hell of a lot more fun doing it to her."

Watch for
the following books in the bold LONGARM
series

**LONGARM AND THE COUNTERFEIT
CORPSE**

212th adventure in the LONGARM series

Available now!

and

LONGARM AND THE MINUTE MEN

213th adventure in the LONGARM series

Coming from Jove in September!